SNAKEWATER
AFFAIR

A SPIDER LATHAM MYSTERY

SNAKEWATER AFFAIR

LIZ ADAIR

DESERET BOOK

SALT LAKE CITY, UTAH

To my friend and hero Mary Etta McCarty, who is, once

again, fighting a battle with an old and malignant enemy

Library of Congress Cataloging-in-Publication Data

Adair, Liz.
    Snakewater affair : a Spider Latham mystery / Liz Adair.
      p.   cm.
    ISBN 1-59038-306-0 (pbk.)
    1. Latham, Spider (Fictitious character)—Fiction.   2. Private investigators—Washington (State)—Fiction.   3. Mines and mineral resources—Fiction.   4. Washington (State)—Fiction.   5. Hazardous wastes—Fiction.   6. Missing persons—Fiction.   I. Title.

PS3601.D35S65   2004
813'.6—dc22   2004000909

Printed in the United States of America   54459
Malloy Lithographing Incorporated, Ann Arbor, MI

10   9   8   7   6   5   4   3   2

ACKNOWLEDGMENTS

I AM GRATEFUL TO MEMBERS of the Barr Road Family Band, who acted as manuscript readers for me. They are: Chris Talley (keyboard), Mark Metge (clarinet), Julie Metge (flute), Edna Harper (baritone), and Wayne Adair (tuba). My daughter and son-in-law, Ruth (viola) and Rich Lavine (baritone), read the pages as they came off the printer and then consented to read the whole manuscript again when I gave the assignment to the band. Shirley White and Jeannie Schmidt also read and critiqued the final draft.

Thanks go to Mick Jolly for some pointers on fingerprints.

Also, thanks to my cousin Joe Smith for teaching me about building and firing cannons. Joe builds them and does Civil War and Living History reenactments. One of his cannons is in the museum in Tucson, Arizona.

My son Wayne Adair is my mechanical guru, both in literary things and real life. Thanks, dear.

I appreciate the enthusiasm of all the people at Deseret Book. They have been helpful and supportive at every turn. I especially enjoyed working with Richard Peterson during the final editing. He is a true gentleman and a wonderful editor.

And thanks to my husband, Derrill, not only for all the Spiderisms, but for help in the genesis of each plot and for a critical eye and ear as it thickened.

C O N F E S S I O N S

THIS BOOK IS MY VALENTINE to the town of Chewelah, Washington, though they may consider it a dubious honor when they see what I've done to the geography of the area. As with the hamlet of Panaca, Nevada, the town of Chewelah in this book is a composite of many small towns I have lived in.

All of the characters in this book spring entirely from my imagination. None are based on real people.

Finally, I must confess that there is no process for holding magnasite ore in suspension in order to transport it by pumping. This is why I love writing fiction: I am not constrained by reality.

IT WAS LATE AFTERNOON THE end of June in 1993. The day had been a scorcher, and Spider Latham's shirt showed damp patches as he sat in the cab of his wrecked pickup. He had the passenger door open with his feet hanging out, and he was screwing the door panel back on when he heard Laurie's three-wheeler coming in from the pasture. She was driving slower than her usual neck-or-nothing tear over the countryside, and he saw that she had his mother perched on behind. While she stopped to open the gate, Spider tried the window, rolling the crank to make sure that it went up and down. Satisfied with the results, he tossed his screwdriver into his open toolbox on the ground and closed the pickup door, standing hands on hips, waiting for Laurie to come abreast.

"Where you been?" he asked as soon as he knew she could hear him.

"Just checking the fence line. Bud is putting his cattle in the north pasture tomorrow, and I wanted to make sure there weren't any places where the fence was down."

"Hello, Mama," Spider greeted the small gray-haired woman who sat behind Laurie on the three-wheeler, clinging tightly to her waist.

Rachel Latham smiled tentatively but didn't reply. Spider glanced momentarily at Laurie and read concern in her brown eyes. He shrugged, just a tiny movement of his shoulders, and then demonstrated the window. "I fixed the oil pan and put in new windows. I think you can drive it now."

Laurie surveyed the crumpled pickup. "Well, it could have been worse. At least we've got something to drive."

"Yeah, well, I've learned not to carry such a high deductible. We ended up with enough money to fix a few things, but I'll have to do the bodywork myself."

"There wasn't much choice. During all that time you weren't working, we were lucky to keep it insured. We were lucky to keep it at all."

Spider Latham had been a millwright at the mine in Castleton for twenty-five years. It was a comfortable living, and he and Laurie had built a house and barn and raised two boys and sent them on missions and to college. But three years ago the mines had closed and Spider, along with the rest of the county, was out of a job. While other men in the tiny Mormon hamlet of Panaca, Nevada, had moved their families out or had gone to Las Vegas to work at the nuclear test site during the week, Spider had hung on, scratching around for odd jobs to try to stay in the valley settled by his great-great-grandfather. He and Laurie sold everything they could, including Laurie's car and all but six of her sleek Hereford cattle. Just when it was looking as if the Lathams, too, would have to leave, the deputy sheriff was killed in an accident, and Spider had been offered the job.

Spider pulled down the brim of the baseball cap he was wearing and looked at the dented cab. "Huh," he grunted, not agreeing with Laurie about luck.

"And we were lucky that you walked away from the accident. Don't forget that."

"Naw, I'll think of that every time I look at the roof of my pickup."

Laurie laughed. "You do that. I'm going to take your mother in and give her a snack. She's been eating so little that I want to make sure I balance the insulin I'm giving her."

Spider closed his toolbox. "Okay. I think I'll get busy on the first of those dents. I may not be able to get them all out, but I'll Bondo what I can't fix, and then get it painted. We've got enough insurance money left to do that."

Laurie nodded and drove slowly over to the back door, where she helped her mother-in-law off the three-wheeler and up the porch stairs. Spider stood watching, thinking that a month ago his mother had been a walking encyclopedia of Latham history, enlightening their days with a continuous stream of anecdotes about life in Meadow Valley, twenty, thirty, forty, fifty years ago, though she couldn't remember what happened five minutes before. And now she had become silent, a docile cipher, unable to express much beyond the most basic of needs.

Walking into the barn, Spider put his toolbox on the workbench and picked up a toilet plunger. He was halfway to the pickup with it when Laurie stuck her head out the backdoor and called to him.

"Yeah?" Spider hollered back.

"There's a message on the answering machine for you."

"Who is it?"

"It's Ace Lazarra."

Ace Lazarra. *Curious,* Spider thought, *how she keeps coming back into my life.* She was so different from Laurie. Laurie was small and quick, with a freckled nose and rough hands from outside work. Laurie was earth and toil and sacrifice and goodness. Ace Lazarra was a long-legged beauty in a designer suit, with a smoky voice and hair in an elegant cut. She moved in moneyed, powerful circles in Las Vegas. While working on a case together she had invited Spider to dinner. He had refused because he was a married man, and she had laughed that husky laugh and said, "I like you, Spider Latham."

Spider changed his course and headed toward the back porch. "Ace left a message for me?"

Laurie glanced quizzically at the plunger in his hand and nodded, standing aside as she held the screen door open for him.

Mother Latham was at the table placidly eating a bowl of cottage cheese. Spider smiled at her as he set the plunger down and punched the button on the answering machine. He got a faint smile in return.

"Hello, Spider." There was no mistaking that voice. "This is Ace Lazarra. I want you to call a man by the name of Brick Tremain. He has need of someone like you. When you talk about money, aim high. He can afford it, and he'll respect the goods more if they are expensive. Remember . . . I recommended you. Don't let me down." Spider jotted down the number as Ace gave it and played the message again to check that he had written it correctly. He looked up to see Laurie standing with the open cottage cheese container in her hand, staring at him.

"What does she mean? Who is Brick Tremain?"

"I don't know. Never heard of him."

"Are you going to call him?"

"Why not? Ace never steered me wrong before." Spider punched the buttons. "She said to aim high. Huh."

A receptionist answered on the third ring, practiced and businesslike. "Brick Tremain Enterprises, this is Erin. How may I help you?"

"Uh, this is Spider Latham. Mr. Tremain asked me to call."

"Just one moment. I'll connect you."

Laurie was still holding the cottage cheese, watching. Spider winked at her, coming to attention as his call went through.

"Brick Tremain here." The voice was smooth and articulate, with just the hint of softening around the edges. But even with that softness, Brick Tremain had the sound of someone who was used to giving orders.

"Mr. Tremain? This is Spider Latham. Ace Lazarra asked me to call you."

"Latham? Oh, yes. I've got something I want to talk to you about. Can you be here in my office tomorrow morning? I can see you at . . . ten-thirty."

Spider looked out the window at the Latham transportation: the county deputy sheriff's mid-sized cruiser and the pickup with the top all crumpled in from a rollover accident up on Finlay's Summit last month. He couldn't drive the cruiser to Las Vegas on personal business, and though he wasn't too proud to drive the mangled pickup around Lincoln County, somehow he didn't want to go to Vegas in it. "Uh . . ." Spider didn't know how to frame an answer.

"Shall I send a car for you?"

"Uh, that would be fine. Do you know where I live?"

"I don't, but the driver will. What time do you have to leave to get here by ten-thirty?"

"Probably about seven-thirty."

"Fine. Expect him at that time."

"You want to tell me what this is about?"

"We can discuss it tomorrow. It's not something I want to talk about over the phone."

"All right. I guess I'll see you tomorrow."

"Fine."

Click.

Spider stood with the phone to his ear for a moment and then hung up.

"So what was that about?" Laurie asked.

"I don't know. He wants to see me tomorrow. He's sending a car for me. Going to pick me up at seven-thirty."

"So that means the driver has to leave Vegas at four-thirty!"

"I imagine he'll be paid for it."

"He's not a shady character, is he, this Brick Tremain?"

"I don't know. I wouldn't think so. Ace wouldn't put me in touch with someone shady. I'm pretty sure."

Laurie was cleaning up Mother Latham's place at the table and bent down to pick up a napkin that had fallen to the floor. "What's this?" she exclaimed.

"What?"

"Your mother's pant legs are damp." She pulled up the material and looked at her mother-in-law's bare leg. "Spider, come look at this."

Spider stood behind Laurie. "I don't see anything."

"Look, there's something making her leg all wet."

"She's not . . ."

"No, she hasn't wet her britches. I don't know what this is. Her legs have been swollen the last few days. The skin has been tight and shiny-looking. It's worried me, but now they seem to be oozing." Laurie spoke a little louder. "Mother Latham, do your legs hurt?"

Rachel Latham's eyes shifted to Laurie's face, and there was a lag between the question and comprehension. Finally the older woman shook her head.

"This scares me a bit." Laurie frowned. "I think I'd better run her over to Cedar to the doctor tomorrow. You say I can drive the pickup now?"

"Yeah. What do you think it is?" Spider gestured toward his mother's legs.

Laurie went to the phone. "I don't know. I don't think it has anything to do with her diabetes, but I don't know." She found the number she wanted written on a card by the phone, dialed the number, and made the appointment.

Spider picked up his plunger and waited for her to complete the transaction. "Do you need me to put this fellow off and take you over tomorrow?"

Laurie shook her head decisively. Her ponytail swished back and forth. "You go on and don't worry about us. Probably this is something that is easily dealt with."

"Okay, then. I'm off to see what I can do with the pickup."

"With a plunger?"

"Old Zorm told me I could get some of the dents out by sucking them with a plunger. I figured it's worth a try before I take the headliner out and start beating it with a hammer."

"Well, purty it up for me, Pa, 'cause I'm going to town tomorrow."

Spider grinned. "I'll purty it up, Ma." He saluted with the plunger and whistled as he headed out to the waiting pickup.

SPIDER WOKE THE NEXT MORNING at six, conscious of the empty bed beside him. He glanced at the bathroom door, but it was open and the bath was dark. Just as he was about to get up, Laurie came into the bedroom, leaving the door open behind her.

"Your mother was up," she whispered as she climbed back in bed. "She's starting to get her days and nights mixed up now."

"How were her legs this morning?"

"They're better. Still swollen, but not so tight, and not weeping."

"Is she back to sleep?"

"I think so." Laurie nestled in, fitting her body into the curve of Spider's. He put his arm around her waist and pulled her close, enjoying the familiar fragrance of the shampoo she used.

"I've got to be getting up," he said.

"Mmmmm." Laurie yawned. "Spider, what did Ace Lazarra mean when she said to aim high?"

"I've been wondering about that, too. I think she meant to ask for lots of money if Brick Tremain wants me to do something for him."

"What would lots of money be?"

"I don't know. Probably her idea of lots of money is more than yours or mine."

"But there's the possibility of some extra money coming in?"

"I don't know if it's a possibility or not. Why?"

"Well, we've got this expense for your mother's doctor. The part that Medicare doesn't pay."

"Deb will pay part of that."

"But we have to pay the rest." She yawned and turned over, her auburn hair spreading out over the pillow behind her.

Spider leaned over and kissed the hair at the nape of her neck, then threw off the covers and sat up. "Well, I'll get up and see what old Brick has on his mind. I can't see that it has any possibility of any extra money for us, though. What would he want done in Lincoln County?"

"Mmmm." Laurie's voice sounded faint. "I'm going to doze until your mother gets up. If that hasn't happened by the time you go, wake me."

Spider agreed and went into the bathroom, trying to make as little noise as possible, so as not to disturb his sleeping wife.

Just at seven-thirty a dark blue Cadillac rolled over the cattle guard. Spider roused Laurie to let her know he was going.

"You look nice," she murmured.

"I debated what to wear. Figured I'd just as well wear a suit and tie. Good-bye, Darlin'. I'll see you tonight." He kissed Laurie, and as he left the room she was sitting up, yawning, with hair all tousled and feet hanging over the edge of the bed.

Spider paused at the service porch and eyed the baseball cap hanging on the peg where his Stetson had hung just a month ago. Glancing out the window at the clear blue sky, he contemplated the discomfort of going hatless, but vanity won over utility. Thinking that if some extra money did come in, he might be able to buy a new hat to replace the one he lost in the rollover last month, Spider strode bareheaded down the porch steps toward the waiting sedan where a young man in a dark blue suit stood holding the passenger side rear door open.

"Good morning," Spider greeted, offering his hand. "Just the two of us? If so, I'll ride shotgun."

The driver blinked and paused momentarily before shaking Spider's hand with an engaging smile. He closed the rear door and opened the front, and as soon as Spider was settled, he walked smartly around to the driver's side.

"Name's Spider Latham," Spider said as soon as they were underway.

"Jade Tremain, at your service, sir."

"You related to Brick Tremain?"

"I'm his son."

Spider looked at the young man with interest. He liked what he saw: Jade Tremain was of medium height and build. He had sandy brown hair that swirled in a cowlick in the front over his right eye, the smallest of gaps between his front teeth, and a sprinkling of freckles on his nose that combined to give him the look of a simple rustic. There was a lively intelligence in his hazel eyes, though, as he turned to look at Spider. "Don't let the chauffeur's uniform fool you. I'm in my father's confidence, and he told me to answer any questions you might ask. It'll save him time later." He put the car in gear and rolled over the cattle guard and onto the gravel road that led to the highway.

"Any question at all?" Spider sat back in the plush seat and pondered a moment. Finally he asked, "How'd you like getting up at four in the morning to come and fetch me?"

Jade flashed the tiny gap in his teeth. "It was three-thirty. And I liked it fine. I saw an awesome sunrise that was worth the price of admission."

"And you work for your father as chauffeur?"

"I'm a college student. I get my bachelor's this year, but I didn't get my education handed to me. My dad believes in people learning the value of work. And, he wants me to know the company and the people from the bottom up. When I'm not driving, I'm in the mailroom. I've already been in the warehouse, and my first job was night janitor. Dad didn't want me thinking I was better than any of the people who give an honest day's work for the company."

"And do you?"

"Think I'm better? No."

Spider didn't speak as they drove past his cousin Murray's place. He let his eyes wander over the house and outbuildings, noting how Slick and Dan, Murray's two cutting horses in the corral out back, raised their heads as the car approached. He saw that there was a sheet of tin on the shed that needed to be nailed down and was mentally making a note to talk to Murray about that when Jade spoke again.

"But I know I haven't learned yet what my dad's trying to teach me. I've been too close to the power of money, I think. People treat you different when you have lots of money."

"I wouldn't know," Spider said dryly.

There was an awkward silence, and then Spider said, "Tell me about your father. What's he like?"

"You don't want to know why he's sent for you and what he's going to ask you to do?"

"Oh, that'll come. First I want to get the lay of the land. Find out who's asking."

Jade shook his head as he pulled up to the stop sign and checked for traffic. Then he turned south on Highway 93. "I'd like to sit in on the conversation between you and my dad," he said, grinning.

"Why is that?"

"You both have your own way of going about things, it seems. I'll admit when I heard I was coming clear out to Lincoln County, I wondered. But he said you came on the highest recommendation."

"Highest, eh?"

"Yup. I think the word honorable was used. That's a word my dad likes."

"So, tell me about him. What does he do?"

"What doesn't he do? He has lots of different business interests, but what is nearest and dearest to his heart is mining. He got his start in copper in the heyday during the fifties and sixties. He amassed a fortune and diversified into different mining interests and other things, too."

"So I take it your dad didn't start out with money? Wasn't born to it?"

"No. His genius is that he comes up with a better mousetrap. Sometimes it's a process, sometimes it's a machine. Lots of times it's just seeing a more efficient way to do something that's been done the same way for a hundred years. Like his magnesium process. A long time ago he was down in Arizona where he saw them pumping coal a hundred miles or so through a pipe to an electrical generating plant, and he got the idea that there might be a way to keep other ores in suspension, so they could be pumped that way too, instead of being hauled by truck. So, he patented a process that he's using at his magnesite mines." Jade went on to describe the process at Snakewater.

"Magnesium," Spider mused. "What's it used for?"

"Everything! It's used as a strengthening alloy, in fertilizer, and in different chemicals. It's even used in medicine."

"Well, I know I've had my share of milk of magnesia. It was my mother's cure-all," Spider commented. "So there's a good market for magnesium?"

"Has been. It's getting a little tighter lately, and it doesn't help that profits are going down."

"What's your father like?"

"He's a hard man in some ways, and a marshmallow in others."

"How is he hard?"

Jade thought a moment. "He has a strict moral code and expects everyone to live up to it. Honesty. Integrity. Hard work. That kind of thing. Hates liars. One thing you learn is you never, never lie to my dad."

"And how is he soft?"

"He believes in second chances. If you're upfront about how you've fouled up, the mistakes you've made, he'll give you a second chance. But if you try to fake him out, you're dead. He's really rigid about that. He runs background checks on people he's hiring, fingerprints them and all. If you've done time or been arrested, that's all right as long as you tell him. If you try to hide it, he'll find out, and you're history."

"Huh," Spider grunted. He was just getting ready to ask why he had been summoned to see the morally rigid Brick Tremain when Jade went on.

"Like my brother-in-law. He did time, you know. He was in prison in California. Served a couple of years for fraud, though he says that he didn't know the place he was working was a front for something else. He got off with a lighter sentence than some of the other fellows because he was a witness against them. When he got out he came to Vegas and went to work for my dad. He was upfront about his past, and Dad gave him a chance. He met my sister and. . . . well, he's my brother-in-law now."

"What's your brother-in-law's name?"

"Stan. Stanley Lucas. We call him Stan."

"Stanley Lucas. And how do you feel about having him as a brother-in-law?"

Jade was quiet, staring straight ahead until Spider began to wonder if he had heard the question. Finally he shrugged. "No one ever asked me that question. I was just sixteen when he married my sister."

"And that was how long ago?"

"Six years. She's twelve years older than I am. She was twenty-eight and . . . well, she's not plain. She has really nice features; she just doesn't . . ." Jade shrugged again. "Stan was thirty-five, and knew how to make himself agreeable. I always had the feeling that Stan came in with a plan, and she was part of it—and his plan succeeded. He married Opal and was made regional manager for BTE."

"BTE?"

"Brick Tremain Enterprises. Stan is over all the mining interests in the western United States."

"How has he done in that position? How long has he been there?"

"He's been there five years. How he's done is part of why you're going to see my dad."

"Oh?"

"I don't know what the problem was. I said I was in Dad's confidence, but that was probably an overstatement. I know there was a problem with the mine at Snakewater. It wasn't as profitable as Dad thought it should be, and he sent Stan up to investigate."

"And what did Stan say?"

"I don't know. He never came back."

Spider's brows shot up. "Never came back?"

"Nope."

"Where had he gone?"

"A little town called Chewelah, in eastern Washington."

"So he's still there?"

"No, the police say that he got on the plane to come home, but he never picked up his luggage when he landed. He disappeared."

Spider frowned. "When did this happen?"

"About a month ago."

"And the police have investigated?"

"Well, that depends on your definition of the word *investigate*. My dad doesn't feel that they have. That's why he wants to hire someone else to look into it."

Spider shifted in his seat. All of a sudden he was uncomfortable, feeling that he was occupying the position as an imposter. He had been deputy sheriff of Lincoln County, Nevada, since last November, hired because the previous deputy had crashed head-on into a cliff. At the time, Spider had been unemployed for two years, long enough for him to jump at the chance for the county job. It didn't pay much, but it allowed him and Laurie to stay on in the house they had built. During the eight months he had been deputy he had solved two mysterious deaths, but he didn't think that gave him any background to poke his nose into a case that "real" police had already investigated.

Spider sat in troubled silence, thinking that he should tell Jade to turn around and take him home. He didn't want to be there under false pretenses. He was trying to think of a way to frame the request when the younger man spoke.

"What happened to your pickup?"

"Beg pardon?"

"I saw your pickup. Looked like you wrecked it. How'd that happen?"

Thinking he was sinking any credibility he might have, he told Jade about his disastrous ride over Finlay's Summit the previous month. The gap-toothed grin grew wide as Jade heard the particulars, and he waited only a moment before regaling Spider with the story of how, at sixteen, he had inadvertently driven his sister Opal's VW bug into Lake Mead. It floated out fifty yards before it sank in thirty feet of water. "Dad was furious because there was the potential for an environmental disaster, with the oil and gas causing a slick on top of the water. But none of it got out. He hired a barge and crane and got it hoisted up. But I wasn't allowed to drive again for a year."

Spider laughed at the picture of Jade abandoning ship and went on to describe his first car: a model A that consisted of chassis, seat, and a windowless windshield with a one-gallon gas can strapped to it for a gas tank.

Jade's eyes danced in appreciation, and they spent the rest of the drive to Las Vegas describing various automotive disasters and enjoying it hugely. It was only when they pulled into the basement parking garage of the twenty-five-floor Heritage Tower that Spider began to feel ill at ease again.

SPIDER TRIED TO ORIENT himself as the blue sedan snaked down into the shadowy gray bowels of the parking garage. He pushed away thoughts of how many tons of concrete and steel were balanced above him and instead concentrated on leaving mental breadcrumbs marking the way back out.

Jade made one more turn into a well-lit section of the garage and pulled in beside a red Yugo with black and orange flames painted on the front. Spider looked at it with interest. "I don't think I've ever seen a Yugo," he mused. "Where's it made?"

"Yugoslavia. That's my car," Jade admitted before he turned off the key.

"That right?" Spider got out and stood looking at the small, square auto. "How big is the engine?" he asked over the roof of the Cadillac.

"Just over eleven hundred CCs," Jade said in disgust. "Pedro in the warehouse has a motorcycle bigger than that."

"That so? Huh. Is it easy to get parts?"

Jade shrugged. "It's basically a Fiat. I guess it's all right. This is the Brick Tremain method of keeping me humble." He pressed the button on the keychain to lock the Caddie's doors and joined Spider in front of his car. "He doesn't want me to feel that I'm any better than anyone else who works for BTE. Never mind that Milan Marovic, my fellow night janitor who spoke very little English, drove a Mustang."

"Well, he probably was paying for it himself. I'm assuming your dad gave you the Yugo."

"There is that. Never look gift horses, and all that jazz."

With that, Spider looked around. "Where do we go?"

"This way." Jade headed to the end of the line of cars where an orange elevator door broke the gray expanse of the concrete wall. He punched the button, and they both stared at the light above the elevator until it lit and the chime announced that the lift had arrived.

They rode up two floors to the ground floor lobby, all tinted glass and deep carpet in muted colors. Just off to the right was a wide corridor with a bank of elevators on each side. Jade led the way to one that had just disgorged three Elvis impersonators and held the door open for Spider, who stood looking after the black-pompadoured triplets in white, spangled, bell-bottomed jump-suits. "There's a booking agent on the fifteenth floor," Jade explained.

"Huh," Spider grunted as he stepped inside.

One minute later he followed Jade out of the elevator and across another wide, soft-carpeted corridor to a single elevator door on the opposite wall. "What floor is this?" he asked.

"Twenty-fourth. BTE offices take up the whole twenty-fifth floor."

The elevator door opened and they stepped into the cherry-paneled interior. "Nice wood," Spider commented.

It was a short ride, and a moment later Spider was standing outside the elevator looking through a thirty-foot wall of floor-to-ceiling glass straight out over the city of Las Vegas to the Spring Mountain Range and Charleston Peak. "Wow!" he said, standing transfixed.

"Yeah. It's quite a view." Jade stepped around him and walked to a receptionist's desk. "This is Mr. Latham, Erin. He's here to see my father."

Erin was young and fresh with short blonde hair and a dimple in one cheek when she smiled. The dimple appeared as she looked up at Jade. He pointed to Spider, and she shifted her gaze to the rangy visitor who had strolled over to the window and was looking down at the street below. The suit he wore fit well, with pant legs beveled down to fit over his cowboy boots. With the mountain peak at his back and his dark hair going salt-and-pepper at the temples, Spider carried an aura of urbane ruggedness that made Erin's eyes widen. She picked up the phone and punched in two numbers. "A Mr. Latham to see Mr. Tremain."

Spider looked up when Erin called his name. "Mr. Tremain will see you now, Mr. Latham. If you will follow me, please."

The carpet on the twenty-fifth floor was a soft purplish gray, and it absorbed the sound of their steps as they walked down an interior hall away from the high panorama of the lobby. Erin opened a door, and as she stood aside to let Spider enter, the dimple peeped out.

"This is Mr. Tremain's personal assistant, Bev Compton. Bev, this is Mr. Latham."

Bev was standing in the middle of the room with a file folder in her hand, and she looked up as Erin announced Spider. She was a striking figure, handsome rather than pretty. She was tall and slender, with a mane of flaming red hair. Her complexion was fair, without the usual freckles associated with redheads. She was dressed in a smart, expensive-looking, kelly-green outfit with matching high heels that showed off shapely legs. She regarded Spider with appraising green eyes, and apparently she liked what she saw because she held out her hand and smiled. "How do you do, Mr. Latham," she said in a soft, breathy voice that was oddly out of place with her commanding carriage and presence.

"Pleased to meet you, Miz Compton." As he shook her hand, Spider wondered how many more people he was going to go through before he finally found out what he was here for.

The office was small but nicely furnished and had about ten feet of window-wall revealing the city in the near distance and mountains and sky beyond. Spider had just a moment to glance at the view before Bev opened a communicating door. "Mr. Tremain will see you now, Mr. Latham," she announced in that soft voice. "Can I get you anything? Coffee? Tea?"

"No, thanks." Spider entered the room, expecting from the son's description a rough-hewn, larger-than-life personage. Instead he saw an older version of Jade. A weather-beaten complexion replaced the freckles, and the cowlick had been somewhat tamed by a hairstylist, but when he smiled, Spider saw the same gap in the front teeth. Tremain was dressed in dark suit pants and a crisp white shirt and tie, and he smiled broadly as he rose to greet Spider, extending his hand. "Come in, Mr. Latham. Thank you for dropping everything to come see me."

Spider shook Brick Tremain's hand, but looked beyond him through the transparent outer wall at the vista. That's quite a sight," Spider said. "I don't know how you get any work done."

"Just over those mountains is a place called Pancake Springs. Ever been there?"

"Don't think I have."

"Most people haven't. That's where I grew up. Middle of nowhere, but I learned about rocks there. Learned to smell copper."

"Beg pardon?"

"That's another story." He looked up at his assistant, who was still standing at the open door. "I think that's all, Bev. Thank you."

"Not at all." She closed the door softly.

"That's quite a lady," said Brick. "I couldn't run this company without her. She runs marathons."

"Really runs them, or are you describing her usefulness to the company?"

"Really runs them. Last month she ran one in Washington. Sky to Sea or Sea to Sky or some such thing. Twenty-six miles. Imagine."

"Can't."

"Have a seat, Mr. Latham." Brick Tremain looked at his watch. "I've got a meeting in half an hour that I can't get out of, so I'll get right to it." He waited for Spider to sit down and then sat behind his desk. "Did Jade tell you anything about this mess?"

"Uh, he told me a bit about the company and your son-in-law, but I don't know what I can do to help."

"Well, here's the thing, Mr. Latham. Can I call you Spider? Strange name, but that's what Ace said to call you. How well do you know Ace Lazarra?"

"Not well. She helped me out on a couple of cases." *Here I go again,* Spider thought. *Sounding like a B-movie.*

"She was pretty impressed with you. When I told her I wanted someone honest that I could depend on, she said you fit the bill." Brick looked at his watch. "Here's the thing. My son-in-law, Stan Lucas, was in charge of mining operations in the western U.S. Things were going downhill, generally, but especially at the Snakewater up in Washington—one of our magnesite properties. Stan thought maybe the superintendent or the bookkeeper was cooking the books, or maybe they were in on something together. So, I sent him up for a look-see. He usually visits each plant a couple times a year, just an in-and-out thing, though he'd been up to Chewelah several times already. Said he was worried about it before I noticed something must be wrong. He was up there for a week and was on his way back, said he would sit down with me and go over what he had found. He said it was something significant. But he never made it home."

"But Jade said it was definitely established that he left Chewelah."

"The police said that he got on the airplane at Spokane."

Spider stirred in his seat. "Uh, Mr. Tremain—"

"Call me Brick."

"Uh, Brick, I don't know what you think I can do that the police couldn't."

"Didn't. All they did was check with the airlines and establish that a boarding pass was given out."

"Well, that shows something. I don't have any idea what I could do. I don't have any experience, any credentials as a private investigator. I'm not your man."

Brick looked at his watch again. "Here's the thing. I want you to talk to my daughter, Opal. After that, if you don't want to go, well, that's that."

He closed his eyes for a moment. "Look, Spider. I don't know what you can do, either. But I want someone to try. I want to be able to tell my daughter that someone tried, someone I can trust. Someone who will give an honest effort."

"When you say go, you mean you want someone to go to Chewelah?"

"No. I want *you* to go to Chewelah. Nose around; see what you can find out. See if you can find the 'significant thing' that Stan found. Maybe that will help us learn what's happened to him. Remember, though, that he never made it home."

"Uh. . . ."

Brick spread his hands wide. "Look, I don't know what to do. I'm at my wits' end and getting no help from the police. Ace said you could help me. And Opal sits there . . ." Brick took an envelope out of his desk drawer and pushed it over to Spider. "I know what you make in a month—that stuff's a matter of public record. I'll pay you that per week, plus expenses. And here's a bonus for agreeing to go. Now, when can you leave?"

"Uh, I don't know that I can." Spider lifted the flap of the envelope and looked inside at the stack of green bills, all one-hundred-dollar denomination. He riffled them with his thumbnail and lost count at thirteen. Frowning, he sat a moment trying to judge his gut reaction, trying to see if things felt right.

Brick broke in impatiently. "All right. I'll double the offer. Twice your monthly salary per week. But the bonus stays the same."

"Well, thank you Mr. Tremain. That's very . . . fair." Remembering Ace's admonition, Spider changed at the last minute and substituted fair for generous. "But there's the problem of the job I have for Lincoln County. I don't know that I'm free to leave."

"I'll make sure that you're free. I have influence that I can bring to bear."

"On a sheriff?" Spider's frown deepened.

"Oh, don't bow up. I'm not talking about bribes. The sheriff can always use a donation to his campaign fund. And there's nothing illegal about him giving you a few weeks off without pay." When Spider's expression didn't change, Brick continued, "Don't tell me you don't know that that happens all the time! It's the American way. You scratch my back, I'll scratch yours."

Spider stood and handed the envelope back. "Well, I'll tell you, Mr. Tremain, I'll talk to Opal, see how I feel. If I decide it's something I want to do, I'll see if I can wangle the time off. But that's between me and the sheriff, and you're not involved. As for payment, I'll accept the bonus and your first offer. I make no promises except that I'll do my best."

Brick smiled. "You drive a hard bargain, Spider Latham." He held out his hand. "Ace was right about you! When can you start? We're already a month behind."

"If I decide to do it, I'll go back today and talk to the sheriff. If he gives me leave, I can begin tomorrow."

"Fine, fine. I'll turn you over to Bev. She'll arrange for transportation—tickets and car and all that. Anything you need or want to know, ask her."

"And I want word from you that I have access to anything I want as far as the outfit is concerned in Chewelah."

"She'll attend to that also." Brick stood and walked to a closet where he extracted his suit coat. Leaving the door open, he put on the coat and regarded himself in the full-length mirror on the inside of the door. Catching Spider watching him, he said, "I'm meeting two senators and a couple of lobbyists for the mining industry. It's a pretty important engagement."

"I wish you success."

"Thank you." Brick looked up as the communicating door opened. "I'm just going, Bev. I need you to take care of Mr. Latham. Get him fixed up with transportation to Chewelah. Credit cards, you know what to do. He wants a letter of introduction from me giving him access to anything up there. And give him the file on everything we've received—police reports, the whole thing. Take care of that, will you?" Brick looked at Spider. "Anything else?"

"That's all predicated on if I can get the time off."

"You'll manage."

"I'll need a ride home today."

"Bev will take care of that, too."

Bev nodded at Spider as she walked across to a door beside the closet. She opened it and stood as doorstop, turning her attention to Brick Tremain. "Here's a list of the names of the people you're meeting and brief notes about each," she said in her soft, breathy voice. "First name is French, so pronounce the end with a long *a* rather than a *t*, like Chevrolet."

Brick took the card Bev handed him and scanned it. Then he put it in his inside coat pocket.

"Got your cell phone?"

In answer, Brick patted his belt where his cell phone was clipped.

"Jade will pick you up at the door downstairs and take you to your meeting. He will come back here, as you are to ride with the senators to the luncheon meeting. He will be at the Luxor to pick you up afterward. I'll make sure that he gets there by three, when the meeting is supposed to be over. He'll be prepared to wait until you're finished if you have something that keeps you longer."

"Thanks, Bev. I won't be back today. Take care of Mr. Latham." Brick sketched a wave to Spider and disappeared into the hallway.

Bev moved to let the door close behind her and smiled at Spider. "If you will follow me, Mr. Latham, let's see what we can do for you."

MR. LATHAM FOLLOWED BEV into her office. "Call me Spider."

Bev had a file drawer open and turned with arched eyebrows. "What did you say?"

"When you say 'Mr. Latham' I keep thinking you're talking about my dad. Call me Spider."

The green eyes blinked. She picked a folder out of the drawer and shut it decisively. "All right." Putting the folder on the edge of her desk, she indicated a nearby chair. "If you will sit down, I will find out what we need to do."

Spider sat. While she was busy elsewhere, he examined a framed poster that hung on the opposite wall behind the desk. It pictured a surging crowd of people, all in running attire with numbers pinned to chest and back. "Are you in that batch?" Spider asked, pointing.

Seated at the desk with a note pad and pencil, Bev looked behind, and her flaming hair followed the arc of the turn like sinuous crimson silk, showing copper highlights in the sun.

"Yes. Can you find me?" she challenged.

Spider stood and moved closer. "Is this like finding Waldo? Are you wearing a red and white striped hat?"

"No, but I'm wearing the number sixty-six."

"What race is this?"

"It's last year's Boston Marathon."

"No kidding! Huh." Spider stood intently, scanning the throng as Bev wrote numbered items on the spiral notebook. "I give up."

Turning her chair around, Bev stood in one fluid motion and pointed to a figure in center backfield, a face and shoulders only; nothing else was visible at that distance and camera angle.

"But I can't see your number!" Spider protested.

"I didn't say you could see it. I only said I was wearing it on that day."

Spider met Bev's eyes for a moment, one eyebrow lifted a fraction. There was the suggestion of squaring about her shoulders and a ghost of a smile on her lips.

Spider was first to look away. "I see," he said in a neutral tone and returned to his seat.

Bev picked up her pencil from the desk, playing with it as she leaned against the filing cabinet and looked down under lowered lashes at Spider. "So," she said. "Are you with us?"

Spider considered a moment. "That depends."

"On what?"

"Well, first, I'm going to talk to Opal Lucas. Then, if I think it's something I ought to do, I'll go back home, talk to my boss about time off."

"And your talk with Opal will be key to your decision?"

"Yes ma'am."

Bev regarded him for a moment, and he returned her gaze. "Okay," she said, sitting at the desk and pulling the notebook to her. "Case closed. We might as well get everything in train right now. It'll save time later. What's the soonest you can leave?" She looked up and forestalled his protest, "If you decide to go."

"If I decide to go . . ." Spider gave the same emphasis as Bev, " . . . and if I can get time off, I could leave tomorrow morning."

"All right, then. I'll get arrangements made for a plane ticket," she glanced up, "refundable, of course. I'll have a car there for you. Motel room. Credit card. Ummm . . . letter of introduction. I imagine you were fingerprinted when you were hired as deputy, so . . ."

"Nope."

Bev looked up, pencil poised on number six. "Beg pardon?"

"I wasn't fingerprinted."

"No background check?"

"Nope."

She leaned back in her chair. "So, how did they know you didn't have a shadowy past?"

"I don't think there are too many 'shadowy pasts' in Lincoln County. Since the mines closed, if you're there it's because you've been there all your life and are bent on staying. Everyone's life is pretty much out in the sunshine. Aren't many secrets around there."

"I see. Well . . ." Bev pushed her chair back and stood up. Spider was beginning to wonder about the soft, smooth voice that was so at odds with the decisive, almost controlling, mannerisms. He wondered if the tonal inflections were natural or assumed, and what it cost her to maintain the façade, if indeed that's what it was.

" . . . company policy is that everyone is fingerprinted. I need to make an ID tag for you, too. My camera is in the shop. Hmmm, let me see your driver's license."

Spider obediently fished out his wallet and opened it to reveal his deputy sheriff's badge. He extracted his Nevada license and handed it to Bev. She took it and examined the picture.

"This is great. I'll just use the picture off this for the ID tag." She sat at her computer and put the license in a scanner. While it was uploading, she tapped the folder on the edge of the desk. "Pre-employment packet," she said. "For if you decide you're with us."

Spider opened the folder, but instead of looking inside, he watched with interest as his license appeared on the screen. Bev manipulated his image to another screen and typed relevant information into spaces provided. When she hit print, out came an official looking document that she fed into a small laminator on the shelf beside her desk. Trimming the rigid plastic ID, she then took a tool out of a drawer and put a metal eyelet through one corner. From another drawer she drew a lanyard that had "BTE" woven into it all the way around, clicked it through the eyelet, and dropped it in front of Spider.

"You haven't even begun your paperwork," she chided.

"I'm too interested watching you do your work."

"I'll leave you alone to do it and go get set up to fingerprint." Pushing her chair tidily in, she left the room, and the sound of her footsteps were lost in the deep pile of the carpet.

Spider got to the matter at hand, and by the time she returned, he was just finishing his W-4 form. Silently, Bev picked up the stack of papers and riffled through them. "Fine," she pronounced as she evened up the edges and put them back in the folder. "Follow me."

Spider trailed out the door, down the hall, and into a kitchen, where a fingerprinting apparatus was set up. "Grab a paper towel," she directed, rolling out the ink. Spider did as she directed, stood where he was told to stand, and tried to relax his hand and not help as she rolled each finger, printing the image in the proper place. He watched with interest as the circular whorls appeared, etched in black ink on the white cardstock, and he tried not to show that this was the first time he had seen the process done. *I need to tell Brick Tremain that I can't do this,* he thought. *He'll be wasting his money.*

"Wipe your hands with the towel, then wash them at the sink. Use this." Bev handed him a bottle of soap, and while he worked at getting the ink out from under his fingernails, she cleaned off her tools and put them away on the top shelf. Spider noticed the ridge in her arms as she lifted the weight of the glass roller board. It reminded him of Laurie's arms when she was stacking hay bales in the barn.

Closing the cupboard door, Bev said, "Now, let's get you on your way to Opal's house." The command was implied as she left the kitchen, and he mentally saluted before following.

"How well do you know Las Vegas?" she asked when he was again seated in front of her desk.

"I can get around all right."

She spread a map in front of him. "This is where we are. When you exit the garage, turn right and go two blocks. Take a right, and you're on Charleston Boulevard. Just stay on that, and you go clear out here, to Moonshadow Estates. There's a big sign; you can't miss it. Turn in at the entrance. Tell them at the gate you're to see Opal Lucas. Take the first right, then the first left then the first right, and it's at the end of the cul-de-sac."

"Moonshadow Estates, through the gate, right-left-right. Got it."

"Okay. Here's what I'm going to do." Bev opened a cupboard and scanned the keys hanging on the inside of the door. "I'm going to give you a BTE vehicle to drive to Opal's. Then you can take it on home and bring it back tomorrow." She held up her hand for silence when she saw Spider about to speak. "If, after talking to Opal, you decide you can't go, then come back here and someone in the mail room can take you home."

Bev selected a set of keys and then picked up the telephone, punching three buttons. "Hello, Maria. Is Jade back yet? Yes, thanks . . . Jade? I want you to meet Mr. Latham at the elevator and take him down to the garage. I've given him the keys to number seven, so help him find it. Okay?" Spider heard something that sounded like "oooowww" coming from the phone. Bev said a soft, "Thanks," and smiled as she put down the receiver.

She handed Spider the keys and turned back to the cupboard, taking out a small strongbox and opening it with a key she had in her pocket. "When did America declare independence?" she asked with her back still to Spider.

"Beg pardon?"

Bev turned around with a credit card in her hand. "When was the Declaration of Independence signed?"

"1776," said Spider, mystified.

"That's the pin number for this card. You can sign for things or get money from an ATM using that pin. Don't lose it, and don't forget the pin.

And bring me all receipts." She handed the card to Spider. "I think that's it. You'll get your letter of introduction tomorrow. I'll get you on the first flight out after noon, so if you're here by ten, Jade can take you to the airport. Better plan on staying a week or more."

"Uh, what about the folder? The information you already have?"

Bev picked up a file out of a basket on her desk and carried it with her to the door. "Jade will meet you at the elevator and get you on your way." Offering him the folder, she said, "Good-bye, Spider. It was nice to meet you."

"My pleasure," Spider said automatically, taking the file in his free hand, but as he walked down the hall the term *railroaded* held new meaning.

Jade was waiting at the elevator, his brow like a thundercloud. He jabbed at the down arrow and stood with his hands in his pockets and his shoulders hunched.

As they stepped into the private elevator, Spider asked, "Something go wrong with your day?"

Jade shook his head but continued scowling. Spider assumed a benign mien and worked on inventing an excuse not to become embroiled in BTE affairs. At the twenty-fourth floor, the doors opened and Spider exited first, crossing to push the summons button on the opposite wall. Jade slouched out after him, and when they were again falling toward the ground, Spider heard Jade mutter something that sounded like, "Red-headed witch!"

Spider eyed him. "Something going on that I missed?"

"She knows I don't like her, and she goes out of her way to needle me."

"Because she asked you to take me to the garage?"

"Because she gave you the brand new Mustang convertible!"

"She did!" Spider grinned, mentally picturing himself driving with the top down, one elbow resting on the windowsill, wind ruffling his hair. "Did she, now!"

"Yes!" Jade was speaking through gritted teeth. "She knows I'd give my right arm to drive that car. But Brick Tremain's son might think he's better than someone else if he drove it. He gets to drive the Yugo. And just to rub it in, I get to send you off in that car."

"Uh, I see," Spider said as they reached the lobby and walked to the basement elevator. He wasn't sure he did, but it had a soothing sound, and it was a sop to his conscience. He, Spider, after all, was going to be driving a new Mustang convertible, while Jade, the boss's son, was left with something less.

They went the rest of the way in silence. When they got to the BTE parking area Jade stolidly led the way past the blue Caddie, past the Yugo with flames, and around a pillar. "There," he said, pointing.

It was the way he said it that got to Spider. Without hope. Spider looked at the red convertible gleaming under the lights at the end of the row. He looked at the bleak young man beside him, held out the Mustang keys and asked, "So what will that Yugo do?"

Jade didn't know at first what he meant. He looked at the keys, looked at Spider, looked at the keys again, and back to Spider, and an incredulous smile split his face.

"You're kidding!"

"Naw. I'm afraid I'll start thinkin' I'm better than other people. I'm better off driving the other one."

Jade grabbed Spider's hand and wrung it. "Oh, thank you, Spider. Thank you!"

"If you sink this one, you're on your own," Spider warned.

"Don't worry. I'll be careful. Here." Jade fished the Yugo keys out of his pocket and gave them to Spider. "You have to push down on the gearshift to get it into reverse," he said, as they retraced their steps. "Sometimes it likes to die when you're stopped at a stop sign, so you have to turn your foot to the side to keep giving it gas while you've got the brake on. And, when you first start it, if it dies, the next time you try, you have to hold the accelerator clear to the floor when you crank it. Let it off the minute it catches." He opened the door for Spider. "I think that's all." He hesitated a moment, his brow clouding again. "You sure you want to do this?"

"Sure. I think I'll make more of a splash in Lincoln County in this than in the other one, anyway."

Spider got in and, after examining the instrument panel and locating the lights and windshield wipers, he put the key in the ignition and turned it. The engine caught quickly, a whiny whir that promised a long ride home. Jade closed the door and stepped away as Spider, mindful to push the gearshift down, put the car into reverse, and backed out. His eyes crinkled as he smiled ruefully, thinking that it was better than hitch-hiking. Only just. Then he set himself to finding his way out of the parking labyrinth.

MOONSHADOW ESTATES WAS a fairly new, upscale neighborhood of large Spanish-style homes with white stucco walls, tile roofs, and cactus-and-gravel landscaping. Spider found the Lucas house and pulled up in front, letting the car idle as he considered the chances of finding someone home. The house had a deserted look. There was a weathered, rolled-up newspaper lying beside a saguaro cactus in the front yard, and all the blinds in the front of the house were closed. When the Yugo sputtered and died, Spider figured it must be time to try the door.

The two-story house had a wrought-iron-fenced balcony that was supported by arches, forming a covered veranda across the front of the house. It would have been pleasant, had it been graced by some flowerpots and wicker furniture, but it was bare, save for little piles of sand that had blown in and drifted up against the walls. Spider was grateful for the shade promised by the veranda, since he had discovered to his dismay that the Yugo didn't have air conditioning. With his suit coat and tie off and the top button on his dress shirt undone, he hoped he didn't look too rumpled. Wondering what he was going to say and missing his Stetson, Spider rang the bell. Usually he would be holding his hat at a time like this, but now he had nothing to do with his hands. They felt large and useless, hanging at his side, and he resisted the inclination to shove them in his pockets.

No one answered. He waited, glancing up and down the street, then rang the bell again. He was rewarded with a sound from inside, and finally the door opened.

The minute Spider saw Opal Lucas he knew he was headed for Chewelah. She had the look of a porcelain Madonna. Very fair, with pale, translucent skin and soft blue eyes, she had hair that was almost platinum. It was the color of his son Bobby's hair when he was a tow-headed toddler, and it hung straight down from a part in the middle. Of medium height, she was rail thin and looked waif-like, dressed in Levi's, a blue scooped-neck tee, and flip-flops. Jade had been right; she did have good features. But she did nothing with artifice or makeup to enhance them, so what one saw, if one noticed her at all, was this pale, serene, sweet-sad presence. Mostly she went unnoticed, Spider figured, and wondered if she wanted it that way.

Opal stood a moment, still grasping the open door, gazing at her visitor. "You must be Mr. Latham," she said finally, holding out her hand.

"Yes. Glad to meet you." He was surprised at the confidence in her grasp.

"Jade called me and told me you were coming over." Her eyes looked past him to the Yugo at the curb. "He said you were a friend." Her eyes twinkled and the corners of her mouth turned sweetly up.

Spider returned the smile. "I figure if your dad trusts him with a Cadillac, there's no harm in him driving the Mustang. Uh . . ." He looked down at the toe of his boot, as if his next line would be written there. "Did Jade tell you what I was coming over to talk to you about?"

"Yes. Excuse me for keeping you on the doorstep. I don't have a lot of visitors, and I'm afraid my manners are a little rusty. Come in." Opal moved back and opened the door wider, an invitation to step inside.

Spider stepped. He found himself in a two-story entryway, with a fountain sitting in the curve of a stairway ascending to a second-floor mezzanine. Banister and upstairs railing were wrought iron, walls were white plaster, floor was unglazed terra-cotta tile, and all was flooded with light from second story windows. The dimensions of the entryway were impressive, but the fountain was dry, and there were cardboard boxes and bundles of pamphlets stacked against the walls.

Opal closed the door and invited Spider to follow her through an archway into the shadowy living room. "If you can see the couch, sit down," she said. "I'll get some light in here. I don't ever use this room, so I never open the drapes."

As the curtains parted Spider was able to see that the room was very handsome, with bold-colored, heavy-framed pictures accenting the neutral tones of carpet, walls, and window treatment. "You have a lovely home," he tried as an opening gambit.

Opal sat in an easy chair opposite him and looked around as if noticing for the first time. "Stan wanted it. He picked it out and had it decorated. He liked . . . likes nice things . . ." Her voice trailed off.

"Uh, I know this is painful for you."

"Actually, it's better to be talking about it. When I'm alone with only my thoughts, things get kind of crazy. I get kind of crazy."

"What do you think happened to your husband, Mrs. Lucas?"

"Terrible things happen to people, Mr. Latham."

"Spider."

"What do spiders have to do with it?"

"No. That's me. I'm Spider."

"I thought Jade said your name was Spencer."

Spider shook his head. "Spider."

Opal sat and looked at him with the still way she had, smiling faintly. "All right then, Spider. And you must call me Opal. I was saying that terrible things happen to people. No one knows that more than I. I don't know why I should think that Stanley, or I, should be immune."

"What do you mean by 'terrible things'?"

"Being kidnapped and sold into slavery."

Spider blinked. His brow wrinkled and he looked through the archway to the lighted entryway, searching for his bearings, thinking things were getting a little too far out of whack here. "Uh, let me get this straight. You think your husband was kidnapped and sold into slavery?"

"No. I said that that is one of the terrible things that happen."

"Here? In America?"

"No. Though we do have things happening here that are near slavery. What I'm talking about happens in Africa. In Mali children are kidnapped, or worse, sold by their parents, and taken to the Ivory Coast and put to work producing cocoa. Thousands of them. Think of that next time you drink a cup of hot chocolate. African children are slaves in Benin, in Gabon, and in Sudan."

"Uh, I didn't know."

"Most people don't."

Spider didn't have an answer, and the silence seemed to stretch out forever. Opal sat quietly, staring at the pattern of the sunshine on the rug, and Spider fidgeted with a wind-up toy that was sitting on the coffee table in front of him. Just as he was thinking he should excuse himself and take the Yugo back to BTE, Opal raised her eyes and met his.

"What I'm trying to say is, I don't know what happened to Stan, but I'm not the only person in the world who doesn't know what has happened to someone they love. If it happens to thousands of parents in Africa, am I any better than they when it happens to me?"

"Do you want me to see if I can find him, or at least find out what happened to him?"

Opal didn't move. She sat with hands clenched in her lap as tears welled up and ran down her pale cheeks. "I would be forever in your debt," she whispered.

"Well, all right then." Spider set the toy back down on the table, then seemed to realize what he had been playing with. "Uh, do you and Stan have any children?"

"That toy belongs to my housekeeper's little boy. Stan doesn't have any children, but I have. Would you like to see their pictures?" A smile lit her face and she stood.

"Yeah, sure!" Spider rose, and when she led the way through the archway into the entry hall, he followed. She continued on into what was meant to have been a formal dining room, but the handsome mahogany table and buffet were piled with more bundles of paper and cardboard cartons.

Spider stepped around a box marked Sunrise Printers to stand beside the pale wisp of a woman who glowed with an inner fire as she pointed with her upraised right hand. There were fifty pictures covering the wall, each eight-by-ten, framing a smiling black face. "These are my children." Pointing to the first on the top row, she said, "This is Malick. He was one of those who worked in the cocoa trade. He was taken as a slave when he was ten. I redeemed him when he was thirteen."

"Redeemed?"

"I bought him back. I work with an international organization that raises money to buy back children that have been sold into slavery—either by kidnappers or by their parents."

"So, you paid money for each of these children? Is that legal?"

"Is slavery legal?"

"No, not here. I would hope it isn't anywhere else."

"And yet it exists."

Spider stepped closer to look at the faces of the children. The smile on the lips didn't always reach to the eyes. But sometimes it did.

"But, if you're the one buying the slaves, aren't you creating a market?"

"And that's a reason to do nothing?" The serenity was gone, and patches of color tinged her cheeks as she spoke with passion. "The market is there, whether I buy any children or not. I'm doing what I can to save as many as I can. I'd do more, if I had more money."

Spider indicated the pictures. "What does it cost? To free a child?"

"Thirty-five dollars."

"You're kidding!"

"No. The price of having your hair done, or dinner out for you and your wife. The price of a child's freedom."

"Huh." Spider let his gaze wander over the thin faces on the wall.

Opal looked at her watch. "Look, Spider, I want to talk to you about Stan, but I've got someone coming in fifteen minutes, and I have to have all these envelopes ready to mail out. Can you help me, and we can talk while we stuff? It's mindless work."

"Yeah. Sure. What do you want me to do?"

"How about if you sit there and put one of these and one of these in the envelope. Then I'll seal them and stack them according to zip code."

"You got it." Spider pulled out a chair and sat down at the table where indicated, next to two stacks of brochures. One was entitled "Modern-day Slavery Fact Sheet" and the other "Slave Redemption Program." Both were put out by an organization called Free the Children. "One of each?" he questioned, getting ready to start.

"One of each."

Spider began, but took a moment to turn the pile of envelopes around for an easier workflow. "When did you last see Stan?" he asked, when he got a routine going.

"It was Memorial Day. We went out on the lake waterskiing with Jade during the day. Then we went home and he packed and left."

"Did you take him to the airport?"

"No, my dad's assistant, Bev, picked him up and took him. She wanted to go over some last-minute details with him. He had asked her to find some information for him before he went up to Snakewater, and they hadn't had time to go over it."

"And do you know that he arrived at Chewelah?"

"Oh, yes. He called me from there once, and he called the office several times and talked to Dad and to Bev."

"But you're absolutely sure he was in Chewelah? There's no chance he was someplace else, just saying he was there? Not . . . " Spider temporized when she started to say something, " . . . that I'm saying that happened. But, when the logical things don't pan out, sometimes you have to look at the illogical."

Opal shook her head. "No, because the mine superintendent called Dad complaining about Stan being there. He was there for sure."

"Did Stanley have any enemies?" *I'm sounding like a grade-B movie again,* Spider thought.

Opal wrinkled her brow in concentration. She grimaced. "You don't like to think of your husband having enemies, but he may have had. He lived a different life before he came to Nevada. He was very open about the mistakes he made before, and some of them were pretty serious. There are people who might like to do him harm, but I think they are all still in prison. He got two years. They got ten. Let's see, ummmm . . . they won't be out 'til next year, I think."

"What about if someone gets time off for good behavior, or out on parole?"

"I don't know about that. I don't know." She shook her head. "Is that possible?"

"I don't know. Might be something to look into." Spider grabbed another bunch of envelopes out of the box and replenished his stack of brochures. "Did Stan tell you what he had found in Chewelah? Did he say he was uneasy or think he was in any kind of danger?"

"No. Those are the kinds of questions the police asked me, too."

"The Chewelah police?"

"No, the Las Vegas police. He apparently disappeared here."

"Then why am I going to Chewelah?"

Opal shrugged. "Dad thinks the key is in Chewelah and in what Stan found."

"Then I guess I need the information that he got from Bev before he went up, don't I? That may be the place to start. Do you have any more envelopes?"

"We're finished! Thank you for helping me." Opal tidied the stacks and placed them in boxes ready to be picked up. "Is there anything else you want to ask?"

"No. I've got the information that Bev had in a file. I'll read that, and I might have another question or two after that. I wonder though, do you have a picture of Stan? One that I could use?"

Opal hesitated. "I have only one. Oh, I have snaps, but only one portrait."

Spider started to say something, but she held up her hand. "No. I know, you need it. Wait here." She jumped to her feet and disappeared for a moment, coming back with an eight-by-ten photo of a handsome man in a glamour pose, one shoulder lowered and looking down with a warm smile on his lips. It was signed in the corner with a broad, bold script: "All my love, Stan."

Spider stood and took the picture. "I'll keep it safe. Don't worry."

"I don't." Opal followed him back to the entry hall. As he turned to take leave, she tucked two brochures in his shirt pocket and patted them. "Put these where they will do some good," she said.

"I know just who to give them to." Spider opened the door and stepped out onto the shade of the veranda.

"Be careful, Spider. I would hate for anything to happen to you because you took my problem as yours."

"I will. Good-bye." Spider offered his hand and she took it.

"Good-bye."

Walking in the sun down the sidewalk, Spider wished he had a short-sleeved shirt on. As he got into the Yugo the black vinyl seat was scorching, and he immediately felt sweat forming in his hairline and on the back of his neck. The engine whined to life on the first try, and as he pulled away from the curb he thought that the flames painted on the hood of the little square car were appropriate. Driving the Yugo was like driving an oven on a roller skate.

Skate 'n' Bake, he thought. *Well, let's get at it.*

C H A P T E R

THREE-AND-A-HALF HOT AND sweaty hours later, Spider pulled into the parking lot of the courthouse in Pioche, county seat of Lincoln County, Nevada, population 3,500. Pioche was a mining town that clung to the shaft-riddled hills like an aging and seedy limpet. It had been a booming and boisterous success twice—once in the nineteenth century, once in the twentieth—but it had been almost half a century now since the last glory days. When the mines closed no one entertained much hope that they would ever reopen.

Spider frowned when he saw that Sheriff Dan Brown's car wasn't in the parking lot. He pulled into a spot in the shade and sat in thought, staring at the high, double-sashed window of the sheriff's office complex until he saw Randi Lee's face, faintly blurry through the eighteenth-century windowpane, peering out.

Spider felt the back of his shirt sticking to him as he got out. Looking up, he saw Randi's brows arch as she recognized who belonged to the Yugo. Grinning at her reaction, he walked to the front of the courthouse and pushed through the large, ornate wooden doors that had helped make the courthouse a regional architectural wonder when it was built well over a century before.

The coolness in the courthouse owed less to air conditioning than to the thickness of the walls and vents in the attic that let a prevailing cross breeze blow the hot air out. Spider nodded at Mrs. Beal emerging from the assessor's office, but he didn't stop to exchange pleasantries. Randi was waiting for him at the door of the sheriff's office, and she was grinning.

"I can't wait to hear the story that goes along with that car," she greeted.

"I'll tell it to you if you help wangle me a couple of weeks off."

Randi was Spider's ally in the sheriff's office. She was tall and raw-boned, with an honest face and direct gray eyes. Underpaid and under-appreciated by the elected official she supported, she cared about the county and the people enough to make sure things ran smoothly, which probably ensured Dan Brown's reelection. She had once suggested to Spider that he might like to run, but Spider had countered that she would do a better job than either he or Sheriff Brown, and he would be glad to organize her campaign.

Randi perched on the edge of a desk and pointed to a chair. "Sit and tell me what you've got in mind."

"I've been asked to go up to Washington state and do some investigating. I need two weeks off. Without pay."

Randi turned her head to stare out the window, and her eyes narrowed in thought. "This have anything to do with that affair last month? The Rocky Ridge thing?"

"Not really. The person who recommended me for this job helped me out there—someone I know in Vegas. But this is something completely different. I'm probably out of my league here—I'm definitely out of my league—but I feel that I need to make a try."

"Your son lives in Washington, doesn't he?"

"Yeah. Seattle."

"Any chance you could arrange to see him while you're there?"

"I don't know. Where I'm going is a ways away from Seattle. Where you heading with this?"

"Well, you might have a better chance of getting the time off if you were taking some personal time to go see your son. Sheriff Brown wasn't too pleased that you solved the Rocky Ridge thing while he was out of town. If you're doing some private investigation work . . ." Randi held up her hand to stop Spider's protestations. " . . . it wouldn't set too well. If I suggest to him that with the money that would go to your salary the sheriff's department could buy a base radio, and if I can get Mr. Higarten to write an article for the paper about the sheriff getting one, then maybe he would see your going in a good light. But you need to let me handle it. You just fill out the time-off requisition and leave it with me."

Spider grimaced. "I was planning on leaving tomorrow. They kinda need to know right away so they can buy the tickets."

Randi got a form out of a file cabinet and gave it to Spider. "Tell them to go ahead. I think I can make it happen."

"Thanks, Randi." He took a pen out of his pocket and began filling out the requisition.

"Now, what's the story about the car?"

Spider chuckled, and when he had checked two boxes and signed his name, he handed the form back and proceeded to tell her the story of Jade Tremain and the Mustang.

Randi laughed at the story, but cautioned, "I hope the dad won't be angry that you went around his back by letting the boy have the convertible. You may be walking into a nest of hornets there. Are you sure you want the time off?"

Spider stood. "Yeah. I need a new hat. Figured I'd get me one with the extra money." He extended his hand. "Thanks."

"Take care, Spider. We need you back in one piece."

"You got it." Spider touched a nonexistent hat brim and headed back out to the Yugo. Grateful for the shade that kept the seats from searing his backside, he got in and drove to Buck's Western Wear, where he bought a new Stetson just like the one he lost at Finlay's Summit. Then he headed back down the hill to Meadow Valley and home.

Spider and Laurie had 120 acres of prime grazing land with a year-round spring that sat three miles down a gravel road off Highway 93 just past Panaca. Spider made the turnoff and went half a mile before the Yugo coughed and sputtered, caught and whirred along again for a few hundred yards, sputtered again, and died. "Great Suffering Zot!" Spider exclaimed. "What's this?"

There was still a quarter of a tank of gas. No warning lights on. No apparent reason for the car to die. Spider pulled the hood latch and got out, fumbling a moment and burning his hands on the hot metal, groping to find the release lever to raise the hood. He stood and inspected the engine, felt the alternator, and checked for loose wires or vacuum hoses. All seemed as it should be.

Spider was so intent, with his head down in the engine compartment, that he didn't hear the approaching pickup until it was just about on him. He straightened up and saw that it was Laurie, coming from the direction of home, with her mother-in-law riding shotgun.

She pulled alongside and rolled down her window. "You're out of gas," she said. "I brought you some."

Spider shook his head. "Naw, it's not that. I don't know what it is."

"Trust me. You're out of gas." Laurie's eyes crinkled at the corners. "A fellow by the name of Jade Tremain called and said he forgot to tell you that it runs out of gas at a quarter of a tank. He said he didn't know if you had enough to make it home. I was heading out to rescue you. Spider, what are you doing driving that outlandish car?"

"You may call it outlandish, but I've got a few other names to call it. It's a long story, and I'll tell you all about it when we get home."

Spider lifted a two-gallon gas can out of the back of the truck and, after locating the gas cap, began pouring it in the Yugo.

"It's lucky I had some gas for the tiller in the barn," Laurie observed.

Spider just grunted. When he finished, he capped the gas can and put it back in the pickup bed, looking up to find Laurie watching him with twinkling eyes. "I'll follow you home," she said and rolled past to a place where she could turn the pickup around.

★   ★   ★

It turned out to be evening before Spider had a chance to tell Laurie about his day. The news she had from the doctor in Cedar City drove everything else from his mind.

"It's congestive heart failure." Laurie had said, and went on to explain that was the cause of the swollen, weeping legs. It wasn't necessarily dire. The doctor had given her some medicine and told her to wrap the legs in ace bandages and keep them elevated as much as possible. And no salt.

Spider felt a tightness around his heart. "Well, that's that. I'll call Brick first thing tomorrow morning and tell him I can't go."

"Why on earth would you do that, after you've made all these arrangements?"

"I can't leave Mother like this."

"Like what? She's been on this downward slide for some time. This is just another stage. The doctor said he's seen people in her condition live on for quite a while."

Somewhat reassured, Spider helped put his mother to bed, and when Laurie left Rachel Latham's bedroom, he hung behind to rock in the rocker and reminisce in a rambling monolog that bore no resemblance to the lively conversations he used to have with his mother.

When Rachel finally dropped off to sleep, Spider quietly joined Laurie in the living room, where she was reading a brochure from the doctor.

"I'll stay if you want me to," he said.

"There's no need. Really, Spider, she's doing fine. I just have to watch the legs and make sure that ulcers don't develop."

Laurie set the brochure aside. "So tell me again, how did you happen to be driving that car? I had an idea you'd be going and coming in a limousine."

Spider told her the story of his day, describing Brick Tremain and his children and the problem they wanted help with. When he told Laurie about Opal, he gave her the leaflets that Opal had tucked in his pocket.

"Spider, all of this sounds fantastic! Missing husbands and slaves in Africa and a paranoid company owner who hires an ex-con but has you, a deputy sheriff, fingerprinted. And what happened to his wife? Opal and Jade's mother? Where is she? And why is he sending you to—where is it? Chihuahua?"

"It's a town just north of Spokane. Chewelah."

"So why is he sending you to Chewelah if they've established that the son-in-law actually left the area?"

"Brick thinks that the reason for the disappearance has to do with something that Stan found in Chewelah. Something that he discovered."

"Well, he's paying you well to go there, even if it's a goose chase. What about this?" She held up Opal's pamphlet. "Do you think this is on the up-and-up? Could it be a scam?"

"If it is, I don't think she's the scammer. But she could be a scam-ee. I don't know if she's been to Africa and seen the children or not. I don't know. She seemed genuine."

"When do you leave?"

"Tomorrow morning. I may be gone a couple of weeks."

"That would be two months' salary! Um. . . ." Laurie looked down, and her cheeks flushed. "I have a confession to make."

Spider raised his eyebrows. "What?"

"Do you remember, last month on Fast Sunday, when you were talking about tithes and offerings?"

"Vaguely. What was I saying?"

"You said that tithing was a commandment, and obedience was expected, and so paying tithing didn't necessarily 'cut any ice' with the Lord. But our free-will offerings, you said, are how we show that we truly love the Savior—by giving of our substance to the poor. That really struck me, and so I doubled our fast offering and matched it with the same amount to the humanitarian fund."

"And . . . ?"

"And the next thing I know, you get two months' salary dropped in your lap. Just when we're going to need extra money for doctors. It's a little bit awesome."

"Yeah, well you need to learn the difference between high-sounding words and putting things into practice. I wasn't necessarily advocating that we do something."

"But what you said is so true! You know, I've discovered in this last reading of the Book of Mormon that it wasn't because the Nephites became rich that the Lord allowed the Lamanites in to chastise them. It's that they became rich and wouldn't take care of the poor. I never saw that before."

"Well, taking care of the poor is a bit more complex than just doubling your fast offering."

"Oh, I know." Laurie fingered the pamphlets. "Like this. I think that we need to give to this place. We can afford to free one child. If it's a scam, then it's like King Benjamin says, we need to give to the beggars and not say, 'he brought it on himself.' We can't not give because we don't know for sure."

"Opal told me to give those to someone where it would do some good. I knew just who to give it to."

"Yeah. But from then on I think we'll concentrate on giving to the humanitarian fund. That's helping people in Africa and other really, really needy places, and we know the money is going to legitimate places."

"You're not going overboard on this, are you? I'm not going to come home and find that you've sold the place and given the money to the poor?"

Laurie chuckled. "No. But I want you to understand, Spider, that I didn't give the money, hoping for a reward. I'm awed by what happened, and frightened that I will remember this when it comes time to give again. I don't want to give with that in my mind."

"Well, it may be in your mind, but I know it's not in your heart, and the Lord knows it too." He glanced at the clock on the wall. "I need to run in to the Junction and fill up that car before they close. No one will be open when I leave in the morning, and I'll be in trouble again."

"I'll get the suitcase out and get you packed. And maybe I'll give Bobby a call and see if he can get over there to see you this weekend."

Spider stopped in the doorway to the hall. "You're going to make an honest man out of me yet, Darlin'! That's the reason I told old Dan Brown that I was going to Washington—to see Bobby." He whistled as he strode through the kitchen, catching the keys off the key-board and stepping through the back screen door into the warm desert night air, thinking that it would be good to see his son again.

SPIDER SPENT A NIGHT troubled by recurring, bizarre dreams where he was on an airplane in his underwear, trying to act suave and carry it off amid the crowd of strangers. He was awakened by Laurie twice, coming or going as she got up with her restless mother-in-law, and Spider went back to sleep only to have the same embarrassing dream again. Finally at five o'clock he got up and padded quietly into the living room where his suit-cases were sitting open, waiting for his last-minute packing. He picked up the folder that Bev had given him and headed into the kitchen. Turning on the light over the table, he sat down and opened the folder. There wasn't much: a computer-generated confirmation of Stan's airline flight home on the fifth and a police report. The official-looking paper from the Las Vegas Police Department was written in terse, third-person prose. What Spider gleaned was that Opal had called the police after the airline had called about Stan's luggage, which was unclaimed from the day before. The report quoted Opal as saying that Stan hadn't been home and hadn't called. When the police said their policy was to wait seventy-two hours, since it was not uncommon for someone to go benignly missing for a day or two, she had called the Snakewater Mine in Chewelah to make sure that he had left when intended. He had. Opal then went to the police department to personally plead her case, and apparently they were as unable to resist her as Spider had been. The laconic writer of the report had checked with the airline and confirmed that Stan had boarded the plane, which was a non-stop to Last Vegas. Next, the policeman had checked with the hospitals and morgue, finding no unidentified males there. In a conversation with Opal he had asked the same B-movie question about enemies, and she told him what she had told Spider, after which he checked on Stan's record and found that he had served time in the California State Prison System at Deuel Vocational Institution. Searching further, he found that the people who were convicted along with Stan were still in prison, so this apparently wasn't a case of someone seeking revenge.

The report did note that an insurance policy for a half million dollars had been taken out on Stan two months previously, with Opal as the bene-ficiary. A check with the insurance agent revealed that it was Opal who had purchased the policy. The police had picked up the luggage from Opal, who said she had touched nothing. An inventory was attached. Spider scanned the list but found nothing out of the ordinary: Clothing, toiletries, two George Strait cassettes, a pound of jerky from Smoky Joe's, a Louis L'Amour novel. Spider made a mental note to ask Opal about the insur-ance and looked up to see that the sun was rising. He closed the folder and stretched. Then he took a sheet of paper and made a list of everything he knew about Stan Lucas's disappearance.

Glancing at the clock on the stove, he decided he'd better get a move on if he was going to make it to Las Vegas by ten o'clock. Showering and shaving as quietly as he could, he finished packing before he woke Laurie. "I'm on my way," he said softly.

"Mmmmm?"

"Have a hard night?"

"Uh-huh. Your mother got up once and fell. It's lucky I heard her. Poor thing, she was disoriented, but she didn't hurt anything."

"I can still beg off this trip. I don't have to go."

"No, that's fine. I think I'll just put an air mattress in there on the floor beside her bed. If she gets up, she'll have to step on me or fall on me. That way I'll know every time."

"Do you need to call the Relief Society president to get some help in here?"

Laurie yawned. "Not yet. I may have to give up my Young Women's calling, though. Annie and the girls are coming tonight to stay so I can go to activity night. We'll see how that goes."

"Well, go back to sleep. I'm gone. I'll call you tonight and let you know how to get hold of me if you need me." Spider kissed her upturned lips and smiled at her as she snuggled down in the covers. "The sun's up. Your chickens will be calling for their breakfast."

"I know." She yawned again. "I'm just going to take a minute and plan my day. With my eyes closed."

Spider chuckled and softly made his way down the hall, picking up his luggage and carrying it out into the slanted rosy rays of the early morning. Grateful for the coolness and contemplating a much more comfortable ride than the day before, Spider opened the Yugo's trunk and hefted in his large suitcase, pushing it back to the back of the trunk. He heard something crinkle and looked in to see that he had mashed a file folder that must have been lying in the trunk. Spider pulled it out from behind his suitcase and tried to smooth it out. The name on the label caught his eye: Snakewater Mine, Toxic Waste. Opening the folder, Spider saw that it contained a memo written to Stan Lucas on June fourth with a cc to Brick Tremain. It was from Tony DeYeso at the Snakewater mine. Glancing at the page, Spider could see that it contained more information than he could assimilate standing in the driveway. He put the folder in the front zipper pocket of his suitcase, wondering what such a document was doing in Jade's Yugo, and made another mental note to ask the young man how that happened. Then he put his carry-on case in, closed the trunk, and was on his way.

He made much better time than he had the day before, pulling into the parking garage at nine o'clock. Successfully negotiating the serpentine path to the brightly lit BTE parking area, Spider pulled into the place where Jade had the Yugo parked the day before. He got out and stood for a moment, wondering whether to lug his suitcases up to the twenty-fifth floor or leave them where they were and pick them up on the way to the airport. He would be banking that Jade wasn't going to go anywhere in the Yugo. Otherwise, he was sunk.

As he stood by the flame-clad car with his hand still on the door handle in indecision, the lights in the parking area suddenly went out, dropping a cover of blackness like a hood over Spider's eyes. He heard running steps coming toward him and turned around, trying to see through the darkness. "What's going on?" he called.

No one spoke. For an answer he was slammed back against the Yugo by the force of a shoulder ramming into his chest. Spider grunted and reflexively put out his hands to push away his attacker, but he was caught by surprise from behind by another assailant who grabbed his arms and pinned them down. Spider struggled to free himself, dragging the dead weight that imprisoned his arms with him as he staggered first to the right and then to the left until he was stopped by a fist slamming into his mid-section. Another caught him on the right cheek, snapping his head painfully around. Spider continued to struggle, pushing against the slug-ger and dragging his arm-anchor. Suddenly he noticed that the darkness was lightening, and he could see the outline of his assailants. A car was approaching, and though it couldn't be seen yet, the rays of its headlights ricocheted around the garage, finally making it to the BTE corner and cre-ating a dingy dusk of the blackness. Spider heard a voice in his ear saying something directed to the slugger, something about stopping, but it was too late, because the punch had already been thrown, and it connected right above Spider's ear, producing a shower of stars. Spider's knees buckled and the darkness surged back. He went down where he stood, out in the path of the oncoming car, as his assailants fled into the shadows.

Spider came to moments later to a breathless voice asking, "Can you hear me? What is your name?" and the whole world was red. Then he real-ized it was a curtain of hair, red hair, he was looking through. He was on the floor of the parking garage, and he was looking at a set of headlights through Bev's hair, which was hanging down as she bent over him. "What is your name?" she asked again.

"Spider Latham," he whispered.

"What happened?"

"I don't know. Two men. The lights went out. They jumped me. Ran away."

Bev looked around. "Are you all right?"

"I think so. Let me sit up."

She sat back on her heels and watched Spider raise himself to a seated position.

"Okay so far," he said.

"I'll help you stand."

"No, that's fine." Spider began struggling to get up and felt Bev's hands under his armpits, firmly lifting him off the ground, practically standing him up. When he was on his feet, he said, "Thanks. When you say you'll help someone, you don't mess around."

"I work out," she said, dismissing his thanks. "Go stand over by the wall. I'll park, and we'll find our way to the elevator and get hold of security to get the lights back on and report this. Brick is going to be furious."

"Well, I'm not too pleased, myself," Spider said, gingerly touching his cheek.

"Brick had extra lights put in to make this place safe. Did they rob you?"

"No. They took off as soon as you drove up. They said . . ." Spider's voice trailed off, and he stood for a moment in thought.

"Did they threaten you? Tell you they wanted something?"

Spider shook his head. "No, but I lost my hat. I'm getting a little tired of this."

"There it is." Bev pointed.

"Thanks. Okay, I'll stand over there like you said while you park your car."

Bev watched as he reached to pick up his new Stetson; then he shambled to the wall and leaned against it for support. Satisfied, she parked her car and turned out the lights, plunging the garage into darkness again. Moments later she emerged from her car with a flashlight in her hand, showing the way to the elevator.

The lights were on in the lift, and by the time they stepped out into the lobby, Spider was feeling better, though his cheek was sore and tender. He continued to improve with added altitude, and when the elevator doors opened at the twenty-fifth floor, he had shaken off most of the effects of his encounter.

"You're going to have a bruise on your cheek," Bev said, looking at him critically.

"Won't be the first."

"Why don't you go have a look in the mirror, maybe put some cold water on that cheek. We can put ice on it if you want. I'm going to go call security."

"All right. I'll just be a minute. There is something I want to ask you before I take off. By the way, who's taking me to the airport?"

"Jade."

"Good. My luggage is in his car."

Bev stopped and looked hard at Spider, and Spider could see the wheels turning as she realized that she had found him by the Yugo and not the convertible. She didn't say anything, but the lids came down partway, hooding the eyes, and she turned and walked silently away. Spider headed for the men's room.

He was glad to be alone as he surveyed himself. He had chosen to travel in Levi's and a short sleeve shirt, and he was able to brush the dust of the parking lot floor off his shoulder and backside. He took a paper towel, folded it and dampened it with cold water, and held it as a compress against his cheek for a moment. Then he took a pocket comb and neatened his hair. Satisfied, he went back out, greeting Erin at the reception desk on his way down the hall.

Bev was on the phone and motioned him to sit down, pushing a folder over to him. He opened it, and inside was an envelope with the stack of hundred dollar bills that Brick had promised as a retainer, along with a letter signed by him giving Spider full access to everything at Snakewater Mines, including personnel records, accounting books, and computer files. There was also a confirmation for his flight reservation with Blue Sky Airlines. Another paper informed him he would be staying at the Gunsmoke Lodge.

Bev finished her conversation and hung up. "Well, they've got the lights back on in the parking garage. Nobody saw anyone suspicious. Too bad it was dark and you couldn't get a good look at them. You didn't, did you?"

"Get a look at them? No."

"So," she said briskly, turning to other things. "You brought the credit card? Still remember the pin? Good. Now, at the Spokane airport there is a Snakewater car parked in parking lot B, space thirty-two. The key will be at the Blue Sky customer service desk. And . . ." she handed him a sheet of paper, ". . . here are the directions to Chewelah. Is there anything I haven't covered? I'll get Jade up here."

Spider read the directions while she made the call to the mail room. "When did you go to Chewelah?"

She frowned. "I haven't been to Chewelah. What would give you that idea?"

"These directions sound like you've been there. 'Get in the left lane after passing Costco . . . turn two blocks past Safeway.' I'd swear you had been there."

Bev shook her head. "I pulled it off the Internet. It's a computer program. It makes a map and gives complete directions."

"You don't say! Huh." Spider folded the instructions and put them in his shirt pocket. "There is one other thing."

"What is that?"

"I'd like a copy of the information that you gave Stan just before he left."

Bev frowned. "What information?"

"You took Stan to the airport because you had some information to give him. Something he had asked you for."

"Who told you that?"

"Opal."

The hoods came down over the eyes again, just for a moment. "I had forgotten about that. Yes. Stan asked me to do some research for him, and I was able to put it together just minutes before he left. It was something that he wanted before going to Chewelah, but I don't know why. I don't even remember what it was about."

"You didn't keep a copy?"

"No. I gave him the original."

Jade spoke from the doorway. "You would have something in your computer. You could find the file."

Bev frowned at Jade, who was obviously pleased at being able to offer that suggestion.

"It's not in my computer. It came in the mail."

"You don't remember what it was about, but you remember that it came in the mail?" Spider tried to keep his inflection neutral.

"That's right." Bev's inflection was definitely not neutral. She threw the statement out and dared him to take issue with it.

Spider didn't take issue, but he let it lie for a moment before standing. "Do you want me to talk to security? Do I need to fill out any forms or answer any questions?"

"Do you have anything to say that you didn't already say to me?"

"No, ma'am."

"That's fine, then. I'll take care of everything. Jade can take you to the plane." Bev picked up the phone and began dialing, her attention on a paper in front of her. Spider took that as a dismissal.

Gathering up the things that she had given him, he picked up his hat and followed Jade out to the elevator. He accepted the young man's thanks for the use of the convertible and kidded him about nearly having to walk home. They kept up a light and superficial conversation as they drove the

Yugo first to the bank so Spider could deposit the cash retainer and then to the airport. Jade had offered to take Spider in the Caddie, but he refused.

As they pulled up to the unloading area at the airport, Spider touched his cheek with his fingertips. The spot was still tender.

"Did you hear that I was attacked this morning?"

Jade was so startled that he forgot to turn his foot sideways, and the engine sputtered and died. He automatically turned off the key and looked blankly at Spider. "Attacked?"

"Yeah. I was down in the garage. Somebody turned off the lights, and two fellas jumped me. They were set to clean my clock, but they ran when Bev drove up."

Jade continued to stare.

"The thing is, it wasn't me they were after."

Jade licked his lips. "What do you mean?"

"I was standing by your car with my back turned and the lights in the garage went out. When Bev was coming, it got light enough for me to see them . . ."

"You got a look at them?"

"Yeah, and they got a look at me."

"Did you recognize them? Would you know them again?"

"It was still pretty dark. But I know they're Hispanic, and I know they weren't looking for me."

Jade swallowed. "How do you know that?"

Spider looked Jade in the eye. "Because they spoke Spanish. I'm a little rusty, but I used to be fluent. One of them used a word—one I didn't learn on my mission—and then he said, 'This isn't him. This one is too old.'"

Jade looked away.

Silence.

"You in some kind of trouble, Jade?"

The young man shook his head, his eyes averted. "It's nothing I can't handle," he said grimly. "I'm sorry you got mixed up in it." Ripping open his door, he strode around and yanked open the trunk. Dumping the suitcases on the sidewalk in front of Spider, he stuck out his hand, finally meeting his eyes. "I'm sorry to leave you like this, but there's something I need to do."

"That's all right." Spider gripped his hand. "I hope you'll go to your father if you need help. You told me yourself that he believes in second chances."

"This isn't a second-chance situation. It's something I have to take care of myself. But thanks, Spider, and good luck."

Spider stepped up on the sidewalk and waved as he watched the little square car drive away, thinking how easy it was for a son to break a father's heart. Then he turned to find the check-in desk for Blue Sky Airlines.

SPIDER HAD NEVER DRIVEN a brand new car before, so he was totally surprised to find that the car in space thirty-two of parking lot B was a plush GMC Yukon with only 440 miles on the odometer. When he opened the door and smelled the newness of leather and vinyl, he muttered to himself, "Spider, you're in the wrong pew."

It was midafternoon by then. Spider drove past the dark, crystal-like stone columns that marked the entrance of Spokane's airport with Bev's instructions on the seat beside him. He stopped for Pepsi and a bag of chips, careful to stow the receipt in his wallet, and then got on Highway 395. Heading north out of Spokane, he marveled at the scenery and wished Laurie were there to see the tall conifers with deeply-textured bark and the succession of shimmering lakes, each with a solitary fisherman sitting still as a statue in a small boat, tied to the lake with a wisp of gossamer fishing line.

Spider wound through the hills, listening to songs from the forties and fifties on the only station he could get, and about the time his odometer hit 500, he dropped down into the Colville valley. It reminded him of home; it was about the same size as Meadow Valley, with mountains rising steeply on both sides. But this valley had the Colville River snaking sleepily through, and the fields were lush and green with new stands of grain.

A sign said, "Chewelah 5 Miles," and Spider could see the town in the distance. It was definitely bigger than Panaca. Probably bigger than Pioche, too. Picking up Bev's instructions, he read them with one eye on the road. "Go through the stoplight (there is only one) and one block past the Safeway store is the Gunsmoke Lodge." Following the instructions, Spider found himself sitting in the shade of a large mountain ash in the parking lot of a motel which, though long in the tooth, made a brave effort at being in good repair. Two, two-story frame blocks of eight rooms faced each other across a parking lot. At the end of the lot was a landscaped park-like area sloping down to a stream large enough to have been called a river in Nevada. At the highway end of one of the buildings, on the ground floor, was the office. Standing outside the door, dressed in Levi's and a black Harley Davidson tee shirt was a tall, strong-looking, middle-aged woman with square shoulders and a square jaw and long, mouse-colored hair. She was smoking a cigarette and chewing gum, and she watched Spider as he got out of the car.

"Good afternoon," she greeted as Spider walked across the parking lot. "Need a room?"

"Afternoon." Spider touched the brim of his Stetson. "Yes, ma'am. I've got a room reserved on the BTE account."

"You new with the company? Haven't seen you here before." She dropped her cigarette on the sidewalk and ground it out, then kicked it into the shrubbery. "Come on in, let's get you registered."

Spider followed in her smoky wake. "Uh, is it possible to get a non-smoking room?"

"All our rooms are non-smoking. Office is too. That's why I was standing outside. I'm Stella, by the way. I'm the maid, but I watch the office for Madge when she runs errands. If you need anything, just let me know. Sign here." Her square jaw worked methodically on the gum as she watched him sign his name.

Glancing at the name, Stella remarked in a husky smoker's voice, "Spider, huh? My dad used to call me Cricket. I was Cricket until I growed up. He still calls me that sometimes." She laughed and put the form in a drawer. "Okay. We have a room for BTE that we pretty much keep free. Mr. Lucas set it up so that we charge a little extra when there are company people staying here, and that way we leave it to be the last one we rent out, just in case someone needs to come up on short notice. Only time we're all full up is during deer season. Mr. Lucas knows that."

"So I'm in the official BTE room, and no one's been in it since the last person?"

"Yeah. That was Mr. Lucas, about a month ago. He's about the only BTE person we ever have any more. Mr. Tremain hasn't been here for years."

"You've worked here for quite some time, have you?"

Stella set a metal key out on the counter. "About ten years. Long enough to get to know a bit about Snakewater people."

"And tell me about the Snakewater people."

"Well . . ." The jaw worked as the eyes went to the ceiling while she thought. ". . . Mr. Tremain cares about making money, but he cares about people too. All people. Mr. Lucas cares about making money, and he cares about people, but just certain ones. It helps if you're pretty." She pushed the key closer to Spider. "It's number eight over on the other side. The end one, ground floor."

"Down by the creek?"

"Yeah. The ones, top and bottom, on the end down there have fireplaces. They're a bit nicer than the other rooms. Have tubs instead of showers, two queen size beds, that kind of thing."

Spider picked up the key. "Well, thank you, Stella. I appreciate your help."

"Anything you need, just ask," she reminded him again.

"I will." He touched the brim of his hat and left the office. After moving the SUV over by number eight, he carried his luggage into the room and surveyed it, wondering what the lesser rooms were like if this was the top of the line. It was done in a fishing motif, with wood paneling that only served to darken the room. The two beds were along the wall that connected to number seven, and the bathroom jutted out into the room, making an alcove wall at the foot of one of the beds, against which was a dresser with a TV on top. The fireplace was on the end wall, between the door to the bathroom and a window that looked out onto the creek. Above the small mantel hung a large framed print of a fisherman in chest waders playing a trout. The fireplace screen was brass, with smoky black metal mesh hanging like a curtain across the front. Beside the screen a set of tools, poker and shovel, leaned tiredly against a brass stand. It might be inviting to sit in front of the fire on a chilly winter evening, but chairs in front of the fireplace would interfere with traffic into the bathroom, and somehow Spider couldn't picture someone thinking of this room for a romantic, fire-lit romp among the bedclothes.

Spider found the collapsible suitcase stand and set his large suitcase on it, taking his suit and shirts out and hanging them on the high tubular shelf that passed for a closet. Smelling a minty fragrance wafting from his suitcase, he found that his mouthwash had leaked a bit, staining a pair of white socks. Lifting out the offending bottle and the socks, he took them into the bathroom. As he rinsed everything in the sink, he noticed a cigarette butt floating in the toilet. Mentally accusing Stella of smoking in the room, he flushed the toilet and turned to hang his socks on the shower curtain rod. Turning back, he was alarmed to see the cigarette butt perilously close to floating over the rim of the toilet, which was obviously clogged. Mercifully it didn't overflow.

Sighing, Spider made sure he had his room key in his pocket and headed back over to tell Stella about his problem, only to find a "we'll-be-back" clock in the window with the hands pointed to five o'clock, which was half an hour away. Spider put his hands on his hips and looked around, hoping there might be a handyman working somewhere. There was no man handy, but adjacent to the office and stowed under the stairs was a utility cart holding cleaning supplies, rubber gloves, trash bags, and a plunger. *That'll do,* thought Spider, and grabbing the plunger, he went to do battle with the facilities in number eight. Realizing that this was the second time this week he'd had a plunger in his hand, he wondered if this were an omen, a sign as to how this project would turn out.

When everything was finally running smoothly, it was too late to go out to Snakewater Mine and hope to accomplish anything. But figuring he would at least get the lay of the land, Spider took the local phone book, which Bev had assured him had a map of the area, and headed out. Referring to the map, he turned on Third Street, which was a block beyond the Gunsmoke Lodge. Third Street became Flowery Trail Drive as the road began ascending the mountain, and he drove about four miles until he got to Snakewater Road, which teed into Flowery Trail. There were four cars stopped at the stop sign waiting for him to pass—workers getting off shift, he supposed. Turning onto Snakewater, Spider nodded at the drivers, who looked questioningly at him. *They'll know who I am tomorrow,* he thought. *It'll be all over the mine ten minutes after I show up.*

He continued along the road, noting the ruggedness of the terrain, the tall conifers, the small roads leading off uphill and down, disappearing into the woods. They had names like Lonesome Pine, Endless Agony, Paradise Lane, Skyline Ridge, Smith Road. Thinking the last name unimaginative, Spider began to wonder how much farther it was. *Are we there yet?* After three miles, in which he passed a score of cars and pickups going in the opposite direction, he finally came to the Snakewater Mine.

Spider drove through the gate in the chain-link fence and pulled to the side of the road, assessing. The mine was a sprawling, impressive affair, a huge chalky scar defacing the green-forested mountainside. As Jade had said, there was a gigantic crusher operating just below the mine area. Farther down was a mill that consisted of a large cylinder set on massive concrete pillars. Spider imagined that it was a ball mill that pulverized the ore into powder that then could be slurried through pipes down the mountainside to the loading facility in the valley, where it would go by rail to the smelter.

There were perhaps six or seven cars left in the parking lot. Someone came around the corner of the office building on a forklift and parked it by a front-end loader, lowering the forks to the ground and hopping off. Narrowing his eyes to see in the distance, Spider noted that it was a woman. She stood at the door to the office for a moment with her hand on the doorknob, looking at him, but then she went in and the door closed behind her, and he was left on the outside, watching. "Huh," he grunted. "I don't know what this is going to accomplish," he muttered, turning the Yukon around. "I almost feel bad about taking old Brick's money. Almost."

The traffic had cleared by the time Spider hit Flowery Trail Drive, and he drove into town looking for a place to have dinner. The two places he had seen when he pulled into the motel closed at two. There was a bar and grill that was open, but Spider drove a little farther, hoping for something that promised to be less smoky. Turning up Main Street, he saw that the Mountain Aire Steak House was serving dinner. Pulling in behind a Stevens County sheriff's car, a mid-size cruiser very much like his own, he sat tapping his fingers on the steering wheel as he stared at the uniformed man in the front seat who was writing something down in a notebook.

Spider hesitated to approach him, thinking he might be busy on something important. *Maybe you just don't want to talk about the wild goose chase this is shaping up to be,* he chided. *You take the money, now do the job.*

Getting out of the car, he ambled up to the cruiser's driver's side window, which was down. The shadow he cast on the notebook caused the writer to look up. Older than Spider, possibly pushing sixty, the officer had white hair balding at the crown and rimless glasses set on a sharp nose in a thin face. He cocked his head back to look at Spider though his bifocals.

"How do," Spider greeted. "Uh, I'm Spider Latham, up from Lincoln County, Nevada. Do you have a moment to talk to me?"

"Cy Chamberlain. Deputy sheriff." Cy closed the notebook and stuck his hand out the window. "I was just going in to have some supper. You had supper yet?"

"Uh, no."

"Is it something we can talk about in there?"

Spider shook the proffered hand and glanced away, grimacing, unwilling to say what he had to say in earshot of strangers.

"I can ask Sugar to give us a table in the banquet room," he said. "She's my daughter. She won't mind, and we can be alone there."

"That would be great." Spider stepped back when he heard the door unlatch.

"Just give me a minute to get out of here." Cy swung the car door open and gingerly turned first one leg and then the other out of the car. It was only then that Spider saw the braces on his legs and the crutches in the front seat.

Restraining the urge to move forward and help, he waited while Cy dragged the crutches out of the car and used them to help him stand. When erect, the older man was about as tall as Spider, but he was thinner and less robust. Spider accompanied him to the curb and again stifled the urge to help as Cy maneuvered up on the sidewalk.

"Where did you say you were from?"

"Lincoln County, Nevada."

"You're a ways away from home, then."

Spider stepped forward to get the door and took off his Stetson as he followed Cy inside.

The Mountain Aire had tried for an alpine look on the outside, with painted white gingerbread around the eaves and window boxes spilling over with vibrant displays of robust verbena and geraniums. Inside it was mostly greasy spoon, though they did have red-and-white-checked oilcloth on the tables and a few framed black-and-white enlargements of old mountain photos. As he waited for Cy to shuffle in, Spider examined a photo of a 1930s vintage recreational vehicle parked by a mountain stream.

"We'll be in here, Sugar," Cy called to a round-faced young woman who was behind the counter, filling glasses with ice and water. She had straight blond hair pulled back and was wearing jeans, a tee shirt, and an apron.

"That's fine, Daddy. Be right with you."

Spider unlatched the accordion door and pulled it open, waiting to sit down at the nearby table until Cy was seated.

Sugar came with menus and water and Cy introduced Spider as a visitor. Cy recommended the chicken fried steak, but Spider ordered a New York cut, medium rare, figuring there wasn't much you could do to ruin a steak.

When Sugar was gone, Cy turned to Spider. "Now, then. What can I do for you?"

Spider took his wallet out of his hip pocket and opened it so Cy could see his badge. "I'm a deputy sheriff, too, though I'm up here on private business. Private for Brick Tremain, that is. He's hired me to come up and look into the disappearance of Stan Lucas."

"Stan Lucas disappeared? When?"

"You know Stan Lucas?"

"He was a fellow that got around. What happened?"

Spider explained the outline of events as he understood them and then asked, "You mean the Las Vegas police never got in touch with you? You didn't know he dropped out of sight?"

"I don't guess they felt they had a reason to, if he made it to Las Vegas. And you say that Brick Tremain thinks Stan found something here that led to his disappearance? Did he give any clue as to what it would be?"

Spider rested his elbows on the table and shook his head, feeling once again that he was out of his league.

"Well, I don't have any hot tips for you, and I won't be able to help you do any legwork." Cy indicated the crutches leaning against a chair. "But I can help you if you need a license plate run or some information like that. And, I've lived here all my life. Sometimes a little background helps."

Spider nodded and just then Sugar arrived with their dinners. He sat up and put his napkin on his lap, eyeing the meat on his plate with a sinking feeling that he disguised with a smile as he said his thanks to the waitress.

"She's a good girl," Cy observed. "My youngest. She was going to college when this happened, and she quit to come home and help me."

"What happened?"

"I had polio when I was ten. Came through without lasting paralysis. Oh, I had to wear braces on my legs for a couple of years, but by the time I was in high school I was fine. But, man," Cy shook his head, "it's come back with a vengeance."

"The polio?" Spider was concentrating on cutting his steak, trying to remember what his mission president's wife had said: "If you hold the knife like this, with your finger along the blade and press down with the point, you can cut through harness leather." He never needed that information in Mexico, where he ate mostly beans, but it was coming in handy now.

"It's called post-polio syndrome," Cy went on. "Muscle weakness. Pain. Man, is there pain! I used to be sheriff here, but they've allowed me to fall back to deputy and have kept me busy doing things that I can do so I can stay on active duty and retire with full benefits. I've got six months to go."

"I've never heard of anything like that." Spider popped a small chunk of steak in his mouth and began to chew.

"It's not real common. Especially since the vaccine came out just a few years after I got polio. There aren't too many of us survivors around any more."

"Ummm." Spider hoped he had the right inflection to express agreement and sympathy, since he was unable to speak. He wondered if this was how harness leather tasted.

Spider made it through dinner, even managing a comment or two between mouthfuls, though Cy did the majority of the talking. He seemed knowledgeable about the people and the area. Gagging down a boot might be a small price to pay for such an ally.

In the end, Spider couldn't finish the steak, so he asked Sugar for a doggy bag before thanking Cy for his time and rising to go. He took Cy's card and put it in his wallet, apologizing that he couldn't reciprocate. He didn't explain that, since the mines closed in Lincoln County, there was no budget for business cards. He left a generous tip for Sugar, paid for his supper, picked up a local paper, and headed back for the motel.

There was a middle-aged couple in number four with a black lab that they had let off a leash to run down by the stream. He was splashing in the water, grinning, with his tongue hanging out of his mouth. Spider stood and watched for a moment and then strolled over. "That's a good-looking dog you got there."

"He's our baby," the lady replied.

"He's just a big baby," the fellow echoed. "Likes to play in the water."

"You just passing through?"

"On vacation. We're from Arizona, going to Canada," she offered.

"The Calgary Stampede," he amplified.

"Uh, I didn't eat all my steak at supper," he said. "Would it be all right to give it to your dog?"

"Sure, sure," he said.

"Yes," she agreed, "but let me give it to him. I don't want him to learn to take things from strangers."

"Good idea." Spider handed her the doggie bag, bid them good evening, and retreated to his room.

As he picked up the phone and dialed his home number, Spider watched the woman call the dog to her and give him the steak. The line was busy, so Spider sat on the bed and took off his boots, stacking the pillows behind him and leaning against the wall. Opening the Chewelah paper, he noticed that the Chewelah Ward was sponsoring a free Fourth of July breakfast at the chapel on Saturday morning from seven to nine. There was an article about the plans for Chitaqua, the summer arts and crafts festival to be held in three weeks, and one about a young couple who had just had their first baby. Spider looked at the accompanying photo and thought how young they looked. There was also a column that Cy Chamberlain had written about police activity in the county. One item concerned complaints made by neighbors living on Dallberg Road about a young man in an older, two-tone, brown and beige pickup that was speeding down the road on a regular basis. Spider smiled as he read that, knowing that everyone in the town would know who the young man was, and that the parents would likely take action and the problem would be solved. He wondered if Sheriff Dan Brown would consider starting that kind of a column in the Lincoln County weekly.

Spider picked up the phone to try Laurie again, but remembered that it was activity night. He checked his watch. She probably wouldn't be home for a couple of hours, so he leaned his head back and closed his eyes and drifted off to sleep. He awoke thinking that he had only dozed a moment because it was still light outside, but looking at his watch, he saw that it was nine o'clock. He dialed again.

Laurie answered and Spider felt the familiar comfort of her presence, even though she was a thousand miles away. He lounged on the bed and asked how her day had gone and how his mother was.

"There was a bit of oozing today," Laurie reported. "I had a hard time getting her to keep her legs elevated. Annie and the girls came over to stay while I went to activity night. I had been thinking that I might need to give up that calling, but it's a lifesaver to have that time out and something else to focus on. Though I may have to kill Brother Bingham. Your mother perked right up when the children came. She knew them, I know, though she didn't speak much. They were hoping for more stories, but she just sat and smiled and watched them color in their coloring books."

"Good. Good. And how was activity night? Why is Brother Bingham marked for extinction?"

"Well, the Beehives were in charge tonight, and they had planned for some dance instruction. It was scheduled for a combined activity. But Brother Bingham is such a gung-ho Scouter that he said the Scouts couldn't come to the combined activity and had them off in another room working on merit badges. The poor little Beehives had done such a good job of planning and had looked forward to this, and they just wilted when there were no boys their age there."

"Huh," Spider grunted noncommittally.

"I talked to Bishop about it, reminding him we're supposed to have a joint activity every month, but he's so grateful to have someone who'll do something in Scouting that he doesn't want to rock the boat. And, he told me he has to cut the Young Women's budget because they're having to buy so many merit badges."

Spider smiled at Laurie's vehemence. It was so unlike his even-tempered wife. "You getting enough sleep?" he asked.

"Don't I sound like it? I napped when your mother napped today. I'm doing fine. It's just that this Scouting thing is getting to me. He's got his wife baking a plate of cookies for each merit badge a kid earns, so they're all working like beavers for the cookies. Then they make a huge deal about the court of honor—almost hire a band. Lots of pomp, and they hand out mega merit badges. If one more person says to me that we have to be giving our Young Women awards and making a big deal about it because that's what the young men do, I'm going to barf. Is that what we're supposed to be teaching them? To do things for awards?"

"Beware of the leaven of the Pharisees," Spider quoted.

"What's that got to do with it?"

"Well, you're getting to the heart of the matter, in your usual sweet way. Yes, we need to teach our young people to serve and to stretch and grow because that's how they become Christian. But sometimes you have to reward with outward things in order for them to learn to internalize the motivation. Jesus accused the Pharisees of doing things because they loved the outward show and told his disciples to beware of that."

"Exactly! Yes, exactly! So, what to do?"

"I don't think there's anything you can do," Spider said. "Scouting is a good program."

"You don't think that the Church could come up with something just as good or better—like the Young Women's program? And cheaper?"

"I don't know. I do know that for young men the age that the Scouts are, the uniform, the belonging, the merit badges are important. Problem is, it's hard to find a priesthood leader who's into Scouting. And, yes, you need to teach them to do things for internal reasons, not for standing up and getting a badge."

"So when you find one, you let him take over the whole Mutual program?" Laurie asked disgustedly.

"Sounds like."

"Well, I had an idea. They're working on their hiking merit badge, so I suggested that we do a hike as a combined activity. I remember from when Bobby was a Scout that they have to do a twenty-miler. I said that we should take a Saturday and all hike up Parson's Canyon to the spring up there. It's about ten miles up, and we can hike in the shade of one side of the canyon on the way up in the morning and the other side in the afternoon. The middle of the day we can spend in the shade of the trees around the spring. We can make a day of it. Those who need the experience for the merit badge can use it, and the rest of us will enjoy the fellowship. And my Beehives will get to spend some social time with boys their age. That's so important," she declared.

"Probably more important to the Beehives than to the Scouts."

"Yes, but the Scouts need to be practicing the social-interaction-with-girls skills that they will so desperately need in a couple of years. They may not get a badge for it, but it's important."

"You're a good Young Women's president, Laurie. Go get 'em!"

She laughed. "Well, I know what the program is supposed to be. I haven't even asked about your day. How was it?"

Spider rubbed the tender spot on his cheek, but he didn't mention what happened in the parking garage that morning. Instead he told her about the drive from Spokane and the beauty of the area. He told her about Cy Chamberlain. He told her about his wrestle with the New York cut. He mentioned that the Chewelah Ward was doing a Fourth of July breakfast.

"Oh, I almost forgot," Laurie interrupted. "Bobby said that he's going to come over to see you tomorrow. He's leaving between four and five and will be there about ten. Here's his number. Call him and tell him where to come to. And you'd better give me your phone number there, in case I need to reach you in a hurry."

Spider gave her the number, knowing why she asked for it. They said good-bye, and he held down the button for a moment before dialing Bobby's number. The answering machine picked up, so Spider gave him directions to Chewelah and the motel and hung up. He sat for a moment, considering the toe of his sock where a hole was starting to wear and thinking what else he needed to do. Then he remembered: Opal. The insurance.

Rustling in the papers Bev had given him, he came up with Opal's telephone number. She answered on the second ring, and he asked her about the insurance policy on Stan that she had taken out just months before he disappeared.

There was silence on the line. "Hello?" he said. "Are you there?"

"I'm here. I was just thinking how odd that must appear. How did you know?"

"It was in the police report."

"Oh." Silence.

"Uh, Opal . . . you want to tell me about it? Why you took out a life insurance policy on your husband?"

"My dad insisted. He drove me down and sat with me while I did it. Insisted that if Stan wasn't going to insure himself, I needed to insure him for my own protection."

"Did you think that was odd?"

"Do you have life insurance, Spider?"

Spider could picture her pale, serene face as she asked the question. "Yes, I do," he answered.

"Wouldn't you think it odd that a man wouldn't want to plan for his family in case something happened to him?"

"Yeah. I guess it is odd. Well, thanks, Opal."

"Is that all you needed to know?"

"Yeah. I'll let you know if I find anything while I'm here. Bye."

Spider hung up and stretched, then got up to close the curtains so he could get ready for bed. As he stood with the cord in his hand, the black lab trotted by with the uneaten steak in his mouth. Choosing a place in the flowerbed directly under Spider's window, he buried the meat. Then he lifted his leg to mark a nearby bush and trotted back around the corner and out of sight.

Smiling, Spider strolled back and sat on the bed. Hearing the TV faintly from the next room, he decided to take advantage of cable access and see what he was missing, since Panaca only got one station that was mostly old reruns. Piling the pillows up behind him, Spider leaned back and picked up the remote.

BY EIGHT THE NEXT MORNING, Spider was approaching Snakewater Mine with both front windows open, trying to air out his clothing. Breakfast in the small nonsmoking section of the Cottonwood Creek Diner had been a losing proposition, as all the farmers who gathered in the center of the room to eat ham and eggs and solve the problems of the world were smokers. Air pollution was not high on their list of world problems.

Making a mental note to find a better way to get a good meal, Spider turned in through the Snakewater gates, observing as he drove to park in front of the office that everyone was already at work and seemed to be moving with a purpose. There were no knots of workers, coffee in hand, who hadn't managed to start the day promptly.

Just as Spider pulled in and rolled up the windows against the dust of the plant, a figure came flying around the corner and bumped against his driver's door, both hands on the window. Startled, Spider looked up to see a face just as surprised as his. It was a young woman, probably midtwenties, with a curly mane of shoulder-length hair and brown eyes that first were opened wide and then covered by black-lashed lids as she stepped away from the car in confusion.

Spider rolled down the window, but before he could say anything, she whirled and was gone as quickly as she had come.

"Guess that was the welcoming committee," he muttered as he rolled the window back up and grabbed his ID tag and the envelope containing the letter of introduction. Getting out of the car, he wondered what he had gotten himself into and wished that he was back in his comfortable Lincoln County niche. Eyeing the office entrance and thinking this felt too much like a missionary door approach, he straightened his back and mentally booted himself in the rear, propelling himself up the steps and through the door marked Snakewater Mine.

His determination caused him to burst into the room a little too forcefully, and he stood facing two surprised people who, hands still on keyboards, turned their heads toward him when he entered. Neither spoke. Both stared, unsmiling.

On the left was a swarthy young man with black hair and eyes and a beak of a nose over a well-tended goatee. He looked to be in his mid- to late-thirties. On the right was a stocky young woman with dark eyes and short dark hair.

Spider closed the door and removed his Stetson. "Uh, good morning. I'm Spider Latham, sent here by Mr. Brick Tremain." He held up the envelope and the lanyard with the badge dangling. "He sent a letter of introduction."

Both people stared a moment longer, then the beaky, goateed one went back to his computer screen, and the stocky secretary managed to squeeze out a tiny smile.

"Hi, there," she said briskly, standing up and reaching out over the counter for the envelope. She opened it and read the letter.

Spider looked around. The office was functional, though small. The counter, which had a walkway through the middle, delineated the office space, and there were banks of filling cabinets behind each of the desks. A couple of odd side-chairs sat against the back wall between two doorways. One doorway had a sign that said "Warehouse" on it; the other said "Superintendent."

"I'm Clara," the secretary said, looking up from the letter. "Spider— is that correct and not a typo? All right then, Spider. I'll take you in to meet John, if you'll follow me." She led him to the door designated "Superintendent" and opened it a crack. "John?"

"Yeah?"

"Spider Latham to see you. Sent by Mr. Tremain. He has a letter." Responding to something from inside, she stepped through and reappeared minus the letter. "Mr. Nelson will see you now," she said formally, stepping aside to allow Spider to pass into the room.

The office that Spider entered was small and spartan. Aside from a sheaf of papers on the desk, there was no paperwork in evidence, and there were only a few books on the bookcase that stood against the wall. Above the bookcase was a large print of a handsome, genteel-looking, nineteenth-century gentleman in a black coat and snowy cravat, though Spider noted none of that at first. The room was dominated by John Nelson, who stood as Spider entered.

He was tall, though not taller than Spider. Where Spider was lean and rangy, he was powerfully built, with broad shoulders and arms that filled out the short sleeves of his shirt. He had sandy hair cropped short, and blue eyes that rested warily on Spider even as his mouth curled into a tight smile. He offered a large, calloused hand and invited Spider to sit.

Spider stuffed the plastic ID tag in his pocket and shook hands. He sat, holding his hat on his lap and watching John Nelson's eyes move word-by-word across the page as he read Brick Tremain's letter. When John tossed the letter back on the table, Spider retrieved it, put it back in the envelope, and stuffed it in his shirt pocket. He looked up to see the other man regarding him levelly.

"I'll tell you, just like I told Stan," he said, "that I don't like people to come sniffing around, acting like I don't know how to run a business. Brick Tremain wants to come, that's all right. He owns the place. But I don't take to some cocky, married-into-the-family, snot-nosed, know-nothing, big-shot coming to look over my shoulder."

Spider studied his hat for a moment, running his fingers around the inside of the brim, feeling the texture of the grosgrain ribbon. "Well, that's plain speaking, and I appreciate it. I don't intend to tell you anything about how to run the business. From what little I've seen—and I'd like to see more—it looks like you've got a—"

Spider was cut short by the sound of rapid footsteps crossing the office and a rap on the door, after which it was immediately opened by the dark-haired welcoming committee.

"John," she said, darting eyes at Spider and back. "Smitty says that the number three conveyor has jumped off and he's shut 'er down. He wants you to come and have a look."

John muttered something under his breath before he stood. "All right, Carmen. Thanks." He grabbed a miner's hat off a hook by the door, said, "Back in a minute," to Spider, and stalked out, leaving his visitor alone with Carmen, who stayed only a moment before leaving the room without a word.

Spider watched her through the open door as she paused to ask Clara if she had picked up the newspaper. When Clara gave it to her, she opened it to the back section, folding it over with a practiced flip.

"Ever think of buying your own paper?" Though Spider couldn't see, he knew it was the one with the goatee asking. Carmen answered with a shrug.

"So what do you find so important that you can't wait to get to the newspaper every morning?"

Carmen had the paper on the counter and was bent over intently, running her finger down a column. She stood up and refolded the newspaper. "My refrigerator is making noises," she said. "I'm looking for a new one." She tossed the paper on Clara's desk and breezed out the door.

From his vantage point in the manager's office, Spider saw Clara look over at her office mate with raised eyebrows. She put the newspaper back on the counter. "I've never seen a person buy a refrigerator in the personals section of the want ads," she said neutrally.

"I wonder what she's got going now," the beaky fellow said.

"You mean who she's got going now." Clara shook her head. "I just wish she'd realize what she's whistling away."

"She doesn't deserve him. The sooner he gets over it, the better."

Spider felt uncomfortable listening to office gossip. He glanced out the window and saw John Nelson standing talking to two men wearing hardhats. One was gesturing north, the other was gesturing south. One would speak, pointing one way; the other would speak, pointing the other. John listened intently to each. Then they all three turned and stooped to look under the conveyor that was beside them.

Almost without volition, Spider stood. He saw a miner's hard hat hanging on the wall by the door and took it, hanging his Stetson in its stead. He nodded at Clara as he passed through the office, but didn't say anything, grateful for the letter in his pocket that gave him authority. *Keys of the kingdom,* he thought to himself as he headed around the building and over to where John Nelson and the other two men were still crouched under the conveyor.

Spider was surprised at the feeling of elation he felt, walking in this mountain setting with a hard hat on his head and a problem to solve. He didn't realize how much he had loved being a millwright, how much he missed it. Even the dust smelled good.

As Spider approached, the three men were coming out from under the conveyor, and he heard one saying, "I keep telling him he can't let it lug down like that."

The other said, "And I keep telling him that it's made to handle those loads. If it won't, it's his job to fix it. We need to maintain a certain level of production, and it's up to him to provide the machines to do it."

"And I can't do it with defective equipment. This has been a dog since the day we got it."

"Uh, good morning," Spider greeted.

All three heads swiveled around. Three pairs of hostile eyes challenged, dared, resented.

Spider extended his hand to the younger production man. "Name's Spider Latham."

There was just a flicker of a glance at John Nelson before an answering hand was extended. "Chet Burnham. Foreman," he muttered.

Spider extended his hand to the older maintenance man, but he turned away. Spider waited a moment, then indicated the conveyor with the thumb of the hand that had been extended. "That conveyor an Ogalvie?"

Chet and John both looked at Spider with interest. The older man still stood with his shoulder turned, but he was listening. It was John who answered. "Yeah, it's an Ogalvie. We upgraded about five years ago. Never had a problem with the old one, but we've had a constant battle with this one."

"I had the same problem with an Ogalvie, and I found that the fix was an easy one."

The older man had turned around now, and disdain and disbelief were written on his face. "You!" he sputtered.

But Chet had a production quota, and he wasn't choosy about where he got help. "You think your fix might work on this one?"

"I don't know." Spider looked at the older man. "It wasn't my idea. I had a fellow worked for me, name of Pepper Gilroy, that figured out the fix. He's a genius that way. You want to show me what the problem is?"

"I'm Smitty," the older man said, suddenly shoving his hand toward Spider. "I'll show you."

Spider shook his hand, then followed him, crouching to walk under the conveyor. "The dang thing starts jerking, and next thing you know, it's jumped off the return rollers and bound up and we have to shut 'er down and rethread. I've welded keepers all along here, see? Doesn't do a bit of good. It gets a herkin' and a jerkin' and that's all she wrote. Hunk a junk!" Smitty spat on the ground.

"Yeah, we had the same problem, and I was doing what you've done.

But old Pepper said that wasn't the problem. Come here and I'll show you."

Spider led the way out from under the conveyor and walked the hundred feet to the end, where the material dropped from the conveyor into the hopper. Squatting down, he moved under the conveyor and motioned Smitty in closer. Smitty squatted and looked where Spider was pointing. Chet and John bent over, watching with interest.

"See these springs here, and this apparatus here? This is the mechanism that controls the tension on the system. If it isn't adjusted periodically, and if these places aren't lubricated, then it's not going to work properly, and you're going to have the problem that you had. There's one at each end. You got a set of allen wrenches?"

"I'll get 'em." Chet started off at a trot.

"And bring a grease gun," Spider called after him.

Chet raised his hand to show that he had heard and kept trotting.

"You a millwright?" Smitty asked.

"I was, for about twenty years. Mines closed."

"What you doing now?"

"Uh, I'm a deputy sheriff."

"You're kidding."

"Naw, I'm not kidding."

Spider took the wrenches from Chet, who had returned. "Can you hold on to that grease gun a second? Thanks."

"You're not here doing official stuff, are you? Sheriff stuff?"

Spider chuckled. "Naw. I'm here as a favor to Brick Tremain. He's a hard man to say no to. Now, Smitty, you see these four places? They've got self-tightening mechanisms, but what with all the jiggling and jolting, they work loose every now and then. So, what you need to do is have on your regular maintenance schedule that you come in and tighten them up. See, they're marked where they need to be. This one was way loose."

Spider quickly adjusted the remaining three and then asked for the grease gun, shooting lubricant in at four locations. "That's it," he said, emerging from under the conveyor, followed by Smitty. "Now, that same thing needs to be done on the other end. You all right to take care of it, or do you want me to come with you?"

"I can handle it." Smitty held out his hands for the tools.

"How much longer you going to be?" Chet looked at his watch.

"Ten minutes," said Smitty, glancing at Spider for corroboration.

Spider nodded and Smitty took off.

Chet took off as well, but stopped after three paces and turned. "If this works, we'll owe you a thanks."

"If it works, I'll accept."

Chet strode off, and Spider turned to John, who had been standing silently by. "I borrowed your hat," he offered, for lack of something to say.

John waved away the implied apology. "Want to see the rest of the plant?"

"I thought you'd never ask."

They spent the next half hour wandering purposefully around, with John explaining the process. In the great whitish yellow gash on the mountainside, front-end loaders were working to load oar into huge hoppers that then fed the fractured rock onto a crusher that then fed the aggregate by conveyors to a huge cylinder, a ball mill that pulverized the gravel into a powder, that was then fed into a vat and mixed with what Brick Tremain called his "secret agent." It was a patented chemical compound that held the powdered ore in suspension long enough for it to be pumped down the mountainside, where the chemical agent was filtered out in giant hoppers. The damp boxcar-size blocks of ore, encased in their filter-fabric baskets, were loaded with a crane onto flatcars and transported to the smelter. The used chemical was pumped back uphill to be recycled a second and third time. Beyond that, it was ineffective and toxic and had to be disposed of.

"That's quite a bit of stuff to dispose of, isn't it?"

"Yeah. And getting someone to handle it is no easy deal. In the beginning, the genius of Brick's system was the fact that we didn't have to be trucking everything. With the conveyors and the slurry system, all the handling was easy and cheaper than conventional methods. But the cost of getting rid of the toxic waste is wiping out all our profit. China's starting to be a player in the magnesium game, and we're going to be faced with shutting down if we can't get production costs under control."

"How many people do you employ?"

"Only about forty. It's not a significant payroll, but they are all good-paying jobs, and in a rural county like this, that means a lot."

They were on the edge of the bluff, where the slurry pipes lined up going downhill and the smaller pipe of Brick's "secret agent" came back up. "So how do you know when the toxic stuff has to be sent out?" Spider asked.

"That's Carmen's job. She's the one who monitors the chemical process. When it comes back up the hill, it goes in this vat. She does a test on it, and if it shows up that it's time to go out, she puts it in barrels and sets it out to be picked up."

"You've got someone who contracts to pick it up?"

John nodded. "All that was arranged by the home office. Apparently, there's a big company that does all the western region's toxic waste disposal. I talked to Stan when he was here about getting some other bids, and he said he planned to do that when Greenchem's contract is up next year."

"How long a contract did they have?"

"Four years."

"Yeah, a lot can change in four years." Spider mused. "New technology. More people in the field. More competition. You might find someone who will do it for less."

"We can for sure."

They were back at the office, and as they entered, John paused at Clara's desk. "I want you to give Spider keys to everything. Front gate, office, warehouse, everything."

Clara was just reaching for a sheet of paper out of her printer, and she paused, arm still outstretched and mouth slightly open. Then, only missing that one beat, she said, "You got it," and opened the desk drawer where she kept all the keys.

John motioned for Spider to precede him into his office, and followed him in, closing the door behind. "Sit down, Spider. I haven't changed my mind. I don't like Brick sending someone up here to snoop around about the way I run my business. But you've helped us out here—"

"Let's let it run a few days before we start talking about what I have or haven't done."

"I can tell by the sound of it. So can Smitty. You fixed it, all right."

Spider traded the miner's hat for his Stetson and sat, holding it on his knee. "I wasn't sent to snoop around about the business. I was sent up because Stan Lucas disappeared."

John sat in the chair behind his desk and leaned back. "What do you mean?"

"Stan Lucas left Chewelah and didn't go back to Las Vegas. I can't believe you don't know this."

"How would we know? The Las Vegas police called to make sure that he had been here, but Tony talked to them. They were in a 'we'll ask the questions' mode, so we didn't know why they wanted the information. Opal called to make sure he had left, but she didn't say why. I didn't know where he was going next; sometimes he flies from here to Montana."

"Tony is . . . ?"

"Accountant. In the front office."

Spider nodded. "When did you last see Stan?"

"Gee, I don't know. When was it? Just after Memorial Day. He was here all week, poking around. He and I got into a brangle because he came in after hours and got into the computer and messed up some of Tony's files. I don't know what he thought he would find. We're networked to the corporate office, and they have access to all our information. I told him to get on out of here, and he said he was flying out early the next morning. Let's see." John picked up the phone and punched a button. "Clara? Can you tell me when Stan Lucas left?"

John moved a pencil to the side of his desk mat as he listened and then hung up the phone. "Clara said that he was to fly out Saturday morning, June fifth. She picked up the car from the airport Monday morning."

Spider waggled his thumb in the direction of the parking lot. "Was it this car? The new one?"

"Don't even get me started about that car. If Brick Tremain wants to know why we're not making any money up here, he'd better look closer to home. We had a perfectly good pickup for people to use back and forth to the airport. But that wasn't good enough for Stan. He put a huge hole in my machinery budget with that car and gave the pickup to Carmen to use. So now I have to replace the pickup, too. He's a real piece of work. I called Brick about it, but he said he wasn't going to meddle. Said Snakewater is Stan's baby and that he'd have to answer for it ultimately."

"Uh, Brick said that Stan told him that he had found something while he was here. Something 'significant.' He was going to bring evidence back with him."

"The only significant thing that he would find was his own hand in the till."

Spider's brows shot up. "What do you mean by that?"

"I mean, buying that car with company money. It's really just for his personal use three or four weeks out of the year."

"You mean no one else drives that car?"

"Not 'til you came. I figure you're from the head office, you can drive the head office's car."

"And you say that Brick knows that Stan bought the car?"

"Yep." The inflection that John gave to the word was hard to read, and his impassive face gave away nothing.

As Spider looked down at his hatband again, thinking, trying to figure out what else he should ask, Clara appeared with a key ring.

"Here you go," she said briskly, dropping the keys in Spider's hand. "They're marked." She looked at John. "Anything else?"

"No, thank you, Clara." He waited for her to leave and then asked Spider, "Now what?"

"I have one more question—just curiosity."

"Shoot."

"Why Snakewater? The name."

John smiled. "The valley used to have lots of lakes and artesian springs all over the place. Tradition is that the Indians saw the artesian water bubbling up, and the way it roiled the water made them think of snakes writhing around. So they called the area Snakewater."

"Huh. I just wondered. Well, if it's all right with you, I'd like to wander around, get a feel for the operation, talk to the fellas. It might help me know what questions to ask. I'll want to talk to Clara and your accountant. I'll be around through next week, I guess, unless there's a reason to go home earlier."

"Suit yourself. I'm here if you need me."

Spider stood and traded his Stetson for the hard hat again, pulling the Superintendent's door closed as he left. As he walked through the office, Clara looked up from her filing and gave him a tiny smile. Tony ignored him.

Spider spent the rest of the afternoon learning the names of the workers, asking questions about the process. He found most were willing to talk about the mining operation. A few were even willing to talk about the superintendent.

Smitty shared his lunch with Spider and talked about the mining operation, the superintendent, Carmen Gage, Stan Lucas, Chet Burnham, and most everyone else within eyesight. He didn't know much about Tony and Clara. They had only come to work for Snakewater this spring. There used to be a husband and wife who worked in the office, but they'd retired and moved to Arizona. Smitty said he had been working for Brick Tremain for forty years, since long before Snakewater.

"Dangedest lucky guy you've ever seen," Smitty said. "Says he can smell copper." He paused and then temporized. "Well, I guess you couldn't call him lucky, when you think about his wife and that girl."

"What about his wife? And what girl? Opal?"

"The white one. Is that her name? Looks just like her mama. Has the same crazy streak, too."

"What do you mean, crazy streak?"

"Brick's first wife, Opal's ma, went crazy. Escaped from the asylum and ran into traffic. Hit by a bus. Tragic, it was. Opal had a breakdown when she was a teenager, but they've got lots better medicine now than they used to have. Her ma had electric shock therapy. I don't think they do that nowadays."

"Uh, no, I don't think so. Tell me about Brick. Is he a good man to work for?"

"Well, I'll tell you, he takes care of his people." Smitty closed his lunchbox. "Yep. He takes care of his people."

Spider stood and thanked Smitty for lunch, and then wandered around for another hour or two. At three he checked in at the office.

"I thought I'd like to go down and see the operation at the railroad. I probably won't be back until Monday," he told Clara.

"Give me your hat," she said, holding out her hand. "I'll put your name on it. It'll be ready on Monday."

Spider handed her the hat, smiling his thanks. He walked over to the superintendent's office and knocked, then opened the door and peeked in. "Just after my hat," he said apologetically. "I'll see you Monday morning."

John was busy with a pencil and paper and looked up only briefly, waving absently as Spider closed the door. This trip through the office, Clara gave him the full-wattage in her smile and called "See ya" as he left. Tony ignored him.

As he opened the car door, Spider smiled at the film of dust that had settled on the dark colored vehicle. Some things never change. As he pulled out of the parking lot he thought of all the conversations he had had during the afternoon and figured that, after he visited the lower plant, he'd probably go see if Deputy Sheriff Cy Chamberlain was free to visit.

SPIDER SPENT AN HOUR AT the lower site, trailing around after Fred Sanborn, a garrulous young man who was determined to teach him every step of the filtration and loading process. Spider nodded dutifully as he got elemental lessons in pushing levers and turning knobs with an extended lecture on the result of each push and turn. He didn't have the heart to mention that John Nelson had already sufficiently explained the process in three sentences from half a mile up the mountain.

Spider was edging away, eyeing the company getaway car he had parked in the shade of the filtration tank, when his guide slammed a lever home and announced that this batch was ready. "Want to watch me load it?"

"Uh . . . " Spider looked at his watch. He looked at the car waiting in the shade. Then he looked at the earnest, sunburned young man, smiling, waiting for an answer to his invitation. "Sure," Spider said. "Why not?"

"You want to watch from here, or do you want to be up at the controls with me?"

"I believe this would be a better vantage point. I'll just stay here."

"All right. I'll go on up." Fred pointed to the cab of a small overhead crane that operated on rails strung parallel to the railroad spur running through the filtration plant.

Spider found a shady place and leaned against the railing, watching the young man climb to his place at the controls and fire up the machine. Fred noted that Spider was watching and waved. Spider returned the wave, and then Fred started gesturing and yelling, apparently telling Spider, step-by-step, the loading process, even though not a word could be heard over the whine of the motor.

Spider had to admit that the young man knew what he was doing. Smoothly, he let down the hoist cable to just the right spot and maneuvered the hook in place to secure the load. Then he lifted it evenly, moving the crane along the rails until he was just over the flatcar, where he lowered the load neatly into its snug berth.

Spider wandered over to where Fred was climbing down the ladder from the cab of the crane. "Well done!" he called as soon as Fred was in earshot. "You've got a nice, light touch. No wasted motion."

Fred dropped to the ground. His grin was incandescent. "Thanks. My Uncle Tim has a wrecking yard, and I've run crane, stacking cars for him, since I was twelve."

Spider held out his hand. "I've got to go now, but it was nice to meet you. A pleasure watching you work."

"Thanks for coming by."

Spider made his escape, striding quickly to the car, lest Fred think of something new to demonstrate. Waving as he drove away, he watched Fred's broad grin in the rearview mirror as he pulled up on the highway leading into town.

Spider checked his watch. It was nearing five o'clock. Bobby would probably be arriving about nine or ten.

Spider slowed as he approached town, looking at the names of the street signs as they came up. Cy said to turn off the highway onto Clay and then turn on Myrtle. Third house on the right. Brick house. There it was, and Cy's police cruiser was in the driveway, sitting in the shade of two large mountain ash trees.

Spider pulled in behind Cy's car just as Sugar came dashing out the door and down the stairs with an apron in one hand.

"Hi," she said as she breezed by. "Dad is out on the back porch. Go on around. They just called me in to work. Gotta go." And she was gone, trotting down the street in the direction of the Mountain Aire.

Cy's house was a modest size with a veranda front and back. It had a well-tended lawn and enough trees to shade the house during the heat of the day. Spider ambled around back, making enough noise to advertise his coming, and found Cy submerged in a hot tub on the back porch.

"That can't be very refreshing on a hot day like today," Spider observed.

"But it's sure good for my old, aching bones. Hello, Spider. What can I do for you? Found your missing fellow yet?"

"Not yet. I've been up at the mine, looking around, talking to folks. I want you to explain some things to me. Give me some background."

"I'll do what I can. Pull up a chair. How about a cold beer?" Cy indicated a bottle by him on the deck.

"Uh, no thanks."

"Soda? I've got Pepsi in the fridge. Right through that door."

"You said the magic word." Spider stepped through the back door into a small, neat kitchen, with white cupboards and gray linoleum on the floor. He opened the fridge and found a Pepsi sitting beside some meatloaf covered with clear plastic wrap. Seeing the leftovers, Spider was suddenly aware that the half sandwich Smitty had given him had long since worn off. Reluctantly he closed the fridge and took his Pepsi out to the back porch, dragging a chair over to sit close to Cy, who turned off the jets so they could talk comfortably with no background noise.

"I've been up to the mine," Spider repeated. "Seems well-run. Lots of automation and use of machines. That's a lot of ore to process with that size crew, but from what Chet Burnham said, they're meeting production goals. A pretty impressive show."

"I haven't been up there for a year or so. But I understand what you're saying. I think John Nelson runs a tight ship."

"I was talking to several of the workmen, and they all said they liked working for John. Some of them added something like, 'in spite of his political views' or 'even though he's a constitutionalist.' What did they mean by that?"

"Mmmm . . . " Cy's brow wrinkled and he slid down in the water with his sharp nose just above the surface of the water and blew bubbles.

Spider waited, amused, as the burbling continued. Finally Cy surfaced and wiped off his face.

"Well, I'll tell you, Spider, it's a hard thing to explain. Do you know anything about citizen militias?"

"Like the National Guard?"

"Kind of, only they're not sponsored by the federal government. They're sponsored by people who think that the federal government has too much power. They form military groups to prepare to fight for their rights."

"Fight who?"

"The U.S. Government. The army. The United Nations."

"You're kidding."

"No. But that's only a part of the story. The term 'constitutionalist' includes people active in a militia. But it also includes others who simply believe that the federal government is repressive and has too much power. They believe they are fostering a quiet revolution by being 'resistors.' They resist paying taxes, including income tax, or being bound by any government regulations. If it's not in the Constitution, they say, it's not lawful for the federal government to do it. They don't recognize federal courts. Instead they advocate the use of 'citizen's courts.'"

"You got many of these people around here?"

"The woods are full of them. These are very down-to-earth people who are mistrustful of big business and big government. They're very resourceful. Some are survivalists. Many are fundamentalist Christians who believe the Apocalypse is near."

"Huh," Spider grunted. He waited as Cy submerged to the nose again and blew a lungful of bubbles out into the hot tub.

"That's the good news," Cy said, emerging.

"Good news?"

"Yeah. Those groups are benign. The militia armies drill and get ready, but they don't do anything but talk. And the resistors really only affect themselves with their resistance to taxes. I figure the survivalists stimulate the economy as they buy their supplies and build their bunkers. It's all harmless enough."

"Yeah? And the bad news?"

"Well, there is a faction that is very anti-Semitic and very racist. They are called white supremacists and even neo-Nazis. We don't have too many around here—they're mostly over in Idaho, and I hope they stay there. They may not do anything more than talk, either, but their talk is searing, very inflammatory, very . . . disturbing."

"So, where does John Nelson fit in all this?"

"I don't know. The thing that binds many of these factions together is the Second Amendment—the right to keep and bear arms. I know he's a hunter. Maybe that's as far as it goes."

Cy slid down into the water and blew a brief stream of bubbles, then suddenly he shot completely upright. "Are you hungry?"

Visualizing another meal at the Alpine Aire, Spider stalled. "Uh . . ."

"There's some leftover meatloaf in the kitchen. If you want to go in and get it started heating up while I find my way out of this rig, we can eat faster."

"I can do that."

"Fix anything else you find in the fridge. I think there's some frozen corn in there."

Spider didn't need another invitation. He scavenged in the cupboards and freezer as well as the refrigerator, and by the time Cy had dried off and dressed, Spider had a dinner of meatloaf, microwaved potatoes, canned corn, and coleslaw set out on the table.

As they ate, Spider gleaned more information about John Nelson. A native of the area, he had left to go to Montana when he was young to work in the mines. He had returned fifteen years ago when Brick Tremain opened the Snakewater and had been mine superintendent from the very first. He had never married, never had any serious girlfriends, though some people said he was sweet on Carmen Gage. She was the only Snakewater employee besides John to have a company vehicle to drive, and even though it was an older pickup, most everyone viewed that as a sign that he liked her.

After supper, Spider and Cy cleaned the kitchen. Then, checking his watch, Spider was floored to find that, even though the sun was still above the horizon, it was already nine o'clock.

"My son is coming over from Seattle to see me," he said. "I've got to get going. Thanks for supper, Cy."

"Thank you. I'd still be working at getting it heated up if I'd been on my own."

Spider left by the back door, waving through the screen at the tall, gaunt figure leaning on his crutches. "Thanks again," he called, then strode around the corner to the SUV, got in, and drove quickly to the Gunsmoke Lodge. A new car, almost a twin of the company car he was driving, was parked at the end of the parking lot with two bicycles on a rack on top.

"I wonder if that's him," Spider said, smiling. He hurried out of the car and to the room, unlocking the door and bursting in.

"Hello, Son," he beamed.

Bobby, clad in shorts and a plaid shirt with sandals, was seated on one of the beds with an open laptop computer beside him. There was just a fraction of a hesitation before Bobby looked up, and before he greeted his father he hit a series of keystrokes and shut the computer. Laying it aside, he smiled and rose, taking his father's outstretched hand. "Hello, Dad."

"It's great that you could come over. Just great! How long did it take you?"

"About five hours, but the traffic going over the mountain was slow. Not bad."

They sat opposite, each on a bed, and visited about generalities.

Wendy was fine. She couldn't come because she had a project due at work that she had to finish. Mom was doing fine, though grandma seemed to be going downhill. Work in Seattle was exciting. He was making all kinds of money. Mom's garden was in and doing well. They had peas the other night.

There was a pause in the conversation, and Bobby leaned over and pulled the computer closer.

Spider cleared his throat, trying to think of something to say to start the conversation again. He looked out the window and saw that it was full dark, and looked at his watch. "You tired?" he asked. "Maybe I'll get a shower."

Bobby fiddled with the latch on the computer. "So, what's the plan for tomorrow?"

"They've got a Fourth of July breakfast at the church. I thought we could go to that."

Bobby made a sour face. "It's probably some missionary effort. Save us!"

"Well, I'll tell you, it's probably the best bet for breakfast in town."

"What time?"

"They serve from seven to nine."

"Let's go as late as we can. I'm on vacation. I want to sleep in."

"All right." Spider gathered his toiletry articles out of his suitcase and went to take his shower. When he emerged from the bathroom, Bobby was seated on his bed with his back against the wall and his feet up on the bedspread. His computer was open on his lap, he had a set of headphones on and a faint smile curled his lips. He didn't notice his father until Spider came over and pulled down the covers, and then he jumped and closed the computer.

Dragging off the headphones he said, "You startled me. I didn't hear you."

"You want to pray before bed?"

"What? Oh, yeah." Swinging his feet off the bed, Bobby pushed the laptop over to the far side and knelt with his father.

"Do you want to be voice?" Spider asked.

"No, you go ahead."

Somehow the carpet felt thinner tonight, and Spider's knees hurt as he gave thanks for the day and petitioned the Lord to watch over his wife and mother while he was away. He remembered to pray for Wendy too, and asked for some generic things before he closed and climbed in bed.

Bobby stood and walked over to turn off the light. "I'm not quite ready for bed," he said. "I'm going to work on the computer a bit longer. I've got the sound off so it won't bother you." He sat back on the bed, put the head phones on, and opened up the laptop.

Spider turned over with his back to Bobby and soon fell into a restless sleep from which he woke needing to go to the bathroom. The clock said two, but Bobby was still riveted to his computer screen. Spider yawned his way into the bathroom, and when he returned, Bobby was in bed.

"Good night, son," he said.

"Good night, Dad."

Soon Bobby's rhythmic breathing told that he was asleep, but Spider lay staring into the night.

SPIDER WOKE EARLY TO sunlight peeping in through a gap in the drapes. Though he tried to close his eyes and idle in bed a while, his mind was whirring, and he got up to escape the thoughts that were playing through his brain in an endless loop.

Bobby was still asleep on his stomach with the bedclothes tangled around him, one shoulder bare and his arm stretched out across the bed. Spider dressed as quietly as he could and eased the door open, narrowing his eyes against the brightness of the morning. Closing the door softly behind him, he wandered across the grass to the creek where he stood listening to the splash and murmur of the dark water and watching the way the sunlight created a dollar's worth of nickel-sized sparkles on the surface.

The shadow of a fish flitted by, and Spider wondered if Bobby might like to spend some time fishing today. *I never took him fishing when he was a boy,* Spider thought. *Maybe I should have. Maybe we should have played more. All we ever did was work: build the barn, build the house. By then they're gone.* Spider sighed. He wished he were home. He needed some of Laurie's positive outlook right now.

The sound of a logging truck going by pulled his attention away from the stream, and Spider strolled across the parking lot to the highway and looked down Main Street. Three gray-haired men in blue vests and VFW caps were taking rolled-up American flags out of the back of a pickup and standing them up in holders set in the concrete of the sidewalks. They had a system, and as the pickup rolled slowly by, the seniors hustled behind, leaving a tricolor guard at attention along the street.

Though it was early, Spider could see that the grocery store was open, so he walked down and bought some deli sandwiches and fruit for lunch. At the checkout stand he saw some lemon drops among the bags of candy hanging at child's-eye level, and remembered that his father always had lemon drops when they went deer hunting. He reached for them but saw some individually-wrapped peppermints hanging nearby. Thinking they would be better to carry in a pocket, he chose the peppermints instead.

Emerging from the supermarket, Spider detoured around the block to the hardware store, but it didn't open until eight-thirty. Deciding he'd better make sure Bobby wanted to fish before he invested in tackle and a license, Spider went back to the motel.

Bobby was up and dressed. "Where'd you go?"

"I went and got a picnic lunch. I wondered if you'd like to go fishing today."

"I brought mountain bikes. I thought we could go riding."

"Me? On a bike?"

"Sure, Dad. It's a great way to be in the mountains. You'll love it."

"I haven't ridden a bike in years. Not since I was a boy."

"Trust me. You'll love it. We'll take the lunch with us."

Spider looked at his watch. "Okay. We'll go bicycle riding. But we've got to skedaddle right now if we're going to make it to the breakfast at the church." He opened the door and ushered Bobby out.

"I was hoping you had forgotten that."

"Nope."

"Let's take my car. It's got the bike rack."

Spider climbed in Bobby's car and looked around. "When did you get this car? It looks pretty new."

Bobby backed the car over to a garbage can and threw the Starbuck's cup that was in the cupholder out the window into the trash. "I just got it a month ago. I wanted something I could put my bike on and take to the mountains."

Spider directed Bobby to the church, and they arrived in time to get a substantial breakfast of ham and eggs and pancakes. They had just finished eating when a sandy-haired man, barrel-chested and slim-hipped, dressed in Levi's and a western shirt, stood and asked for everyone's attention. He had the ruddy, weathered face of someone who spends time outdoors, though the skin above his hat-line was pale. He thanked everyone for coming and introduced the program: the ward band would play and then Brother Munson would give a patriotic talk. After that, Sister Peterson would give the closing prayer.

Bobby rolled his eyes, but Spider folded his arms and prepared to enjoy the program. He loved homemade Fourth of July celebrations, "the worser the better," as his mother used to say, because something that is polished and perfect has no character.

The band had lots of character. There was a drummer, two trumpets, a trombone, a saxophone, two clarinets, and three flutes. The players ranged in ages from ten to sixty, and the intonation was all over the place too, but they played "America" with gusto and conviction, and Spider felt tears stinging his eyes.

Brother Munson was about seventy years old. He approached the mike slowly and spoke in a soft, reflective voice about fighting in the South Pacific during World War II and about being captured and put in a POW camp. He told of the privation and cruelty of his situation, of the inhumanity all around him, and the despair that he suffered. Then he spoke of liberation, of seeing the American flag in the hands of a young GI as the allies broke open the gates of his prison. Then he sat down.

Spider reached for his handkerchief and dabbed his eyes.

Bobby leaned over and whispered, "Let's go."

Spider held his finger to his lips and pointed to Sister Peterson, who was approaching the microphone. He folded his arms and assumed the attitude of prayer and heard Bobby sigh before he, too, bowed his head.

As soon as the amens rippled around the room, Bobby was on his feet. "Let's go."

"In a minute. I just want to say a word to the bishop."

Spider made his way to the sun-weathered gentleman and introduced himself. "I just wonder, Bishop, if anyone in the ward takes in roomers. I'm only going to be here a couple of weeks, but it would be great to be staying in a home and have some home-cooked food."

Bishop Garner blinked, and then a grin spread over his face. "Well, isn't that something! Yes! I was just talking to Sister Minnow, and her roomer left yesterday. She was worried about getting someone in to replace him. And here you are! Come on over here, and I'll introduce you."

Spider followed the bishop to the kitchen where a merry, gray-haired crew was washing dishes. The chatter stopped for a moment, and all stared at the stranger standing by Bishop as he beckoned to Sister Minnow. They all heard the transaction for quarters made, and they all congratulated plump, pink, little Sister Minnow over her good fortune when she returned to the kitchen.

Bishop walked with Spider back to the cultural hall. "Sister Minnow's a widow," he explained. "Her husband worked at the mine. He died last year and didn't have any insurance. She does sewing and takes in roomers to help make ends meet. You'll like living there. She's a good cook."

Spider thanked the bishop and looked around for Bobby. He was nowhere to be seen, and in fact all the people had melted away, leaving two young men to put away the folding chairs and tables. Nodding hello to them, and feeling guilty for not helping, Spider made his way across the hall to the door.

He found Bobby in the parking lot, sitting in his car.

"I thought you'd never come," he said grumpily. "Look, we're practically the last car in the parking lot."

"Oh, the cleanup crew is still in there. It's not that I'm so long in coming, it's that the others left to go see the parade. Want to take the time to see it?"

"You're kidding, aren't you? No, you're not kidding. Thanks, but I've just had my quota of small-town-Fourth-of-July for the day."

"All right, but you may be sorry some day that you didn't take time to go."

"Yeah, right."

"I think if you turn down this way we can get onto Flowery Trail Drive from there. It goes up into the mountains—unless you had a place already picked out."

"No. That sounds fine." Bobby took the street his dad indicated.

"All right. Now, turn right here. Right." Spider pointed.

Bobby waited for a slow-moving log truck to go by and then pulled out behind it. "I wonder what's backing traffic up," he muttered.

Spider figured it out before Bobby did. He noted the people lining the streets, the barricaded side streets, the salt water taffy that came flying through the air to land on the windshield. "Uh, I think we're in the parade."

"What!?"

"I guess the parade gods just weren't going to let you miss this one. Smile and wave." Spider smiled and nodded to the people on the side.

"Don't be ridiculous! Did you do this on purpose?" Bobby slid down in his seat.

"Naw. I didn't know where the parade was going to be. I'm as surprised as you. Hey, I bought some candy this morning!" Searching in the grocery bags, Spider located the peppermints and ripped the package open. Spying two toddlers on the sidelines, he sent a couple of candies sailing to land just in front of them. Grinning, he watched the young mother help them pick up the sweets. "I love a parade!" Spider exclaimed as he continued to nod and wave. "Howdy. Howdy."

"Will you stop that!"

"What? And have people think we don't know any better than to blunder into a parade?" Spider threw three more candies. "I think, though, that you can probably turn out at this next intersection coming up. The barricades are over to the side. You might want to sit up so you can see. I wouldn't want you to run over anyone."

Bobby sat up straighter, and even managed to sketch a small wave or two before the escape route presented itself. Quickly he maneuvered past the barricade and took off down the side street as Spider threw two last pieces of candy out the window.

Spider directed them the back way to Flowery Trail Drive, and as they began to climb the mountain, he asked, "Would you mind stopping up at Snakewater? I may not have another time when no one is there."

Bobby sent his father a searching glance and then shrugged. "It's all right with me."

They drove to the mine, and Spider used the keys he had been given to open first the gate and then the office door. Bobby followed him inside. "What are you looking for?" he asked.

Spider looked slowly around. His heart sank. "I don't know."

"I don't think I really understand why you're here. What are you doing?"

Spider sat on the edge of Clara's desk and told Bobby the story of why he was in Chewelah. Bobby's eyes got wider, and he said, "That's amazing! You're a private investigator!"

"Nope. A private investigator would know what he's doing. He would come here today with an idea of what he's going to find and how he's going to find it." He eyed the metal cabinets against the wall. "In the movies they always look through the files."

"In the movies you see in Panaca, which are all forty years old, they do. Nowdays they look in the computer files." Bobby went to Tony's desk and turned on the computer.

"But would you know what you were looking for?"

"Well, let's talk about it. You're here because Stan said he found something significant while he was here. Do you think he was searching the file cabinets or the computer files?"

"That's right!" Spider exclaimed. "He was in the computer, and it made Tony mad because he said he fouled some things up."

"Do you know when he was here? The date?"

"He flew in on Memorial day. That's May thirty-first. Left on June fifth."

"Okay. If I can get in here, we'll see if there were any files that were created or amended in that time. I wonder what his password is. Hmmm."

Spider stood silently as Bobby typed a series of patterns. Finally he said, "Got it!" and the computer began booting.

"How did you do that?"

"I saw this picture on the desk—looks like it's his wife and baby. I tried first one name and then the other, then both together."

Spider looked at the picture Bobby indicated. It was of a pretty, brown-eyed woman holding a tiny infant. "All our love, Edie and Arial," it said on the bottom.

"Okay. I've got a list of things that were created or amended in that time frame. Let's have a look. I'll just pull them up, going down the line. If you see something interesting we can print it out and you can look at it later. How about this?"

Spider looked at the document, but it was a payroll spreadsheet that had no significance that he could see. "Nope."

"This?" It was a purchase order for a case of oil absorbent diapers.

"Nope."

"This?"

It was a familiar document, though it took Spider a moment to place it. "Huh. I've seen this one before. In fact, I've got a copy of it. Huh."

"What?"

"I can't see anything significant about it. But I intended to look at it again and didn't. I just realized that. Something happened, made me completely forget it. Go on."

"What happened?" Bobby asked.

"Uh. . . . "

"What?"

"A couple of guys jumped me in the parking garage in Vegas. Rung my bell pretty good."

"You're kidding!" Bobby was incredulous.

"Naw. Go on."

Sending his dad a concerned look, Bobby clicked twice. "This?"

A questionnaire for the Associated Miner's Safety Team Award popped up. It had to do with how many days since a lost-time accident, how many lost-time accidents, and how many accidents requiring more than first aid had occurred in the last year. Spider shook his head. "I can't see that this would have anything to do with Stan."

"Let's look at the next page, where they list the accidents. Anything there?"

Spider looked at the names. Earl Minnow, Sister Minnow's husband, Spider supposed, was listed as needing a splint on his finger early the year before, but none of the other names were familiar. He shook his head.

"How about this?" Bobby asked, bringing up another file.

"Nope."

"This?"

"Nope."

They went through the process until Bobby had opened each document. "The problem is, your man could have found something when he was looking at the computer files, but if he didn't change it or alter it in some way, it wouldn't show up in this date range."

"He said he found something significant, and he was bringing it with him."

"If he printed it out, it wouldn't change the 'date modified.' Bobby said. "If we knew what it was about, we could find it. But we've got to know what to search for."

"Maybe it wasn't anything in the computer. Maybe it was something that came in from somewhere else." Spider stood. "Let's not spend any more time here today. I'll have to work it out some other way."

Bobby closed down the computer. They locked up the office and then locked the gate behind them before heading back up Snakewater Road.

"Where shall we ride?" asked Bobby.

"You're the bicycle man. You tell me."

"It's not a bicycle, Dad. It's a mountain bike. There's a difference."

"Aren't you glad you don't have any friends around, so I don't embarrass you?"

"You don't embarrass me," Bobby said. "I'm glad to have you going out to ride with me. You're going to love it! I brought my old bike for you. It's a good bike—I paid $1,500 for it."

"Huh." Spider thought of his crumpled pickup and what $1,500 would do there.

"Like I said, it's a good bike, but I couldn't resist this new bike. I just got it yesterday. This is my first trip with it." Bobby beamed with pride.

"Do I dare ask what it cost?"

"Well, it was a little expensive. $2,400, but you'll see when you ride it—I'll let you have a turn on it—you'll see that it's worth it."

Spider pointed to a road taking off to the left. "How about turning up here? Skyline Ridge. That sounds like we might get to a nice view, doesn't it?"

"Skyline Ridge it is." Bobby turned off, and they ascended at a steep angle for a while and then traversed, staying on the shady side of the slope. "Let's park and take the lunch, head up this road here. It looks like it might top out on that ridge."

Bobby pulled off the road and began to take the bikes off the roof rack. Spider got out and helped where he could, standing uncomfortably, holding his designated bike until Bobby was free to coach him about shifting.

"I can't believe that you never had a bike with gears," Bobby said, handing his dad a helmet.

"Believe it," Spider said grimly. "Not only that, but the brakes were on the pedals." He squeezed the handles and watched the resulting braking action. Swinging a leg over, he asked, "And you say I'm not to shift while coasting?"

"That's right. You'll get the feel of it. If you shift soon enough you won't lose your momentum, so don't wait until you can't pedal any more before shifting."

"Can't pedal any more?" Spider muttered to himself, watching Bobby pull on his biking gloves.

"Here we go!" Bobby took off up the dirt road.

Spider followed after hastily fastening his helmet. Resisting the urge to stand up and pump, he used the gears instead and was pathetically grateful for each level stretch. They toiled along, stopping periodically for a drink from Bobby's water bottle, and Spider found that rather than weakening, he was growing stronger, more able to handle the inclines. After about an hour they topped out into an area that had been clearcut, and the view that had been hidden by forest was revealed.

"Wowee!" yelled Bobby. "Will you look at that!"

"Yee-haw! That's what I call a view."

"You want to sit here and have lunch?"

"Don't mind if I do." Spider sat gratefully down on a stump and pulled off his helmet. Dragging his handkerchief out of his pocket, he mopped his brow. "Don't mind if I do," he repeated.

Bobby hung his helmet on his handlebars and dug around in the saddlebags of his "old" bike, bringing out sandwiches and apples. They sat silently munching as they contemplated the vista spread out before them, mountain range after mountain range, clear into Canada.

Bobby leaned back against a stump. "Have you heard from Kevin lately?"

"It's been a couple of months. He's never been too good at writing, and the Mexican mail is usually slow."

"Has he told you anything about what he's doing?"

"Not much."

Bobby threw his apple core across the road. "I'm a little worried about him. He's getting involved with the plight of the Indians—have you heard about what's going on? They're starting to be militant, demanding rights. They've even got a military organization called the Zapatistas. Have you seen them on the news? They wear ski masks to hide their faces, and they're fighting the federales."

"I read about them in the paper a while back. Is Kevin getting mixed up in all that?" Spider looked intently at his son.

"I don't know. The dig that he's on isn't too far from where the fighting is. He's talked about working with a relief organization on his time off. Helping the Indians. I don't know if he's involved in the political stuff or not, but I'm a bit worried about him."

"Has he mentioned the Zapatistas?"

Bobby shook his head. "Not by name."

"Your brother's got a good head on his shoulders. I wouldn't worry."

Bobby gathered the sandwich wrappers and put them in the plastic grocery bag, which he stowed in the saddlebags. "You thought the view was the cherry on the top," he said. "But it isn't. Put on your helmet."

"Are we going back down now?"

"Yeah. Remember, right hand is the back brake. Back brake goes on first. Not the front."

"Brakes on the handlebars. Right is back brake. I got ya." Spider put on his helmet and got his bike ready. "My bottom is going to be sore," he announced.

"It'll be worth it. Ready?"

"Ready."

"Don't think you have to keep up with me. Take your time."

"Sez you!" But Spider's retort was lost. Bobby was already gone, crouching over his handlebars, peddling hard downhill.

Spider was right behind. "Yee-haw!" he hollered. "Yee-haw!" When a bug flew in his mouth, he decided he could do without the yee-haws, but he rode with his teeth bared, whether in a grimace from fear or a grin from pleasure he wasn't quite sure. It just felt natural.

They stayed neck and neck all the way down, and when they reached the car and dismounted they hugged and slapped each other on the back. "You're right," Spider said. "That was the greatest!"

"Didn't I tell you? Didn't I?"

"It was the greatest!"

They put the bikes back on the top of the car and rode down, reliving the precipitous descent, praising and kidding each other by turns. It put Bobby in such charity that he could even joke about the Chewelah Ward band and the parade.

It was late afternoon when they got to town. There was a classic car show in the park, so they loitered around looking at the restorations. They had supper at the cheerleaders' fundraising barbeque, and then Spider left Bobby to wander the car show while he went back to the motel to call Laurie.

"How are things?" she asked.

"I was going to ask you the same thing."

"We're doing all right. Your mother is still getting up in the night, so I'm just staying in there with her. I'm sleeping on the floor, and if she gets up, it wakes me up. During the day, I find if I sing to her, she will sit with her feet up, so I got my old guitar out, and I've been practicing. I decided I might as well be accomplishing something. She's heard 'Strawberry Roan' about fifty times today, and I can finally play it pretty well."

"Well, good for you! Bobby's had me out on a bicycle, and my back-side feels like I've just had a ride on old Strawberry."

Laurie laughed, and Spider told her about the Chewelah Ward breakfast and about the parade. She enjoyed it hugely. "Oh, I'm glad you're having a good time, you two."

"I've got another place to stay—a place where I can get my meals. I'll let you know the phone number just as soon as I know."

"All right. Hug Bobby for me."

"I will."

Spider was smiling when he hung up the phone. He went back to the park to find Bobby, and they meandered around looking at cars until dusk. Then they followed the advice of one of the locals and drove up to a bench above town to watch the townspeople set off backyard fireworks purchased at the nearby Indian reservation. Bobby said it didn't compare with what the city of Seattle did for the Fourth, but Spider thought it was pretty impressive.

When they got to the motel, Bobby wanted to bring the bikes inside. Too many people in town, too much drinking going on. He didn't want to give someone an easy target. Spider helped him, and then they took turns showering and got ready for bed. Bobby said he wasn't sleepy yet. He'd just sit up a while and work on his computer after family prayer. As they knelt, Bobby consented to be voice, but immediately afterward he plugged the phone cord into his laptop, put on the earphones, and became lost in whatever was on the screen.

Spider got in bed and turned the other way, pulling the covers up around his ear. He closed his eyes, but his mind wouldn't turn off. He remembered Bobby sitting there talking about Kevin. "I worry about him," Bobby had said.

Spider didn't worry about Kevin. He worried about Bobby. Kevin was getting involved in poor people's troubles. Spider wasn't sure what Bobby was getting involved in, but he didn't think it had anything to do with poor people.

"I DIDN'T BRING ANY SUNDAY clothes. I didn't know you'd want to go to church." It was Sunday morning and Bobby was dressed in the ever present shorts and a striped, button-down shirt.

Spider looked up from shining his boots and stared at Bobby, trying to think of a reply.

"I thought we could take another ride up the mountain this morning," Bobby continued. "I feel closer to God in the mountains than in fast and testimony meeting, anyway."

Spider continued to stare. Things were feeling surreal. Was this really his son saying these things?

Spider finished buffing the second boot and put his shoeshine kit back in the ziplock bag. Taking his tie, he stood to look at himself in the mirror rather than at Bobby and said, "Son, you do what you want to do. I've got several things on my plate right now that are getting beyond my ability to handle, not the least of which is a mother who's fixing to die. I don't want to get myself in a position where I don't feel able to go to the Lord and ask for help."

"Grandma? Dying? I didn't know."

"Well now you do." Spider slipped the knot snugly up under his chin and regarded the results in the mirror. Then he dug in his suitcase for his scriptures and laid them on the bed. "So, I'll see you back here before you leave for home?"

"No. Wait. I'll go with you. I've got something I can wear." Bobby grabbed a pair of chinos out of his suitcase and headed for the bathroom. He emerged minutes later in the pants, but barefoot, and searched frantically in his suitcase for a pair of socks to wear with the loafers he had in his hand. The socks were found, and finally Bobby was ready.

They walked the six blocks to the chapel without speaking, entering just as the opening hymn was being sung. Spider joined in, but Bobby sat with his arms crossed and stared straight ahead.

Spider was interested to see people in the congregation that he had met at breakfast the morning before. He spied Sister Minnow sitting in a pew with two other older sisters. Brother Munson sat at the very back with his wife, a tiny lady whose stature was diminishing with osteoporosis. At the sacrament table were the two young men who had been putting away tables and chairs.

After the sacrament song, Spider opened his scriptures to the Book of Alma and read that father's words to his son: "Suffer not yourself to be led away by any vain or foolish thing;" and he wondered at how words written two thousand years ago could still be so true. Spider used the meeting, as one or another ward members stood to bear testimony, to ponder the bond that sons and fathers have, and how both are so vulnerable to heartbreak by the other. He stole a look at Bobby, who was leaning forward with his elbows on his knees, resting his forehead in his hands.

A tall, willowy teenage girl with straight golden hair hanging past her shoulders came forward and spoke hesitantly but earnestly about the youth conference she had just attended. Spider was drawn from his reverie by her sweet conviction as she spoke of the classes she took and new friends she made and how her life was brighter now because she knew she was loved by her Savior. She was followed by another girl, short and bouncy, whose nervousness led her to be too flippant, but who managed to pull it out at the last minute and express a firm and dynamic testimony. Then one of the boys at the sacrament table suddenly stood. His companion looked at him in surprise, and he looked surprised at himself, but he made his way bravely to the podium and adjusted the microphone.

He was all elbows and Adam's apple, a tall, gawky boy with curly hair and acne and an inarticulate earnestness that was painful to behold. Spider found himself willing the young man to complete his sentences, mentally helping him with words to describe his youth conference experience. There had been a concert by a group that played contemporary Mormon music, accompanying themselves with guitars and a rhythm section. They sang about discovering God, about understanding the Atonement, and the tongue-tied young man was somehow able to communicate that they touched each and every listening heart. "And when they were done," he said finally, "we gave them a standing ovulation."

Spider blinked, wondering if he had heard correctly. No one else in the congregation betrayed by so much as a flicker that the young man had missed the verbal mark. No one, that is, except Bobby, who stood and edged past Spider and three other people to gain the aisle and leave the chapel.

Spider turned around several times during the rest of the meeting to see if he had perhaps returned and stayed at the back of the chapel, but he wasn't there. Spider went alone to Sunday School and Priesthood Meeting. He stayed after the block to ask Sister Minnow if he could move in that evening and got directions to her house. Then he went back to the motel, wondering if Bobby was still there.

He was. He was back in his shorts, putting his new bike up on the top of the car. "I waited until you got back to leave. I wanted to say good-bye."

"I wondered where you went," Spider said, trying to keep his tone neutral.

Bobby snapped the latches down. "I couldn't take any more of that pap," he said. "What a bunch of mental midgets!"

"Uh, are you putting me among that number?"

Bobby didn't say anything, but his movements were jerky, and he yanked open the hatch of his SUV to throw his helmet in. He wouldn't look at his dad.

"Son," Spider said softly. "What's going on here? You come over, you're not wearing your garments . . . "

"I'm on vacation," Bobby said. "Nobody wears garments on vacation."

"Nobody? Did I miss something? Has the question been changed to ask if we wear the garment night and day, except on vacation?"

"Educated people. People in the upper classes. You wouldn't understand."

"Being a mental midget, I guess I wouldn't. Do educated people, educated Mormons, drink coffee too?"

Bobby's head snapped up and his eyes blazed. "It's decaffeinated. And yes, educated Mormons do drink decaffeinated coffee. What's the difference between that and your beloved Pepsi Cola? You're being a hypocrite, you know, calling me down for having a cup of decaffeinated coffee."

"Come inside," Spider said. "Let's not be brangling out here in front of everyone." He led the way and, in a moment, Bobby followed. "Sit down, Son," Spider invited, and then he closed the door and sat on his bed, facing Bobby.

"I want to tell you about me and the Word of Wisdom. You have the same privilege of working out in your mind what it means to you, but I want you to know where I stand. I believe that the Word of Wisdom was given to us to mark us as a people, like circumcision was given to Abraham to mark the children of Israel. The medical people have never established whether circumcision is or is not beneficial to health. But it surely marked the people as true to the covenant. That's how I feel about the Word of Wisdom. You're right. If it was just a matter of caffeine, the decaf coffee would be okay and the Pepsi wouldn't. Neither would hot cocoa and Hershey bars. The prophet interpreted the Word of Wisdom, and I keep it as he interpreted it, and I do that with my whole heart because I feel that in doing that I mark myself as part of the covenant. Health claims can come and go about the benefits or non-benefits of coffee or wine—it doesn't matter."

"And if the prophet reinterprets it?" Bobby interrupted.

"Then I'm there. But it seems to me that when we extrapolate, we get to be like the Pharisees, making lists of what we can and can't do. How many steps can we walk on the Sabbath? Can we save the ox in the mire? What foods have caffeine and can't be partaken of? Can we eat refined sugar?"

"Well, you're the one who made a big deal out of a Starbuck's cup."

"And with reason. Seems to me like it's a symptom of something else. When you can't sit through a church meeting . . ."

Bobby stood. "With some kid talking about a standing ovulation, for crying out loud!" He grabbed his suitcase and put it on the bed.

"He's sixteen. I remember when you were sixteen and giving a talk at that FFA convention, you said that Limosine cattle were erotic breeders, instead of erratic breeders. No one walked out of that meeting."

Bobby strode to the bathroom to get his toiletry articles, brought them back, and dumped them in his suitcase. He grabbed the chinos that were lying on the bed and folded them hastily.

"There's more to this than you're telling me, isn't there?"

Bobby stopped with the pants in mid-fold. "What do you mean?"

"I think you're into something that's sucked the Spirit out of your life."

Bobby hadn't moved. "What do you mean?" he asked again.

"Well, I'll tell you, Bobby, the other night, before you came, I was watching TV. You know what we've got at home, with the one station showing old reruns. We don't see many of the new shows, so I wasn't ready for the smut and nakedness and sordid ugliness that's available now. It fair curled my hair, and I couldn't watch it. Couldn't watch it."

Spider paused a moment. As Bobby stood, still holding the folded pants, his face began to turn red.

"But I'll tell you, Bobby, I caught a glimpse of what you had going on your computer, and it scared the living daylights out of me. You may be able to hide from me and Mom, but there are others, among them your unborn children, that you can't hide from."

Bobby flung the pants into the suitcase and piled his loafers in on top. Yanking the zippers shut, he said, "I gotta go." He grabbed the suitcase and almost ran from the room, throwing the luggage into the open back of the SUV and slamming down the hatch. "I gotta go," he repeated, not looking at his father, who had followed him out.

Spider felt tears welling up in his eyes. "Son, don't go like this."

"I gotta go. Bye." He was in the car and out the driveway, headed back to Seattle, leaving his father standing in the parking lot feeling gutshot.

Finally Spider turned and trudged back to the motel room. Without enthusiasm, he packed his own suitcases and set them by the door. It was only then that he noticed that Bobby, in his haste to leave, had left his old bike behind.

"Huh," Spider grunted. "He'll have to come back to get it." With his heart a little lighter, he set out to move to Sister Minnow's.

★   ★   ★

Sister Minnow was a flutterer. Small and plump, with large upper arms and a full bosom, she had graying hair that curled around her face and wore blue-tinted trifocals perched on a small button nose. She trailed after Spider as he carried his luggage to his bedroom, demonstrated how the blinds closed, and showed him the French doors that opened to the back lawn.

Her house was like she was: small, older, dowdy, but in good repair. Spider's room had been the master bedroom with private bath when Brother Minnow was alive. Now Sister Minnow occupied a tiny cell at the end of the hall. The third bedroom was her sewing room.

The rest of Sunday was heavy going. Spider found himself playing again in his mind all the things that he had said and that Bobby had said, trying to see if things would have been different if he would have said something else. When he called Laurie, he tried to be light and breezy, but twice she asked if something were wrong. He said he missed her, said he didn't seem to be getting anywhere on this case. He couldn't talk about Bobby yet; the subject was too painful.

He unpacked his suitcases, put his clothes in the drawers and closet, and stowed the luggage under the bed. Just before putting away the smaller suitcase, he took the file folder out that he had found in Jade's Yugo. Holding it in his hand for a moment, he was tempted to read it, but decided that he would keep the rest of the Sabbath free from work and went out to sit in the backyard under a willow tree and read about the conversion of Alma the younger. Fastening on the phrase *the Lord hath heard the prayers of his servant, Alma, who is thy father,* Spider muttered, "That's it!" and strode back into his room to begin to make his case, asking the Lord to help his son.

SPIDER WAS UP EARLY MONDAY morning with the found-in-the-Yugo folder opened, reading the memo from Tony DeYeso that he had previously only glanced at. In dry, businesslike prose, Tony said that, in an effort to hold down costs at Snakewater, he suggested they either change toxic waste disposal providers or renegotiate a new price. He had done some research and found companies who could provide equal service for less money. A comparison spreadsheet was provided.

Spider looked at the spreadsheet and whistled. Greenchem, the company that was currently handling the toxic waste, charged $120,000 per month to dispose of Brick's used-up "secret agent." By comparison, five other companies were listed, none of which would charge more than $40,000. Spider mentally did the math and saw that would be a savings of almost a million dollars a year. He wondered who was responsible for the contract with Greenchem, and was in the middle of castigating himself for forgetting about this folder when he heard Sister Minnow sing out, "Breakfast."

She had pancakes and eggs steaming on the table, and as he ate, she fixed him a lunch. "I'm giving you Earl's lunch box," she said. "Feels good to be packing a lunch in it again."

"I appreciate it. How many years did Earl work at the mine?"

"He was there from the first. It was such a blessing for him to find that good-paying job."

"Did he like working for John Nelson?"

"Oh, yes! He was a good boss, even though he's a constitutionalist."

"I never heard of a constitutionalist before coming here. Is this blue-berry syrup?"

"It's huckleberry. I make it every year when the huckleberries are on. I'm not sure I know what a constitutionalist is. They don't pay income tax, I think. Arvella Taylor, who used to work in the office at Snakewater, was a friend of mine. She said that John filed some sort of a paper that said he wasn't going to pay. He wasn't sneaky about it."

"Huh. And the Taylors left just a while ago?"

"Just after the first of the year. They got that swarthy I-talian fellow in to take Lem Taylor's place. I wouldn't trust him as far as I could throw him."

Spider lifted an eyebrow. "How so?"

"From California, he is. Los Angeles. Lives right next door." As Spider turned around to look, she pointed with the bread knife in her hand. "That way. Something havey-cavey going on at that house, I can tell you."

"What makes you say that?"

"Well, they keep to themselves. Never a hi or hello. And he leaves at night in his car—sometimes very late, and is gone about twenty minutes and comes back."

"Maybe he gets hungry and goes out for something to eat?"

She snorted. "Where would he get something to eat? At that time of night, everything's closed." She shook her head knowingly. "I think it's drugs."

"Drugs?"

"I think he's selling drugs, late at night."

"What in the world would make you think that?"

"Well, he's from Los Angeles."

Spider waited for more proof, but apparently Sister Minnow thought that was sufficient. He finished his pancakes just as she finished packing the lunch and set it on the table.

"That was a great breakfast," Spider said. "And thanks for the lunch. I'll be off now."

"Dinner is at six. Pot roast. We're having company. A gentleman I'm doing some sewing for is going to have supper with us."

"I'll be here."

Spider grabbed the files that Bev had given him, along with the one he was reading that morning, and headed to the mine, joining the stream of cars going up Flowery Trail Drive. As he parked the car and walked to the office, several of the workers called him by name and greeted him. When he entered the office, Clara smiled a sunny good morning and handed him a hard hat with his name on it.

"Thanks, Clara. Good morning." He turned to address the accountant. "Good morning, Tony."

Tony growled something inaudible and didn't raise his eyes.

Spider spoke to Clara. "Is John in?"

"Yes, but he's on the phone. Better give him a minute."

"That's all right." Spider set the folder down in front of Tony and opened the cover. "This memo that you wrote, dated June fourth . . ."

Tony finally looked up. "Yeah?"

"Uh, you want to tell me about it?"

"It's pretty self-explanatory. We've been taken for a ride on the toxic-waste express. We can get the same thing done for less."

"How long has Snakewater used Greenchem?"

"I don't know." Tony pointed to the list of companies. "I do know that all of those companies have heard of each other, but not a one has heard of Greenchem."

"John's off the phone," Clara announced.

Spider picked up the folder, walked to the superintendent's door, and paused before opening it. "Can you get me a phone number and address for Greenchem?"

"I can get it for you," Clara said.

"Thanks." Spider tapped lightly on the door and then opened it. "May I come in?"

"Yes, come in. Sit down. Was that you in the parade on Saturday?"

Spider laughed. "Yeah. I gave my son a bum steer. I don't think he ever will forgive me." He deposited his Stetson and the hard hat on the chair by the wall and sat in the one in front of the desk.

"We used to wash up one of the big loaders and put it in the parade. Fill the bucket with worker's kids, you know, and let them throw candy. We didn't do it this year. I guess because Earl Minnow was the one who was in charge of it. He's gone, so nobody took over."

"I'm renting a room from his wife," Spider offered.

"That so? She's a good cook."

"Yep." Spider laid the folder in front of John and opened it up to reveal the memo Tony DeYeso had written.

"Did you see this before it went out?"

John took time to read the memo. "I did. But, it's not the first time someone's told Brick Tremain that what we're paying to get rid of what they call toxic waste is exorbitant. Besides, the government can't constitutionally require us to do that. There is nothing in the Constitution that says anything about toxic waste."

"Uh, this isn't the 'significant' thing that Stan said he was bringing back, was it?"

"I don't know how it could be. Brick would have had a copy by Monday, anyway, since we sent a copy to him by mail." John tapped the bottom of the letter where it said "cc: Brick Tremain."

"Do we know that the copy was sent?"

John picked up the phone and punched two buttons. "Clara, could you come in here a minute?"

Clara appeared and John showed her the memo. "Can you verify that Brick Tremain was mailed a copy of this?"

"Sure." She left the room for a moment and came back with a file folder marked "Greenchem." In it she found a copy of the memo. "We faxed it to him and sent a hard copy. Both were sent out on the date the memo was given to Stan." She showed the fax face sheet and the copy of the envelope addressed to Brick Tremain that were stapled to the copy of the memo.

"Who gave it to Stan?" Spider asked.

"Tony did."

"Handed it to him?

"That's what he said."

Spider looked at the date again. It was dated the day before Stan left. Friday. He left Saturday morning. Spider tried to remember if Brick said when he got the call from Stan saying he had found something significant. *I've got to start writing things down,* he thought to himself.

"Is there a phone I could use? Maybe I'll call Brick and see if he actually received a copy of this memo."

"You can use the one at the counter," Clara offered. "Come on out. I'll put you through."

Spider followed Clara through the office, walking around Carmen Gage, who was standing at the counter with the newspaper opened, running her finger down a column, her lips compressed in concentration. She obviously didn't find what she was looking for. Her brow was furrowed, and her lips were pouty as she folded the paper back up and threw it on the counter.

"No refrigerator today?" asked Tony in mock concern.

Carmen sent him a fulminating look and slammed out the door.

"Whew!" said Clara, dialing her phone. "Someone's not happy. Okay," she said to Spider, "your number's ringing."

Spider picked up the phone and went through two receptionists to finally get to Brick Tremain.

"Hello, Spider," Brick greeted. "Do you have any news for me?"

"Uh-uh. Just a question. The day before Stan was to have returned to Vegas, a copy of a memo was mailed to you. A memo from the accountant up here, Tony DeYeso, to Stan. What I'm wondering is, did you get that memo?"

"You'll have to be a little more specific. I get lots of memos. I forget the majority of them after I deal with them."

"This would have been some information on the cost of toxic waste disposal. Tony did some cost comparisons and figured you were being overcharged about a million dollars a year for toxic waste disposal."

There was a long pause. "I never got that particular memo."

"It was faxed and mailed. Both."

Silence on the other end.

"Uh, how does the fax work on your end? Does it come directly to your office?"

"No, it comes to Bev's office. She deals with some things and sends the stuff I have to see to personally on to me. But, if her fax line is busy, it rolls over to a fax in the mail room, and they route it on in to her office."

"So the hard copy that came in the mail would have been opened in the mail room? Or would it have been sent to Bev to open?"

"It would have been opened in the mail room. We have a clerk in there that opens the mail and decides who gets what. If she's not sure, she makes copies and routes them two or three different places. Things like memos and correspondence get copied and go immediately in the files. If it came in, either by fax or mail, we should have a copy in the files. I can find out if it's there."

All of a sudden, Spider felt uneasy. "I'd rather you not do that right now, Brick. I'll call you in a bit and talk to you about that. You going to be in later on today?" Spider scribbled a phone number on a piece of paper. "Good. I'll call back soon."

As Spider hung up and turned around, he saw that Tony and Clara were both clicking away furiously at their keyboards. He wondered if he imagined it, or did they begin just as he said good-bye?

Tucking the paper in his pocket, Spider went back to John's office, tapped on the door, and peeked in. "I'm going to be away for a while. I may not get back today. Is there anything you want me to do? Anything you've thought of that might have a bearing on all this?"

"Did you tell Tony and Clara what you told me? That Stan had disappeared?"

Spider entered and shut the door. "No, I didn't."

John picked up the phone and punched two numbers. "Tony, will you come in here?"

Tony entered and at John's indication sat in the chair in front of the desk. Spider moved around to the corner behind John and leaned a shoulder against the wall, watching blandly as Tony sent him a resentful look.

John spoke: "Tony, did you know that the reason Spider is here is that Stan Lucas disappeared on his way home from Chewelah?"

Tony's olive complexion took on an ashy hue, and his Adam's apple bobbed as he stared mutely at his boss. His eyes moved warily from John to Spider and back to John. "I didn't . . ." he began, then cleared his throat. "I didn't know."

"I didn't think you did. You have any idea what may have become of him? Why he might not have gone on home?"

Tony shook his head.

"All right, Tony. Will you ask Clara to come in?"

Tony nodded and left the room, to be replaced momentarily by Clara. She sat in the chair when invited and looked quizzically from one to another.

John asked her the same question he had asked Tony, and she cocked her head on one side, looking intently at Spider before answering. "I thought something must have happened—like maybe they were investigating him for business malpractice or something. But no, I didn't know that he'd dropped out of sight. But, did he disappear here? In Chewelah?"

"No, they know that he flew out of Spokane. You picked up his car at the airport."

"Um, that's right. So, if he left Chewelah for sure, why is Spider here?"

"He's trying to find out if something that happened here might have led to his disappearance."

"You mean if some jealous husband might have followed him to Las Vegas and bumped him off?" The minute Clara said that, she got a stricken look on her face and the blood rushed to her cheeks. She dropped her eyes to her lap and mumbled, "I'm sorry, John. That was not a good thing to say. I'm sorry."

There was an awkward silence before John said, "All right, Clara. That's all."

She fled from the superintendent's office, and John sat stolidly, staring at the door as Clara closed it softly behind her.

Spider moved over to pick up his Stetson from the chair by the door. "Uh, is there something that I missed here? Does this have anything to do with Carmen, because someone told me that you and she . . ."

"I didn't follow Stan to Las Vegas and do away with him in a jealous rage, if that's where you're heading," John said grimly.

"I wasn't heading anywhere. There are undercurrents here that I'm feeling but that I don't understand."

"Well, don't worry. I don't think this particular undercurrent has anything to do with Stan's disappearance."

"Why don't you tell me about it, anyway." Spider sat down.

John spread his huge hands and shrugged his massive shoulders. "What's to tell? I offered marriage. She chose a fling with a married man."

"And so she doesn't know either? That he's disappeared?"

"No. But she'll find out. It'll be all around the plant before the afternoon is over."

Spider continued watching John as he tried to think through this revelation.

"You can tell her if you want," John said abruptly. "She's none of my business anymore."

Spider stood again and put his hat on. "Nope. I'll want to talk to her later, but there are a couple other things I need to do right now." He picked up the hard hat and saluted with it. "I'll be back. Probably tomorrow."

John waved a dismissal and sat with shoulders slumped, staring ahead, until Spider closed the door and left.

Tony didn't look up, but Clara held out a piece of paper to Spider. "Here's the Greenchem address and phone number. Tony says he's tried the number several times. All he ever gets is a recording."

"That so? What were you calling about?"

Tony met Spider's enquiring glance with a belligerent stare, but he looked away first. "I was trying to find out why the last check hadn't cleared."

"When was it written?"

"I mailed it a couple days before I wrote that memo. It ticked me off that we were paying out that kind of money when I didn't think we needed to. So after I mailed the check, I started doing some research."

"Huh," Spider grunted. He looked at the address Clara had given him. "Division. Is that the street I came through from the freeway? I ought to be able to find that easily enough. Thanks." Spider included Tony in his good-bye. "I'll probably see you two tomorrow. Okay if I hang this hat here?"

Clara nodded, so Spider left his hard hat on a hook by the door. She waved as Spider went out the door, but Tony stayed on task, eyes on the paper in front of him.

Spider drove first to Sister Minnow's. He was relieved to see that she wasn't home, thinking that he could probably accomplish more without the distraction of her fluttering around him. He called Brick Tremain on the number he had been given, and got through directly.

"What happened to your two receptionists?"

"I gave you my cell phone number. We can be sure we're private. I got the feeling you wanted to say something that no one else should hear."

"What I didn't want was for you to be advertising the fact that there was a memo that had disappeared. I wondered if there was a way to check and see if it was in the file without doing that."

"There was. I just went to the file clerk and asked for the Greenchem file. I checked. The memo you're looking for isn't there."

"Huh. Okay. Now I've got another question. Do you remember when, what day of the week, it was when Stan told you he was bringing something 'significant' back with him?"

There was such a long pause that Spider said, "Brick? You there?"

"I'm trying to think. I can't remember for sure, but it seems like it was towards the end of the week. But I can't remember."

"The memo wasn't written until Friday, and it was going to be sent to you anyway, so I can't see how that could be the significant thing he was bringing home."

"Only I never got a copy of it."

"Yeah. There is that." Spider thought a moment and then asked, "Does Jade work in the mail room?"

"Why do you ask?" Brick's voice had an edge to it.

"I wondered where to get a hold of him. I wanted to ask him a question about his Yugo."

Brick chuckled. "He told me that you traded transportation with him last week."

"Yeah? I'm glad he told you about it."

"Just call the main number and ask for him. They'll put you through to the mail room."

"I'll do that in a minute. I wanted to ask you another question, two questions, really."

"Go ahead."

"Who negotiated the contract with Greenchem?"

"Stan did. He said that at the time they were the best he could do, and he investigated them all. We've talked about it, and he has said since that he felt he shouldn't have gone for such a long contract. In the last four years there have been advances in technology that have brought down the price of dealing with the waste, according to him. He said he was trying to renegotiate, but because there was only six months left on the contract, Greenchem wasn't willing. That's what I know about it."

"So this memo, the one you didn't get, wouldn't have been a surprise to you?"

"Well, yes it would, because I had no idea there was that much difference. Stan made it sound like it might be twenty thousand dollars a year that we would be saving by renegotiating."

"Huh. Okay. The last question has to do with spreading the word about Stan's disappearance. Why weren't the people at Snakewater told he had disappeared?"

"But they were told!"

"Who told them?"

"The police talked to them. And I imagine that Bev told them."

"Apparently the police only asked questions. They didn't say why they were tracking his movements. The people at Snakewater thought the police might be investigating business malfeasance. And Bev didn't let them know, either."

"Just for the record, did they think that was possible, the malfeasance, from what they've seen of Stan?"

Spider took a moment to answer. "Uh, I think you should ask the Snakewater people directly. I got the impression that they did, but they didn't come out and say so."

"Figures," Brick muttered.

"That's all the questions I had right now. I'll be in touch."

"Call this number, and you'll be sure to get me."

"I'll do it. Bye."

Spider rang off, dialed BTE in Las Vegas, and got through immediately to the mail room where a warm female voice answered, "Mail room."

"Uh, can I talk to Jade? This is Spider Latham."

The affirmative reply was somewhere between yes and jess—just a hint of an accent, almost undetectable.

In just a moment, Jade came on the line. "Spider? Is that you?"

"Hi, Jade. How're things going?"

"What do you mean by that?"

Puzzled, Spider paused. "It's a way of greeting someone. You know, how's it going? How do you do?"

"Oh. Yeah. I'm fine. Yeah. I thought you were talking about when I left you at the airport and said there was something I had to take care of."

"Uh, no. Just how's it going."

"Fine. What can I do for you?"

"Well, when I put my suitcase in your car the morning that I left home, I found a file folder in the trunk. I just wondered how the file folder would have gotten there."

"A file folder? What kind of a file folder?"

"It was a folder with a memo in it. It was from someone here in Chewelah, written to Stan. I need to know how it got in the trunk of your car."

"Are you sure about this, Spider?"

"Dead sure."

"I haven't a clue."

"Has anyone else driven your car?"

There was a pause. "Just Maria."

"Who is Maria?"

"She's my . . . she's my coworker here in the mail room. Actually," he laughed, "she's my boss."

"Well, if you remember anything, or anything strikes you as the way it could have happened, will you call me?" Spider gave him the number at Sister Minnow's and Snakewater.

Jade didn't give much encouragement but said if he had any bright ideas he would call.

Spider said good-bye and set down the phone. Then he made sure he had the Greenchem address and his lunch and headed off to Spokane.

SPIDER SAW VERY LITTLE OF the scenery on the drive to Spokane. His mind was spinning as fast as his wheels, working at the problem of the disappearance of Stan Lucas. On a hunch or a whim or a last-minute idea, he drove past the strip mall that had the address Clara had given him for Greenchem and headed to the airport instead. Parking in the metered section, he crossed the street and walked through the check-in area, looking for the ticketing counter for Blue Sky Airlines.

Blue Sky was an up-and-coming economy airline. The only frills they had were ample leg room and an excellent track record for on-time flights. There were no movies, no meals, no beverages, not even a tiny bag of peanuts.

There was a short line at Blue Sky and two people at the counter, so Spider worked his way up quickly. The agent, an attractive woman of about thirty-five with long brown hair and eyes that picked up the sky blue of her uniform, flashed a wide, welcoming smile. "Do you have a ticket?"

"Uh, no. I'm not flying today." Spider took his wallet out of his back pocket, opened it, and laid it on the counter to reveal his badge. "I'm deputy sheriff of Lincoln County, Nevada. Spider Latham."

The clerk leaned over and examined his badge. Her nametag said Cherie Taylor.

"I need to say that, even though I'm a deputy, I'm not on Lincoln County business right now. I'm going to ask you for some information, but it's for a private investigation, not sheriff's business."

Cherie reached over and, with her fingernail, hooked a plastic-covered card and pulled it out of the slot under his badge. "Is this a temple recommend?" she asked.

"Uh, yes, it is."

"You're LDS?" she asked.

"Yes, ma'am."

"So am I! I'm Cherie Taylor," she said smiling. "You said Nevada. Where in Nevada are you from?"

"It's a little town called Panaca. Just west of Cedar City, Utah."

"I had a roommate in college from Pioche. Is that close?"

Spider nodded. "Eleven miles. What was her name?"

"Tiffany Wentworth. Do you know her?"

"I'm related to her! Her dad is my second cousin. Well, well. Isn't it a small world!"

The wide smile flashed again as Cherie agreed that it was. Then she said, "Let's see what you need to know, and I'll see if I can help you."

"Okay. On June fifth you had a passenger named Stanley Lucas fly from here to Las Vegas."

Cherie turned to her computer and clicked first her mouse and then her keyboard, scrolled down, clicked, scrolled, clicked, and at last she said. "That is correct. It was a round-trip ticket originating at Las Vegas, ten A.M. on June first."

"I just need to make sure that that passenger did indeed fly from here to Las Vegas."

"The return flight was at seven A.M., on the fifth," Cherie said, reading from her screen. "They would have started collecting boarding passes thirty minutes before that. This shows that they scanned Stanley's boarding pass at six-forty. So, your passenger did get on the plane with plenty of time to spare."

"That's a pretty good indication that he made the flight, then? There's no chance that he got off again and the plane went off without him? Maybe someone needed to talk to him or something like that?"

Cherie grimaced. "Well, there's always 'attendant error' as far as that goes—someone gets off, there's a crisis of some sort—nervous flyer or such that they have to attend to—and the passenger doesn't make it back. Because he's turned in the boarding pass, they assume he's there when they take off. However . . ." she studied the screen as she scrolled down, "this flight was full. They normally, in a case like this, count empty seats so they can let stand-bys have them. They would have noticed the discrepancy when they had given out all the boarding passes and they still had one extra seat. I would imagine the person sitting next to him might have said something, too. That person got on just after him, so they would have had a few minutes there together. Then if he would have gotten off, most probably the seatmate would have called the attendant's attention to the fact that he didn't make it back before takeoff." She looked up at Spider. "I think we can safely say that this passenger made the flight to Las Vegas."

"This seatmate. What about him or her?"

Cherie shook her head. "I can't give you his name."

"Was it a local person?"

"I can tell you that it was a round trip ticket, from Los Angeles to Spokane, with a change of planes in Las Vegas, both ways."

"What would I have to do to find out the name of the seatmate, possibly get an address so I could talk to him?"

"Mmmm. I don't know. I've never had to deal with that. But . . ." she scrolled and clicked again, intently hunting through menus and clicking several times until something fed out of the printer behind her. She handed it to Spider. "I think if you call this number, they can let you know how you get that information."

Spider looked at what was printed on the page, then folded it and put it in his shirt pocket. "I do appreciate your help," he said.

"There's one more thing." Cherie's brow wrinkled in thought as she tapped on her keyboard again. "I know the agent who gave out the boarding passes, Jerri Huntsman. She would have been at the gate until the plane left. I'll ask her if she remembers anyone deplaning before departure."

"Could you?"

"Yes. But, there's a hitch. She's on vacation this week. I'll talk to her the minute she comes back. Where can I call you?"

She gave Spider a piece of paper, and on it he wrote Sister Minnow's number and the Snakewater number, and for good measure his home number, too. Then he gave it to Cherie. "Anything she can remember would be good."

Cherie folded the paper and tucked it into her purse under the counter. She held out her hand. "Good luck, Brother Latham."

"Thanks." He shook her hand and touched the brim of his Stetson. "I'll be in touch."

She smiled a farewell and turned to the next customer.

"Well," Spider muttered to himself. "That was a waste. I don't know what I thought I was going to find that the police hadn't already uncovered."

He stalked disgustedly down the corridor and out the door to the parking lot where his car was sitting in the sun. He rolled the windows down for a moment and turned the AC to high as he drove back to the freeway. Getting off on Division, he easily found the building that had the Greenchem address in large numbers on the side, but none of the signs on the strip-mall awning could be construed as being associated with toxic waste disposal. There was a sewing machine shop, a stamp-and-coin dealer, a discount shoe store, a tutoring center, a sandwich shop, and a Mailboxes and More.

Spider parked in the parking lot and left the motor running as he examined the building. There were no upstairs offices. There was nothing to indicate that Greenchem was sharing an office with any of the businesses, unless . . .

Spider turned off the key and got out of the car to stroll slowly along the sidewalk, looking in each window, beginning with Old Sew-and-Sew, Your Bernina Dealer. When he got to Mailboxes and More, he stepped inside, examining the bank of mailboxes to his left. "Uh-huh," he muttered. "Could be."

"Can I help you?"

Spider looked over at the counter to see a slender young man with spiky purple hair and a pierced eyebrow, clad in a baggy black tee shirt with the arms cut out and even baggier black pants.

"Uh, yes. I've come about Greenchem . . ."

"Well, it's about time!" The clerk disappeared behind a wall. "The mail has been piling up and spilling over," he complained, "and I wondered when someone was going to come in and get it. I've called your number three times, and it's a long distance call each time. Don't you ever check your messages?"

"Uh, that's not my department."

"Well, don't be surprised if you find the phone charges added to your bill." The clerk reappeared with a cardboard box stuffed with mostly ads and junk mail and plopped it on the counter in front of Spider, who hesitated only a moment.

"Much obliged," he said, picking up the box. "Sorry about being late."

"You need to read your contract, man," the purple-haired clerk chided.

"I'll make it a point." Turning, Spider walked out of the store and got in the car, stowing the box on the passenger seat. Watching the Mailboxes and More door in his rearview mirror, he quickly drove out of the parking lot, turning north on Division for another mile until he came to a shady park. Pulling in, he stopped under a tree and sorted through the mail, which consisted of a month's worth of advertisements and five letters. There were two pairs of letters from Chewelah, none of which had a sender's name on the envelope. One pair had a street address, and the other two had a box number for a return address. The fifth letter was apparently the check that Tony had mailed.

Looking at his watch, Spider saw that it was past noon, so he turned off the car and carried Earl Minnow's lunch box to a picnic table. He sat munching a roast beef sandwich as he watched the children playing on the swings and slide. There was one little boy, about three years old, who reminded him of Bobby when he was that age. He was holding something, looking intently with his little head bent over his cupped hand, his mouth pursed in concentration. Spider had seen Bobby in just such a pose, peering at a grasshopper he had caught.

With that memory, all the pain and sorrow of the weekend came flooding back. All of a sudden Spider wasn't hungry anymore. He put the half-eaten sandwich back in the lunchbox, and then he tried to outrun the oppressive, black cloud of grief and worry about his younger son by driving too fast back to Chewelah.

Spider wasn't successful in shaking the pall of depression, and by the time he reached the Minnow's, it felt like he had an elephant sitting on his chest. When he pulled into the driveway, he could see Sister Minnow in the kitchen and could hear her humming through the open window. Feeling that he would implode if he had to make conversation with her, his eye fell on Bobby's bike, parked by the side of the house. It was like a lifesaver thrown to a drowning man. He was out of the car in a minute, carrying the bike over to stuff it in the back hatch. When Sister Minnow called out to remind him that supper was at six, he hollered that he'd be back in time. Then he jumped in the car and headed for Flowery Trail Drive.

Turning onto Snakewater Road, he intended to ride up Skyline Ridge again, but when he passed Endless Agony, something pulled him up that road. It wasn't as good a road as Skyline Ridge, petering out to two tracks on a narrow roadbed fairly quickly and falling off more steeply at the edges.

Spider pulled off to the side and parked, taking the bike out of the back. The helmet was still slung on the handlebars, so he tossed his hat in the front seat and put it on. As he put his leg over the saddle, he realized he was sorer than he thought. "Take my mind off other things," he muttered as he began ascending the steep hill in granny gear.

Spider was soon puffing, but he pushed on. His thighs began to burn, but he wouldn't slack. On and on he ground, sometimes so slowly on the steep grades that he was surprised he was able to keep the bike upright. He began to look ahead and pick out a tree or a boulder by the side of the road and challenge himself to make it that far, and as he pumped, he'd repeat, "Dear Lord, help my boy. Dear Lord, teach my boy. Dear Lord, save my boy." It was a litany that he chanted, a bicycle prayer-wheel that spun and spun, now slow, now faster as he clawed his way up the mountain.

Somehow, in the agony of a heaving chest and burning legs, it began to seem that Bobby's salvation rested on Spider's stamina, so when he reached the aimed-for rock or tree, he'd set himself another goal, feeling that if he could make it to the top, he could save his boy.

He did reach the top. It took him almost an hour, and when he finally came to the end of the road, a little grassy cul-de-sac in the middle of the woods, he almost sobbed in relief. Getting off the bike on rubbery legs, he wobbled over to a rock and sat down, with heart pounding and chest heaving. As he sat doubled over with his head between his knees, a fitful breeze whispered by, and the coolness it brought was like a soothing balm.

Spider was beyond thirsty. Cursing himself for being inept, going off without a water bottle, he tried to dredge up some moisture for his cottony mouth. Then he remembered his cousin talking about how the cowboys managed on long, dusty cattle drives. "A cowboy don't carry no canteen," he said. "He takes a button off his shirt and sucks on it 'til he gets to the next watering hole." With fumbling fingers, Spider dug in his pocket for his folding knife and cut the bottom button off his shirt. Popping it in his mouth, he was surprised to find the saliva running, and immediately his throat didn't feel so raw.

Taking off his helmet, Spider maneuvered the shirt button into the pocket of his cheek, then lay down on a shady, grassy spot and closed his eyes. He felt his heart rate slow and his breathing ease. The strength slowly flowed back into his limbs, and the elephant seemed to have gone someplace else to sit.

After a while Spider sat up and looked around. He was surrounded by trees, straight and tall, and the sun was canted far enough to the west that the whole side of the mountain he was on was in shade. He stood, put the button in his pocket, and clamped his helmet back on. "Now for the cherry on the top," he said aloud.

Endless Agony was a steeper road than Skyline Ridge had been, and it was more primitive. Here and there little gullies had eroded, sometimes down the middle of the road, sometimes cutting across. Spider didn't descend with the same abandon that he had while riding with Bobby, but he was still clipping along, with the same teeth-baring grimace of Saturday. He felt the wind on his face, and it seemed to blow away the black cloud that had followed him from the park in Spokane.

He was nearing the bottom. In fact, through a break in the trees he could see the car, made tiny by distance, parked below. Since the road was getting better and he was nearing the end, he eased up on the brake and felt the speed increase.

There was another gap in the trees, and Spider was looking down to see if he could see the car, rather than keeping his eyes on the road. He didn't see the boulder jutting up like a ramp, didn't know what had happened until he was catapulted in the air and his front wheel landed in a little gully that headed right for the edge of the road. He tried to brake, but in his panic he forgot where the brakes were. As he spun the pedals uselessly backward, he shot out into nothingness, out over the tall larch and fir trees, still astride his bike, hollering, "Not agaaaaaaaain!"

Somewhere, after gravity took over, Spider realized he needed to divorce himself from the metal bars of the bike, and he pushed himself away, trying to remember what his bull-riding, cowboy cousin said about falling safely. Tucking into a ball, he prayed for himself this time, and he felt the concussion and give as he hit first the smaller, top limbs and then the lower, larger limbs that made up the conifer canopy below him. Finally there was the concussion that had no give to it, and he felt the wind driven from his lungs before everything disappeared.

IT WAS A CLASSIC "WHERE AM I?" situation. Spider came to and hadn't a clue where he was or how he got there. He knew he was hurt. His shoulder ached and his knees and elbows were both on fire. He lay face up, head downhill, looking up at the tall, straight conifers above him. As consciousness returned, he became aware of a strong musky smell and a low, gnarling sound close by. Lifting his head he saw, above him, just a few feet away, in front of a dense tangle of bushes and undergrowth, a cougar, crouched and ready to spring.

"Whoa!" Spider cried as he tried to scramble to his feet, using arms and legs that had forgotten the basic rules of movement.

"Pull your shirt up over your head!"

Spider tore his eyes away from the cougar to see who was calling to him. It was a woman, bare from the waist up, standing with her arms inside her shirt, holding it like a sail above her head. It made her look seven feet tall.

"Get out of here, you nasty cat!" she hollered.

Spider managed to crab over to a tree and drag himself upright. He felt a stabbing pain in his shoulder as he reached down to get the tail of his shirt. Trembling with weakness, he was afraid that the cougar would pounce while he was tangled up in his clothing, but he tore the shirt open, heedless of the buttons popping and, grabbing the tails, dragged the shirt over his helmet as he was told.

Holding his arms over his head was agony, but he found the strength to holler, "You! Cat! Scat! Get out of here!"

The cat continued crouching, the tip of its tail flicking back and forth, rumbling low in its throat. Spider took a step forward, waving his shirt-sheathed arms back and forth. "Get on out of here! Scat!"

The woman came over to stand near Spider, stamping her feet and hollering. Spider joined her, and they waved their arms and yelled in tandem as the cougar continued crouching, head low and teeth bared. As he held his arms overhead, Spider grabbed hold of a dead, low-growing branch, thinking he could break it off and use it as a club if he had to defend himself or the woman beside him. There was a booming crack as it came away in his hands, and as the sound resounded through the woods, the cat whirled and disappeared in the undergrowth.

"Ahhhhh. He's gone." The woman sighed and dropped her arms. "Whew."

Spider dropped his own arms and turned to thank his companion. At sight of her bare torso, he averted his eyes and worked at putting his own buttonless shirt back on. Then he judged that it was safe to see who had come to his aid.

She was long-legged and tall, dressed in shorts and, mercifully, the tee shirt she had now donned. The planes of her face were classic, and it occurred to Spider that she must have been a beauty when she was young. But now there was a tracing of spider-web lines on her brow, at the eyes, and around the mouth. She pushed her long blonde hair away from her face and smiled at Spider. "I saw your crash. I was afraid you might be dead."

"If you hadn't come along, I might have been dead—and eaten. Thank you!" He unbuckled the strap under his chin and took off his helmet. "How did you know what to do?"

"Um, cougars are a problem around here. I read about that in the local newspaper. I've never tried it to see if it works before. Are you okay?"

"I don't know. I haven't had time to take inventory." Spider leaned forward and looked down at his knees through the holes in his torn Levi's. They were scraped and bloody, but there were no deep gashes. Both elbows were scraped as well, and his shoulder hurt when he moved it, but there didn't seem to be anything broken. "I think I'm all right, though I don't understand why."

"Neither do I."

"The tree branches must have slowed me down. I remember hitting several of them."

"And these are larch trees. They lose their needles every year, so it makes the ground under them pretty soft."

They both looked up, marveling at how far Spider had fallen. Then they turned and smiled at each other. "My name's Spider Latham," Spider said, holding out his hand.

"Honor Wise," she said, taking his hand in a firm grasp. "How do you do?"

"I wonder where my bike landed." Spider looked around. "It can't have gone far."

"I see it over there. It landed about where our friend was crouching."

Spider walked over to it. "Oh, crud!"

She joined him as he picked up the bike and looked at the bent fork. "I think it can be fixed."

"Yeah. I imagine. But it's a borrowed bike, and besides, I'm not looking forward to carrying it all the way back to the car."

"Oh, I think we can manage something else. I was on my ATV, going up the road when I saw you go sailing off. I turned around and rode down here to find you. We can put you on the front and your bike on the back, and we'll do fine. Come on."

Spider grimaced as he lifted the bike, but he carried it to where she stood by a four-wheeler with a tote tray front and back.

"Lay it across the back and bungee it on." She got in the saddle. "Then you hop on front."

Spider did as he was told and rode, humbly and thankfully, perched on front all the way down to the road.

"I hope you'll come in and let me put something on those abrasions before you take off. That way you can sit a while and we can make sure you're not going into shock before you get in a car and start to drive."

"Where do you live?"

She gestured down the hill. "Just below where you parked your car."

"I don't remember a seeing a house. I thought the place was deserted."

"It's a ways off the road." She stopped at his car and opened the hatch as Spider took the bike off and came to stow it in the back. "So what do you think? I've got some chamomile tea in the fridge."

"Sounds good to me." Spider resumed his perch, hanging on as Honor drove down the road a ways and turned off on a winding driveway that led through the woods to a clearing.

"That's your house? Wow!"

It was a simple, clean, log-cabin design, with both the front and back walls of the two-story living room area made completely of glass.

Honor braked to a stop and switched off the engine. "I need lots of light," she said. "Come on in."

Spider looked around as they entered. There was a loft on the back side of the living area, with a drafting table and lamp sitting on it. Against the windows under the loft, was a rack of narrow shelves, spaced about a foot and a half apart, each lined with two-inch flower pots.

Spider wandered over to the window. "You got a thing about cactus?"

Honor laughed. "Well, yes I do. One of the ways I support myself is by propagating cacti. I sell them to mail order catalogs."

"You're a cactus farmer!"

She laughed again. "I guess I am. Sit down and I'll get my first aid kit."

She left the room, but Spider didn't sit. He wandered around looking at the framed pictures on the wall. They were watercolor paintings of wild flowers, plants, and ferns, meticulously drawn and beautifully colored, and each labeled with the Latin name.

Honor arrived with a tray on which she carried her first aid kit and two tall tumblers filled with ice and a pale amber liquid. She handed him a glass. "I didn't put any sugar in. I hope you don't mind."

"That's fine." Spider took a sip and then indicated the drawings with the tea glass. "These pictures are marvelous!"

"Well, thank you. That's another thing I do. I catalog and draw native plants of the area for the Smithsonian."

"Do you now! And are these some of the things you've sent to the Smithsonian?"

She shook her head. "I used to live on the Olympic Peninsula. I did these when I lived there. It's a bit of home that I carry with me. Come and sit down."

"So you're not native to the area here?"

"Well, yes I am. But I married and moved away. My husband was killed in a logging accident, and I came back here to be near family. Drop your drawers, please."

"Beg pardon?"

"Drop your pants," Honor repeated. "I need to be able to clean those knees, and the best way to do it is if the pants are out of the way."

"Ah, that's okay. I'll—"

"Are you afraid I'll make a move when you're vulnerable?"

"No, but . . . "

"Drop 'em."

"Ah, . . ." Spider looked down at his shredded Levi's. How about if we just cut them off?" Spider countered. "They're pretty much past saving already."

Honor looked at him quizzically for a moment and then smiled. "All right, Mr. Modesty." She took a pair of scissors out of her first-aid kit. "I suppose you want to do it yourself."

Spider answered her smile and held out his hand. "'Fraid so." He sat in the straight-backed chair that Honor had set for him and worked with contracted brows as he gingerly snipped away the blue denim fabric, letting the pant legs fall to the floor around his feet.

"It's not beautiful," Honor commented, "but it will do." She scrubbed both knees with a bacteria-killing soap and spread antibiotic ointment on them, and then she had him lift a foot to pull away the discarded bottom. "I think it was a mistake not to have you take your boot off," she said between clenched teeth, tugging hard until it finally came free.

Spider agreed and took off the other boot, allowing Honor to slip off the other pant leg.

"All right, now let's have a look at those elbows."

Spider allowed her to doctor the abrasions on his arms, grimacing as she scrubbed each before applying the ointment. "These are going to get ugly as they heal," she observed, "but I don't think they're bad at all."

"They don't feel too bad," Spider lied.

"How's the shoulder?"

"Seems to move all right. It'll probably be sore for a while." Spider looked down at his shirt, held together by a single button. "Um, do you have any safety pins?"

Honor went yet again to her trusty first-aid kit, handing him a large one. "Come back up in a couple of days. I'm also a massage therapist. I can help get that soreness out."

"Is there anything you don't do?"

She laughed. "Well, it beats working nine-to-five." She put her first-aid things away and wrapped up the severed pant leg bottoms. "If you don't want these, I'll keep them for patches."

Spider shook his head. "I don't want them."

Honor laid the denim on a shelf and drifted to a couch by the front window. There was a hummingbird feeder hanging from the limb of a tree close by, and a tiny bird with an iridescent hood was sipping the sweet syrup. "Come sit over here," she invited.

Spider brought his glass and sank into an easy chair opposite, feeling the coolness of the leather on the back of his bare knees. "I keep thinking I've met you. Have I?" Spider queried.

Honor shook her head. "I don't think so, but I know who you are. You were in the parade last Saturday."

Spider grinned and shook his head. "I'll never live that down."

She took a sip of her drink and said, "You know my brother. Maybe you see some resemblance."

"Who is your brother?"

"John Nelson."

"Ah." Spider nodded. Then he couldn't think of anything to say.

"John was ready not to like you," she said. "But I think he does. He said you fixed the conveyor at the mine."

"I seem to do a better job fixing things than . . ."

". . . riding a bike?"

Spider smiled. "Yeah. That, too."

They sat in companionable silence for a moment, watching the shimmering iridescence of the hummingbird as it hovered near the feeder. Then Honor raised her arm and pointed. "Look there."

Two deer, a doe and a fawn, were picking their careful way across the edge of the clearing, pausing to listen and test the air every few steps.

"She's right to be wary," Spider said softly. "I hope she doesn't run into our feline friend."

"Me, too," Honor whispered.

As they watched the deer slip back into the forest and disappear, Spider sighed and stood. "I need to be on my way. I promised my landlady that I'd be back for supper. I do thank you for coming to my rescue."

"I'll run you back on the ATV."

"No. The walk will do me good. Work a few kinks out. It's not that far." He crossed to where she sat and took the hand that she raised to him, looking down into her clear blue eyes. "And thanks for the first aid."

She smiled, and the hairline wrinkles in her cheeks deepened. "I think you'd rather have faced that cougar again than drop your pants."

He squeezed her hand and released it. "Just about. Don't get up. I can let myself out." He did so and waved to her through the window as he crossed the clearing, aware of the figure he must present in cut-off knee-highs and cowboy boots.

The driveway was winding but level and provided a pleasant walk through the woods, but when Spider got to the road, the incline of the short walk to the car had him winded and weak. Reaching the car, he looked through the back window at the bent bike and shook his head. Then he got in, turned the Yukon around, and drove back to Chewelah at a sedate pace, singing,

> *I'll bet all my money the man ain't alive*
> *That can stay with old Strawberry*
> *When he makes his high dive.*

★   ★   ★

There was a new Dodge Ram pickup in Sister Minnow's driveway when Spider arrived, and a stocky, fifty-ish Confederate soldier sitting alone in the kitchen, sweating around the hairline and wringing his hands.

And I was worried about my appearance, Spider thought. Aloud, he said hello and introduced himself. "Where's Sister Minnow?" he asked, looking around.

"She's in the bathroom, and she won't come out."

Spider frowned. "Is something wrong?" He glanced at the clock, and it was half an hour to dinner time.

"I didn't think so. We was in here joking and having a good time. I come over in my uniform to show it off, and she was right proud of it. She made it for me, see?"

"Isn't the wool a little warm for summer?"

"Yeah, it is. But it's got to be authentic. But anyway, she was working on dinner, making the gravy, see?"

Spider nodded, though he couldn't tell where this was leading.

"And she said the gravy was lumpy, so she was just going to pour it through a strainer to get the lumps out."

Spider nodded, comprehending the situation all at once. In the sink sat a sieve full of lumps, and beside the sink sat the pot that had contained the lumpy gravy. Sister Minnow must have neglected to put something under the sieve as she poured the gravy through, and it appeared that, while she managed to save the lumps, the gravy had gone down the drain.

"She burst into tears and went into the bathroom, and I can't seem to say anything that will get her out."

"Huh," Spider grunted. "Well, sometimes the only thing to do is to let time pass and never mention it again. But, we can try rescuing the situation."

Spider walked to the end of the hall, followed by Johnny Reb. He knocked on the bathroom door. "Sister Minnow? Are you there?"

Silence.

"Sister Minnow, I was just talking to . . ."

"Phil," the soldier supplied.

"Phil, and he was saying how he loved barbeque beef. I told him I bet you know a great recipe for some barbeque sauce we can put on that nice pot roast you've got on the stove. What do you think?"

Silence.

Spider shrugged and gave the hands-up, "I tried" gesture. Phil shook his head, and they had just headed back to the kitchen when they heard the bathroom door open. As one, they turned to see a teary-eyed, red-nosed Sister Minnow emerge.

She cleared her throat. "I believe I can make some barbeque sauce," she said in a damp voice.

"That would be great!" said Phil. "I love barbeque beef!"

Luckily, Sister Minnow was too involved in her own problems to notice Spider's appearance, and he escaped to his bedroom where he showered, grimacing at how the hot water hurt when it hit his elbows and knees. When he was presentable, he joined Sister Minnow and Phil in the kitchen.

As they sat down to melt-in-your-mouth pot roast with an excellent barbeque sauce, Sister Minnow told Spider that Phil belonged to the Sons of the Confederacy.

"We do Civil War reenactments," Phil added. "There's one next month over in Montana."

"He's making a cannon," she shared proudly.

"Made a cannon," Phil corrected. "I finished it today and figure to fire it off tomorrow for the first time. I asked Agnes to go with me. Want to come?"

Spider considered. "Why not? I've never seen anyone fire a cannon."

"Neither have I," confided Phil.

They made good inroads on the pot roast, but Spider saw with satisfaction that there were leftovers that could go into his lunch bucket tomorrow. Then he panicked, remembering that Sister Minnow would find the uneaten lunch. He encouraged them to go sit out back by the stream, saying he'd do the dishes. Sister Minnow resisted, but finally, pink with pleasure, she allowed herself to be escorted by her perspiring dinner guest, and they went out to sit by the stream in the cool of the evening.

Spider quickly dashed out to his car and retrieved the lunch bucket, disguising as best he could the fact that he hadn't eaten much. Then he cleaned the kitchen and went to his room to call Laurie.

Her report was a bit sobering. His mother's legs were swollen and weepy, even though Laurie had wrapped them and made sure that they were elevated all day. "Your mother spoke today. She said, 'You don't know what it's like not to know who you are.' It about broke my heart. I've been singing hymns to her all day, but making up words to fit." Using the tune of "Come, Come, Ye Saints," Laurie sang, "You're Rachel Latham, your husband's name was Bill. You were born in Meadow Valley . . . It seems to soothe her to hear all the old names—her brothers and sisters and mom and dad. If I sing it she pays more attention than if I say it."

"Well, sing on, Darlin'. I do wish I was home to help you."

"No, it's all right, Spider. Though I think I'm going to have to give up my calling in Young Women. I'm pretty much tied here."

"Yeah, I know," Spider agreed sadly.

Neither one spoke for a moment, and then Spider, trying to inject a lighter note, said, "I went up mountain biking today to blow out the cobwebs."

"Oh, you did! How was it?"

"I saw a lot of country. Saw a cougar."

"No! Did you? How far away was he?"

"He was pretty close."

"Scare you?"

"Made me a bit nervous. But he took off."

"Well, be careful."

"I will. I'm going to work a bit now, and then I'm going to bed. I didn't sleep too well last night."

"What was the matter?"

"New bed, probably."

"Okay, take care. Love you."

"Love you, too. Bye."

Spider put down the phone and sat a moment, thinking. Then he got a sheet of paper and made a new list of everything he knew about the disappearance of Stan Lucas, which wasn't much more than what he'd previously written. Wondering if there was any reason to stay any longer in Chewelah, he finally went to bed. It took him a while to get comfortable because of the tenderness of his shoulder, elbows, and knees, but he finally got up and took some aspirin, and then was able to drop off to sleep.

CHAPTER

SPIDER WAS DRAGGED OUT of sleep by the pain in his shoulder. Someone was poking it and calling his name. "Brother Latham! Brother Latham!" The room was dark, but the night-light in the hall cast a muted beam through his open bedroom door.

Spider opened his eyes to the sight of Sister Minnow in curlers and a pink terry bathrobe, looming over him and jabbing his injured shoulder with her index finger. Automatically, he caught her hand to forestall any more damage. "Sister Minnow?"

Her eyes, which were wide already, widened more as she felt her hand pinned in Spider's grip. "Brother Latham! You're hurting me!"

Spider was wide awake now. He released the hand and got up on one sore elbow to look at the clock. It was half past one. "I'm sorry, Sister Minnow. What are you doing here?"

"It's him. He's done it again."

"Who?"

"That man. The swarthy one. From California."

"Tony? Tony DeYeso? Your neighbor?"

"Yes!" She went to the window and peeked out. "He left about ten minutes ago. I want you to go over and confront him when he comes back. Tell him the neighbors are tired of this shifty, sneaking around in the middle of the night. If he can't find some honest occupation, we don't want him around here."

"Sister Minnow, the man is an accountant."

"That's his cover. No telling what he's up to in the middle of the night. We don't want his kind of people in our town."

"What kind of people is that?"

"Drug dealers."

"Aw, sister Minnow. I highly doubt that Tony is dealing drugs. Besides, it's a matter for the cops. Call Cy Chamberlain tomorrow, tell him your concerns, let him take care of it." Spider lay back down and pulled the cover up around his shoulder.

"And a lot of good Cy would do with those two gimpy legs of his. No, you're young and strong. Just go tell him."

Spider didn't move.

Neither did Sister Minnow. "Just go tell him," she repeated.

Spider sighed. "I can't get up while you're in the room."

"I'll leave. But hurry! He's never gone more than twenty minutes."

Sister Minnow left, closing the door and leaving Spider in darkness. "Great Suffering Zot!" he muttered. "The woman is crazy." He snapped on the light to locate the pants and shirt that he had draped over the back of a chair and his boots at the foot of the bed, then he turned the light off again, wanting his eyes to be accustomed to the dark. Dressing in haste, he opened the bedroom door to find Sister Minnow hovering in the hall, just outside. "You wait here," he said. "I'll go out through the French doors."

"Be careful!" she said in an urgent whisper.

"Yeah." Closing the door, he paused until the shapes in the room became clearer before letting himself out onto the back lawn. Sister Minnow's house sat in the dimmest reaches between two streetlights, and there were few porch lights on this late at night. A half moon was the best that Spider could hope for to light his way.

What am I going to say? Evening, Tony, I was just out for a stroll . . . and what have you been doing? Feeling ridiculous and more than a little put-upon, Spider crossed the creek on a narrow, arched footbridge and angled through a clump of trees toward the dark DeYeso residence. At that moment, Tony's gray sedan pulled into the driveway, and Spider automatically stepped behind a tree.

The car lights went out. Tony got out of the car and opened the back door, leaning inside to pick up something heavy. With one eye on him, Spider tried to make his way quickly to the sidewalk through the murky night-shade of the trees. Still a bit blind from looking at the headlights, he blundered into Tony's recycle trash bins. The quiet serenity of the night was destroyed by a huge clatter as he kicked the bin, and aluminum cans bounced and rolled. Spider was barely able to keep his balance, and as his arms flailed, he kicked the bin a second time and stepped on another can before finding solid, unencumbered ground. During the time he was off balance he was aware of another sound rending the night-quiet, but he didn't get a chance to puzzle over what it could be, because he was suddenly tackled and taken to the ground. Sliding along on a searingly painful shoulder among the clattering cans, he fetched up against the bin and reacted instinctively. He was on his feet, crouching to face his assailant, who was standing in the moonlight with his fists clenched and ready. Spider circled warily, crunching another can as he did so and causing a wail from the box on the top of the car.

Spider turned his head to peer in the direction of the noise, but in doing so, he left himself open to a right to the jaw that dazed him and sent him clattering among the cans again. During the time it took for him to hit the ground, Spider finally worked out what Tony's midnight drives were all about. Still lying on his back, Spider held up his hands, palms forward. "Wait, Tony! Wait! Is that a baby?"

It wasn't a box on top of the car. Spider could see that now. It was a car seat.

Tony was standing over Spider with his hands still clenched. "Yes, it's a baby, you meddling dung heap. I had her asleep, and now she's awake."

"Well, beating on me isn't going to get her back to sleep. I can maybe help you there."

"I don't need your help."

Spider's hands were still outstretched. "Well, my first was colicky—cried all the time. I learned a trick or two. Be glad to try."

Silence. The hands unclenched. Tony stepped away.

Spider gritted his teeth against the pain in his shoulder as he got up, rubbing his jaw. "Let's take her inside, see what we can do."

Tony didn't reply, but he picked up the car seat and led the way. When they were in the house, Spider asked him to turn on one lamp only and to keep the room dim. "Did you change her before you left?"

"Yes. And I fed her, too. There's no reason for her to be crying."

"How old is she?"

"Two months." Tony lifted the baby out of the car seat and laid her on the table. She had a mass of black hair, and as she cried, her little clenched fists fanned the air in the neighborhood of her ears.

"She's got a temper, doesn't she?"

"Like her dad," Tony said, ruefully.

"Well, let's see what we can do. Have you got a receiving blanket?"

"Is that one of the thin ones?"

"Yeah. Come here, little one," Spider cooed. "Come here . . . is it Ariel? Come here, Ariel." Spider picked up the baby and held her in the crook of his arm as Tony went to get a blanket. When he arrived with it, Spider spread it on the table and laid the baby in the middle.

"Now this is swaddling. A baby this young feels secure if she's all swaddled up. See, tuck this end in here, with her arm down inside, and then this one comes over, pinning the other arm down."

"Won't she feel restricted?" Tony asked. "She doesn't like it, you can tell. She's crying."

"She's been restricted for nine months in the womb. She's not used to much freedom yet. Now then," Spider put the baby on his shoulder.

Holding her tightly, with his mouth next to the baby's ear, he softly hummed "O Ye Mountains High," while patting her gently on the back and doing knee-bends. The baby continued to cry, but gave signs of wearing down.

"Do you have a heating pad?" Spider sang to Tony.

"A heating pad?"

Spider nodded.

"Yeah, I'll get it."

When Tony returned with the pad, Spider didn't break rhythm as he sang, "Put the pad in her bed and turn it to low and we'll wait for the bed to get warm."

"In her bed?"

Spider nodded as he continued to bob and hum, and the baby stopped crying.

Tony disappeared down the hall, and when he reappeared, Spider turned so he could see the baby. "Are her eyes closed?" he whispered.

"Yes. How'd you do that?" Tony answered softly.

"This is the easy part. The hard part is getting her in the bed. If it's cold, it'll wake her up. That's why you put the heating pad in there, to warm it up. Makes a smooth transition. Where's her bedroom?"

Following Tony down the dim hall to a room with a white crib and a nightlight, Spider whispered, "Pull the heating pad out of there." Then he eased little Ariel down onto the warm sheet. He put her on her side and rolled up a receiving blanket to prop against her back. Then he put another folded blanket over her. "That should do it," He whispered.

The two men stood looking at the sleeping infant, and Tony straightened the edge of the blanket with a smile curving the corners of his mouth. "Thanks," he said softly.

Spider led the way out of the room and Tony shut the door before following. He flapped an arm in the direction of the front yard. "Sorry about what happened out there. I'd had such a rough time getting her back to sleep. I finally had to take her for a ride. That's the last resort, but it always works."

"You have to do that often?"

"Couple of times a week. Actually, every time my wife has to work late and I'm the one to put the baby down, it happens."

"Where does your wife work?"

"At the hospital. Sit down for a moment, will you?" Tony pulled out one of the kitchen chairs and turned on the light. "Whoa! Did I do that? Your jaw's kinda swollen. And your arms! Did you do that out there?"

Spider sat and gingerly touched his face and then worked his mouth. "Naw. The arms happened earlier. As for the jaw, I don't think anything's broken. It might be sore for a day or two, but that's all right."

Tony laughed. "I was so mad at you for waking her up! By the way, what were you doing over there, banging around in the beer cans?"

Spider grinned. "I was out to catch a drug dealer."

"So what are you, an undercover cop? Are you just pretending to be looking at Snakewater?"

"No, that's real. It's your neighbor, Mrs. Minnow. She's convinced that, because you're from Los Angeles, you must be selling drugs. She's seen you leave late at night, and she made me come over here to see why."

Tony threw his head back and laughed, remembering the baby at the last minute and turning the hearty roar to a muffled snicker. The black brows and beak of a nose were more attractive when set in a merry face, and Spider felt himself warming to this young man.

"So, you must have moved here just before Ariel was born," Spider said conversationally.

"Yes. We came here for a new start. I was offered the job, and we felt that my wife could get a job anywhere with her nursing skills, so we took it. She went to work a couple nights a week when the baby was a month old.

"She's a pretty baby."

"She's the best thing that ever happened to me, aside from marrying her mother. The best." Tony looked down at his hands for a moment. "I haven't been very much help to you. I've been resenting the fact that you've come. But if I can help you, I will."

"Uh, thanks. But right now I'd better head back. Sister Minnow will be wanting a report."

"She's your sister?"

"No. No. She belongs to my church. We call each other brother and sister."

"What are you, Pentacostal?"

Spider shook his head. "Latter-day Saints. Mormons. I do have one question before I go."

"Shoot."

"How did you happen to write that memo about Greenchem?"

"Well, it was obvious that we were being overcharged," Tony said. "I saw that as soon as I came to work for Snakewater. I did some research to find industry standards as far as price. It took me all of about an hour. If Stan was any kind of a businessman, he'd have done that too before signing that exorbitant contract."

"You said you didn't know who signed the contract."

"I'm assuming, since he's been over the mining interest for five years, that he was the one who negotiated with Greenchem. The head honcho, from what John says, pretty much leaves it to Stan. Says it's his baby."

"Had you seen Stan before this trip?"

Tony thought a moment. "Once before. He stopped in overnight on his way back from Montana. That's when he bought the Yukon. Everyone figured he just stopped in to see Carmen. He didn't talk to anyone about business."

"Going back to the memo. Clara said you handed it to him, rather than sent it."

Tony nodded. "Yes. I had it on my desk to give to him on Friday, but he didn't come back to the mine, so after work I went by the motel."

"He was there right after work?"

"No. I came home and had dinner and then ran it over. Carmen was just leaving."

"So you gave him the memo. What did he say?"

"I can't remember the words." There was a pause before Tony went on.

"But it was something about people knowing their places, and for me not to be trying to curry favor with Brick. Then he shut the door in my face."

"Huh. And you didn't see him again after that?"

"No."

Spider stood. "I appreciate you talking to me about this. I can't believe that this memo was what Stan said he was bringing with him. It's a puzzle. And I hate puzzles."

He held out his hand. "We better get to bed. I'll come over and help you clean up those cans in the morning, when it won't wake the neighborhood."

Tony clasped Spider's hand and then walked him to the door. "Don't worry about it. You'd better go put some ice on that jaw. You'd never guess that I passed my anger management class. But I did."

Spider chuckled. "Babies will do that to you."

Tony turned the porch light on, and Spider walked back by way of the sidewalk, sighing as he saw Sister Minnow's anxious face in the window, because he knew he'd lose another hour of sleep while she fluttered. But it was almost worth it. *Who'd a known old Tony had such a soft spot?* he mused, rubbing his sore jaw. *Yep, it was almost worth it.*

CHAPTER

17

SPIDER WOKE FEELING LIKE he had been beaten with a shovel. It took superhuman effort just to throw back the covers and sit on the edge of the bed, and every muscle and joint in his body screamed "Don't!" as he contemplated the bathroom door. It was only because of his faith in what a hot shower would do that he was able to stand and creak his way across the floor.

Undressed, he peered at himself in the mirror. The jaw wasn't too bad. A bit swollen, but it wasn't too noticeable. The bruise on his cheek had faded to a yellow smudge, the arms were pretty scabby around the elbows, and the knees looked worse. Spider turned his back to the mirror, grimacing at how his neck hurt when he looked over his good shoulder. There were bruise marks like whip-lines where he had hit the larch branches on the last leg of his bike trip yesterday. "Coulda' been worse," he muttered, shuffling to the shower. "Coulda' been dead."

Spider's faith in hot water was justified, and after steaming up the bathroom, he found he could move a little more easily. With only some minor difficulty he dressed and joined Sister Minnow for breakfast. She was bustling around, and it was only as he was leaving that she saw his arms and said, "Oh, dear!" Spider grabbed the lunch bucket, and headed for the car.

"Don't forget," she called after him. "We're doing the cannon this afternoon."

"I'll remember," he promised. As he set the lunch box on the passenger seat beside him, he noticed the box of mail from yesterday. Wondering what law he was breaking, he picked up one of the envelopes and examined the return address. There was no name on it, just a street address that he didn't recognize. By flattening the envelope with his fingers, he could make out figures through the paper but couldn't read them. Tapping the letter on the steering wheel, Spider thought for a moment. Then he tucked it and its twin in his pocket and drove to the hardware store, where he bought a map of the county.

Spider spread the map out on the hood of the SUV and found that the address was on a bench across the valley from the mine. He marked his route in pencil, repeating aloud the names of the roads he would travel.

The first turn he made was from the highway to a blacktop road. The second was from blacktop to well-maintained gravel. The third was from well-maintained to marginal-but-graded gravel. The fourth turn left him on two faint wheel tracks deep in the woods. Spider paused, but the signpost confirmed that this was indeed the road he was looking for, so he forged ahead. Every now and then he would see a mailbox, and the numbers kept climbing, so though he saw no houses, he was still willing to believe that at the end he would find the address on the envelope.

The woods were dense, with the limbs of the trees on each side of the lane meeting to form a leafy bower. He was beginning to feel oppressed by the shade when finally he came to a mailbox with the right number. It was set beside two grassy tracks that took off uphill to the right. Sighing, he made the turn and drove slowly over the ruts and bumps.

Rounding a turn, Spider found himself in a clearing—an open, forty-acre meadow. Sitting at the upper edge was a cabin with a covered porch surrounding it. There was a green pickup parked in front and four hound dogs asleep on the porch. By the time Spider pulled up in front, the hounds were in the dooryard to greet him, setting up a two-tone, dipthong ruckus and bringing out the cabin's occupant.

Spider got out of the Yukon and allowed the canine crowd to sniff at him before making his way through. "How do?" he greeted, looking up at the man on the porch. "Name's Spider Latham."

The cabin's tenant was about forty. He was small and wiry, with long blond hair pulled back in a pony tail, a cookie-duster moustache, and piercing blue eyes. "Bryan Wilson," he offered, "but most people call me Cougar."

A strong smell of body odor wafted toward Spider. "And why is that?" he asked, hazarding a mental guess.

"'Cause I hunt cougar. You been in a fight?"

"Wrecked my bike."

"I used to ride a Harley. You gotta be careful."

"Uh . . . yeah. Are there many cougar around here?"

"Are there? Hoo boy! Don't you just know! Those espresso-drinking city folks over in Seattle didn't like the idea of us hunting the poor defenseless cougars with dogs, so they passed a law against it. Tightened up the season. Only allow so many licenses, all that claptrap. So naturally, the numbers is mountin', like rabbits."

"Yeah. I saw one yesterday. Up by Snakewater."

Cougar spat on the ground. "A fellow just outside of Chewelah shot one in his backyard. His little girl was playing in the sand box, and he couldn't scare the cat away. So he shot him. I don't know what it's going to take before those Starbuck-suckers get the idea that this is not an endangered species."

"Uh, I don't know either." Spider rested one boot on the bottom step. "Say, Cougar, I need to ask you something. Did you write these two letters?" Spider held them out.

Cougar took them and frowned. "Yeah, I did."

"Can I ask why you were writing to Greenchem?"

"I was sendin' in my hours, just like I always do, ever' two weeks."

"Hours for what?"

"For pickin' up the barrels!"

"Ah. So you're the one that picks up the toxic waste at Snakewater."

"Yeah. Easiest job I ever had." He spat on the ground again. "They give me a shiny new pickup with a lift gate on it." He gestured to the truck parked next to Spider's vehicle. "Oh, I got to slap some signs on when I use her for work, but otherwise it's mine to use. I go twice a week up to the mine and pick up the barrels, deliver them to the drop-off, and they pay me a thousand dollars a month. If I hadn't done it for nigh onto four years, I'd say it's too good to be true."

One of the hounds was pressing against Spider's leg. He leaned down and rubbed it behind the ears, asking, "How'd you get the job?"

"Fella come t' me. Drove right up to the house. Said he knew I was on disability, didn't get out much. He had a job he knew I could do. Wanted me to keep a low profile, not talk to people about the job."

Spider's brows went up. "Why did he say that?"

"Well, the way I figger, the mine super don't take too kindly to having to spend the money for toxic waste disposal."

"That's John Nelson?"

"Yeah. He didn't want me getting crosswise of John. And, he didn't want a bunch of yahoos pesterin' him for jobs when they found out how cinchy this one was."

"So you kept a low profile?"

"Wasn't hard," Cougar said. "I generally keep t' myself. Only time anyone comes around is when there's a nuisance cougar that they want me to track with my dogs. Lately that's been quite a few."

"I can believe it!"

"Say, how'd you get those letters?" Cougar asked.

Spider climbed two of the three steps and pointed at the Spokane number. "Uh, there was a glitch at this address. I picked them up, and I'll make sure they get to the main office. This isn't the address of the main office. I just wanted to come by and let you know the reason you haven't been paid."

"You work for Greenchem?"

"Naw, I work for BTE, for the fella that owns Snakewater. Trying to get this thing straightened out."

"Well, thanks! I was beginning to wonder. I only had a problem one other time. I called the number they gave me when they hired me, and I got an answering machine at first. But someone called me right back. It was a gal and I mean to tell you, she got things straightened out right now."

"Did you call about not receiving this last check on time?"

Cougar shook his head. "I was just about to."

"Uh, I wonder. Would you mind if I kind of stood by while you make the call? I want to see if there's someone in the main office right now."

"No, fine. Come on in. We'll make the call." Cougar Wilson spat once more and then led the way around the veranda.

As he followed, Spider noticed that the lumber for the house was rough-sawn, but the workmanship was solid and square. "You build this house?"

"Yeah. Been at it for ten years, building as I've had the money. I camped in the woods for eight years until I had enough to buy the property, then camped here for another two while I saved the money to frame it and add a roof. I had a fellow with a portable sawmill come, and we logged off a few acres and milled it right here."

Spider looked around at the lonely landscape, with the sunny meadow climbing up the mountain and woods taking over after that. "Where do you get your water? Did you drill a well?"

"There's a creek that runs by over there. I sank a barrel for a catch basin, and I pipe it down from there."

"Does it ever freeze up in the winter?" Spider asked.

"Oh yeah. But I have storage barrels in the living room that I keep full. I can go a long time on a little water."

Following Cougar downwind, Spider didn't find that hard to believe. "You said you're on disability. You able to do the heavy work of building?"

Cougar held the door open for Spider to enter the house. The living/dining/kitchen room was a modest size, with sparse, rough-hewn furniture, a wood cook stove and a pot-bellied stove in the middle of the room. There were two cougar pelts tacked to the wall and another two laid out as rugs on the floor of the living area.

"Oh, my disability isn't physical," Cougar said in answer to Spider's question. "Or at least it didn't end up being that way. I had a pretty rough childhood, and it's left me so I can't be around people very much. Can't work with people. I was in several foster homes after they took me away from my real parents."

"You were taken away from your parents?"

"Yeah, when I was six. My mother had an affair with another man, and I was the result. My dad—my mother's husband, I mean—hated me, and my mom was ashamed of me. They put me in the hospital a couple of times. Broke my nose once. Broke my leg the next time."

Spider didn't know what to say, but Cougar went on with his tale.

"One of my foster parents arranged for me to have an SSI grant when I turned eighteen. I get a check once a month from Social Security."

"But you seem like a pretty genial fellow. You're obviously industrious. I would think someone would be lucky to have you work for them."

"Oh, with one or two other people, I do all right. But I get nervous if there get to be many more than that. I tend to freak out." Cougar set the envelopes down and scanned his telephone directory written on the board walls above the phone.

"Isn't there a problem with this Greenchem job? Won't that affect your grant?"

Cougar dialed a number. "Would if I reported it, but I don't."

"I see." Examining the wall behind the phone, Spider found the Greenchem listing and tried to commit it to memory.

The answering machine picked up. "This is Cougar Wilson. I've sent in my last two time cards and haven't received anything yet. I hope you will check into the problem and make sure that I receive both checks that are due me. Thanks and 'bye." He hung up and shook his head. "Nobody there."

"What's the name of the fellow who hired you?"

"Steven Greene. He owns the company."

"What's he look like?"

"I guess he's my age, maybe a bit younger. Medium height and build. Reminds me of Paul Newman in old movies. He's real self-assured, well dressed. Looked pretty outa-place out here. City fellow. But nice. Made sense."

"Huh," Spider grunted.

"I seen him at Snakewater once. He was talking to that gal that sets the barrels out for me. He didn't see me, but I saw him."

"Will you let me know if he gets in touch?"

"How?"

Spider picked up a pencil hanging on a string by the phone and wrote his name on the wall with the same three phone numbers he had given Cherie Taylor.

"Does that say Spider?"

"Yeah, you're a Cougar. I'm a Spider."

Cougar laughed, revealing several missing teeth. "I'm a Cougar, you're a Spider," he repeated, laughing again.

Spider picked up the letters. "I'll hang on to these and get them to the main office so you can get paid." Stuffing them in his pocket, he turned to go when a shiny red child's rocking chair caught his eye.

"You got kids?" he asked.

Cougar thought that was funny, too. "I got kids?" he echoed and laughed again. "No! But in my first foster home, they had a little rocking chair like that. I loved it. I used to sit for hours, looking out the window and rocking. I thought I'd like to make rockers like that, for kids that are having a hard time."

"So you're going to make more of these?"

"Already have." Cougar stepped to an inner door and opened it to reveal a small store room stacked high with rockers of all different sizes and colors. "There are some fellas who come and get them 'round Christmas time and give them to needy children."

Spider gazed in amazement at the rainbow of rockers and then turned to his fragrant companion. "I'm proud to make your acquaintance, Cougar." He shook his hand and then patted the letters in his pocket. "I'll make sure you get paid what you're owed," he promised.

"I'd appreciate that."

Walking through the door and around the veranda, Cougar trailed behind Spider, chuckling and muttering, "You're a Cougar and I'm a Spider." He stood on the veranda surrounded by his dogs as Spider got in his car and turned around, and waved as he drove away.

Spider watched in his rearview mirror. *I don't quite know what to think about that,* he mused. *I hope I get to meet this Steven Greene. I know this: He's going to do right by Cougar Wilson, or I'll know why.*

With that determination, Spider headed down the hill, hoping that Cy Chamberlain was at home.

CY WAS ON THE BACK PORCH, sitting on a chair by the hot tub untying his shoes. "Morning, Cy," Spider greeted. "You busy?"

"I was just going to soak my bones." He eyed Spider, taking in the swollen jaw and the scabby arms around his elbows. "You been causing trouble around here?"

"I'm embarrassed to say that I took a tumble on my bike."

"You all right?"

Spider rubbed his jaw. "A little sore, but nothing that I'm going to complain to you about. I wondered if you could help me."

"What d'ya need?"

Spider tossed one of the letters with the post office box return address in Cy's lap. "I need to know the name of the person who wrote that letter. Can you talk to the postmaster and get that for me?"

"Dunno. I can try. Where'd you get this?"

"Well, that's another thing. I need you to go with me to Spokane and help me find out who set up for Greenchem to get mail at the address on that letter."

Cy looked up at Spider. "So this address isn't really . . ."

"No. It's one of those mailbox places. I went in the other day to say I came about Greenchem, and before I could say anything else, the clerk gave me all the mail and said I should check the box more often. I didn't open any of it, and I intend to give it back, but first I want to find out who wrote this one."

"So what do you want me to do first?" Cy asked.

"Come with me into Spokane. You can talk to the post office when we get back."

Bending slowly over, Cy began retying his shoes.

"I'm sorry about your bones," said Spider.

"Don't be. This is going to get me out of writing that stupid newspaper column."

Spider shoved his hands in his pockets to restrain himself from offering to help. When Cy was through, Spider made idle conversation as he walked slowly beside the older man out to the Yukon. Closing the door after Cy's laborious entrance, Spider got in and headed for Spokane.

As they visited on the way, Spider found out that Cy was a widower. His wife had been dead five years, he said. They had been married thirty years when she died suddenly of cancer. It was a good marriage, but she was not the love of his life, he confessed. As a young man he had loved someone, but she had chosen another and moved away. Cy paused, then said he didn't know how he happened to mention that. He had had a good marriage and didn't think about the other much at all.

Spider told Cy about Laurie and about having his mother live with them. He told about his sons—Kevin working as an archeologist in Mexico and Bobby working in Seattle for an outfit that had something to do with computers. Cy asked if Bobby was making lots of money and Spider said he thought he was. They both shook their heads.

When they got to Spokane, Spider drove to the strip mall and parked in the handicapped space in front of Mailboxes and More. Keeping pace with Cy, Spider carried the box as they crossed the parking lot and entered the store. The spiky-haired clerk was not on duty behind the counter.

Instead there was a short, heavy woman in a blue flowered tent dress. Spider set the box down on the counter and nodded, taking off his Stetson and setting it by the box.

"Afternoon, ma'am," Spider greeted. "I was in yesterday, and the fellow you had working gave me this box of mail for Greenchem."

"Oh, I know he did. I was so upset with him! Get a clue, I told him! How could you do that? This mail is always supposed to be forwarded!"

Cy was leaning on his crutches, but even with that and the slight stoop to his shoulders, he still looked official in his uniform. "I'm deputy sheriff of Stevens County," he said. "And this is Spider Latham, deputy sheriff up from Las Vegas. We've come to talk to you about the person who arranged to get this mail here."

The woman threw up her pudgy hands and backed up, all three chins quivering as her eyes widened. "Las Vegas! That's where he said to send the mail!"

"Who said?"

"Mr. Greene. The man who rented the box. He wanted us to forward anything that came in, to Las Vegas once a week."

"How long has this been going on?" Cy asked.

"Several years. Three, maybe. Maybe four."

"Why didn't this get sent out?"

"Because I was gone for a month taking care of my mother. I left suddenly, and my son said he would take care of things, but I forgot to tell him to send the Greenchem mail, and it just piled up. I was going to take care of it as soon as I got home, but I found that he had given it to someone that came in. Someone in a cowboy hat." She frowned at Spider. "You had no right to take that," she accused. "That's U.S. Mail."

"We need to talk to Mr. Greene," Spider said. "Can you give us the address in Las Vegas where you send the mail?"

"I don't know if I should."

Cy weighed in again. "Well, you can give it to us now, or we can go through the legal process and get it from you, which will probably entail you taking a day to come up to the courthouse in Stevens County."

Her broad brow furrowed. "I can't afford any more time off! I can't be away any more. Here. . . ." She grabbed a recipe box from the back counter and rifled through the cards, pulling one out and making a copy of it. "Here's where he said to send everything." She handed the copy to Cy and pulled the box of errant mail to her. "And I'm going to forward this right now." With that, she marched ponderously to the room behind the mail boxes and didn't return.

Spider looked over Cy's shoulder at a copy of Mailboxes' standard forwarding-request form signed by Steve Greene.

"Great Suffering Zot," breathed Spider.

"What?"

Spider glanced up and saw the blue flowered tent hovering near the mailbox room door and jerked his head in the direction of the door. Cy nodded and followed him, snail-like, out to the sidewalk.

"What did you see?"

"The way Mr. Greene signed his name. I've seen that S before. See how he makes it almost like a figure eight that's kind of leaning over?'

"Yeah?"

"That's the way Stan Lucas makes his capital S."

Cy whistled. "You got something we can compare it with?"

"Back in Chewelah I do."

"Let's go!" Cy cut his travel time back to the car in half and flung first his crutches and then himself through the door Spider held open for him.

Spider got in and turned toward Chewelah, but neither spoke. Both were mulling over this piece of information, wondering about the implications. Finally Spider broke the silence: "So, what do you think? If Stan is Steve Greene, then is he the company that contracts to get rid of the toxic waste? That means that he negotiated the contract with himself."

"Looks like. Why would he do that?"

"Because his price is about three times as high as any one else in the business."

"Aha."

Both men chewed on that for a while.

"Does this have anything to do with him disappearing?" Spider mused.

"Could be. But what?"

Spider shook his head and they traveled again in silence.

Cy was the first to speak. "Let's say Brick Tremain got wind of what Stan was doing and got angry. Maybe he was angry enough to kill him, or have him killed."

"After making sure that his daughter took out an insurance policy on him for half a million dollars," Spider added. "I don't know. It sounds okay until you meet Brick."

"Who else would care?"

"John Nelson cares," Spider offered.

"That sounds okay unless you know John."

More silence. Spider was the one who broke it this time. "Jade would care."

"Who's Jade?"

"Brick's son. But I can't see him either."

Cy sighed. "Sometimes it turns out to be the one you couldn't, or wouldn't, see. If that's what happened, if Stan's been killed, we can't rule anyone out."

Silence again. They were passing a lake, and someone in a red kayak was gliding over the glassy surface, dipping first one side of the paddle in and then the other.

"Maybe Stan meant to disappear," Spider mused. "Tony DeYeso wrote a memo to Stan the day before he left, saying that the toxic waste disposal rates were exorbitant. He sent a copy to Brick. Maybe Stan knew the jig was up and decided to get out of town while the getting was good."

"So he flew to Las Vegas and then got on another plane or some other form of transportation and left. Could be."

"Okay. Suppose he wanted to avoid the heat. Why? Was what he did illegal?"

"Unethical, maybe. Illegal? I don't know."

Both men were lost in thought until they dropped down into the valley and could see Chewelah in the distance. "I need to go back to Vegas and see what's at that address," Spider declared.

"What address?"

"The one the lady at the mailbox place gave us."

"Good idea."

"Could we find out if he flew out of Las Vegas on another plane?" Spider asked.

"Same name?"

"Maybe try both Stan Lucas and Steve Greene. Do you have a way of doing that?"

"I'll find a way," Cy said. "But I might not be able to come up with anything this afternoon."

"Yeah. But first let's go by and look at the signature on that picture, and make sure I'm not up in the night about this."

Spider drove to Sister Minnow's and left the motor running with the air conditioning on while he dashed in and got the folder that he had brought from Las Vegas.

Back in the car, he pulled the eight-by-ten photo of Stan Lucas out of the envelope and showed it to Cy.

"Has the look of Paul Newman, doesn't he?" Cy asked. "Same nose and chin."

"Does he? I can't see it, but a fellow I talked to this morning said the same thing about Steve Greene. Look at the *S* and compare it with the one from Mailboxes."

Cy placed the copy of the card up by the signature on the picture. "Looks the same to me!" he declared.

"What are the odds that they're not the same guy?"

"Pretty slim, I'd say."

Spider stowed the picture and sample signature in the folder and put it in the backseat. Then he drove the six blocks to Cy's house. "I don't know that it still makes a difference, but if you'd find out about the name and address on that letter, I'd appreciate it," he said.

"I'll do that right away and then get started tracking whether Stan left Las Vegas. When are you heading back?"

"I'll see when I can get a flight. I'll call you if I'm going to leave tonight."

"Fair enough. Gosh, but it feels good to be back in the saddle!"

Spider laughed. "Even if the saddle's on an old nag?"

Cy hauled himself out of the car. "Old nags still know the paces. They may be slow, but they still know the paces."

"I guess," Spider agreed. When Cy managed to get the door shut, he drove away, watching in the rearview mirror as the deputy sheriff eagerly inched his way up the sidewalk.

Sister Minnow was home when Spider got back, so he entered his room through the French doors in back. Munching on a roast beef sandwich out of the lunch box, he sat on his bed and used the phone to make arrangements to fly to Las Vegas early the next morning and pick up a rental car. Then he lounged back on the bed and dialed home.

Laurie answered on the third ring.

"You sound tired," Spider said, concerned.

"How can you tell? All I said was hello."

"That's all you need to say. Are you getting enough sleep?"

"I don't think so. I'm so afraid your mother will get up and wander or fall down with me not hearing her that I never feel as though I go soundly to sleep. If she moans in her sleep or even rolls over, I wake up."

"Sounds to me like this is getting to be too much for you to handle."

"There's a big difference between being tired and not being able to handle it. I'll manage. I made it through Bobby's colic, didn't I?"

"Oh, that reminds me," Spider said, chuckling. "I had a chance to use my crying baby technique last night." He told Laurie about skulking over to spy on Tony DeYeso and the resulting kerfuffle. Laurie enjoyed it hugely.

"You've made my day." Her voice came smiling over the wire. "Laughing must be good for you. I don't feel nearly so tired now."

"It's not the laughter, it's the power of my personality."

"I believe it. I hear your mother stirring, hon. I've gotta go. Thanks for calling me. I needed that."

"Love you," Spider said.

"Love you, too. Bye."

Just as Spider hung up the phone, he heard someone pull in the driveway. It was Phil, towing his cannon on a trailer behind his pickup. Spider ambled out to look. Sister Minnow, dressed in a long dress and sunbonnet, came hurrying out too. Phil, already damp from perspiration, stood proudly by.

"I thought we were going after work," Spider said.

"I took the day off. There were some things I had to make so we could go shoot it off. I just got done, so I thought I'd come on over to see if we could go earlier."

"All right by me," Spider said, walking around the big gun. "Where'd you get the barrel?"

"A fellow over in Coeur d'Alene makes them. In the eighteen hundreds, it would have been made of bronze, but this one here is made of a seamless steel tube with cast iron poured around it. It's the same size and weight, but a lot stronger and safer."

"Where'd you get your wheels?"

"I made them."

"You did?"

"I had a fellow up around Colville put on the bands. He has a forge and does stuff like that. But I turned the hubs and turned all the spokes."

"You did a fine job. It's beautiful!"

"I brought the instructions. I figure you could read them on the way, and we can figure it out when we get there. It can't be that much different from an old muzzle loader, and I've shot one of them."

Feeling that it was probably a lot different, Spider took the pamphlet from Phil and opened it to the place marked instructions. "Did you bring all these things that it lists here?"

"Yep."

"Welder's gloves? Did you bring those?"

"Yep."

"What do you need welder's gloves for?" Sister Minnow asked.

"Spider is going to read it on the way," Phil answered.

"Say, Phil, did you ever play with carbide when you were a kid? You know, put it under a tin can with water on it and wait for it to explode and send the can sky-high?"

"Yeah. We done that all the time."

Spider grinned. "Me, too. Well, let's get on out and see what this baby will do."

SISTER MINNOW SAT BETWEEN Phil and Spider in Phil's pickup truck, with her voluminous petticoats spread over onto Spider's lap as they traveled. He concentrated on reading the instructions for firing the replica of the mountain howitzer they were towing on a car trailer.

"Okay, the minimum size crew you can have is three. That means you're part of the crew, Sister Minnow."

"I am! Oh, dear."

"Yeah. You have one in the front who uses a corkscrew—did you bring one of those, Phil?"

"Yeah, I made one."

"Okay. The corkscrew gets any foreign objects out of the barrel. Then he swabs it down with something wet. And then he puts the powder and ball down the barrel and rams it home. Is that me?"

"I figured you could do that," Phil confirmed.

"The powder monkey—that's you, Sister Minnow . . ."

"Powder monkey! Oh, dear."

"Your place is twenty feet behind the gun. You make up the charges and then, when you get the signal, you bring them to me."

"What's the signal?"

"I haven't come to that yet," Spider said, reading on. "Okay. Next is you, Phil. You're behind the gun, and while I'm swabbing and putting in the charge, you stand at the back with your finger over the hole. This is where you wear the welding gloves."

"What hole?" asked Sister Minnow.

"There's a little hole in the back," explained Phil. "That's how we light the cannon off."

"Yeah, Phil. You put one of the caps in the hole—no, first you take your ice pick and pierce the bag that's holding the powder. That would be the charge that I've rammed down the barrel."

Phil's brows knit. "I stick the ice pick through the hole?"

"Yeah. Through the hole and into the bag that holds the powder. You've got to make sure that the primer can ignite the powder. You did bring the primer, didn't you?"

"They said to use caps from shotgun shells. I got some from the reloading store up in Colville."

"All right." Spider read on, "When you've got the primer placed, you take the lanyard and stand away from the cannon."

"What's a lanyard?" asked Phil.

"It's a cord. A string. Did you bring one?"

"No. I wonder if it's important."

"I think it is." Spider glanced out the back window into the bed of the pickup. "You got anything like baling twine or a rope or anything in the back?"

"No. Shoot! I thought I had everything on the list."

"I have some narrow lace on the bottom of my petticoat," offered Sister Minnow. "I could rip that off. I'll bet I've got ten yards of it."

"What do you think?" Spider asked Phil.

"If it does the job, that's fine, as long as it doesn't get back to the rest of the Sons of the Confederacy."

"I don't know, Phil," Spider said. "They'll probably all want lacy lanyards if they find out you've got one."

Phil didn't see the humor. "It's not historically accurate," he said and pointed out the window. "There's where we'll fire it off. In that field." Turning onto a lane that skirted some woods, he pulled over and parked.

The fenced field was about twenty acres, with short grass and dried-up cow pies giving evidence that it had recently been used as a pasture. Surrounded on three sides by forest, there were red and black "Posted No Hunting" signs nailed to trees every couple hundred feet.

"Why did you choose this place?" Spider asked, getting out of the truck and helping Sister Minnow down.

"Belongs to my grandfather." Phil stood with his hands on his hips, looking around. "I figured there wouldn't be any problem about firing on someone else's property. I think if we get it off the trailer we can swing it around and fire that way, since that's the long side of the field."

Spider helped Phil set up the ramps to roll the artillery piece off its low trailer onto the lane. Climbing up on the trailer, Spider examined the howitzer more closely. The wooden wheels and spokes were painted lime green and stood about as high as Spider's waist. The stubby barrel, about a yard long and too massive for Spider to get both hands around, sat on a lime-green framework attached to the axle. The two-inch bore was a black hole in the middle that Spider chose not to peer into.

Phil stood on one side of the barrel and Spider stood on the other, and together they heaved, one hand on the barrel support, the other pushing against a wheel spoke.

"How much does this thing weigh?" Spider grunted.

"The barrel weighs about three hundred pounds," Phil answered. A vein was standing out on his temple. "Here she goes!"

As the howitzer rolled down the ramp, Spider followed, picking up the tongue and using its momentum to heave it around so that the trajectory would be parallel to the road, facing the forest opposite.

"I think we're about twenty feet away from the pickup," Spider observed. "That's where Sister Minnow can stay. Where is she, by the way?"

"I'm over here taking the lace off my petticoat," she called from the other side of the pickup.

"Good." Spider pulled the book of instructions out of his pocket. "Plastic sandwich bags? Aluminum foil? Did you bring those?"

"They're in that plastic bucket."

"Are you going to use balls? Did you bring some?"

"I brought five. Cast them myself," Phil said proudly.

"Here's your lanyard," sang Sister Minnow, emerging with a bunch of lace in her hand.

"Put it on the cannon," Spider said, "then come over here and we'll put together one of the charges. You'll do the next one, Sister Minnow."

She saluted and then giggled, picking up her skirts to trot to the cannon and back.

When they were assembled around the tailgate, Spider laid the open instruction book down, reading through the steps as he performed each part of the process.

"Where's the gunpowder? It says to put four ounces in a plastic bag and seal it. How much is four ounces of powder, do you think?"

"A pint's a pound the world around," quoted Sister Minnow.

"A pint of what?" asked Spider. "A pint of water would weigh more than a pint of marshmallows."

"A pint of anything you would measure for baking. Sugar, flour, shortening."

"How many ounces in a pint? Sixteen?" Spider started shaking gunpowder into the plastic bag.

"Four ounces would be half a cup. I would say about that much."

Spider gave her the sandwich bag. "Will you seal this for me? Now, where's the aluminum foil?"

Phil got the box of foil out of the back of the pickup and gave it to Spider, who tore off a good-sized piece.

Laying it on the tailgate of the truck, he rolled it up to make a tube and folded one end to seal it. "It said to make a tube two inches in diameter. Then we put the gunpowder in the bottom . . ." Spider held the tube, and Sister Minnow dropped in the bag of powder " . . . and then the ball. Where's the ball?"

Phil held up a lead sphere about the size of a baseball and dropped it into the tube on top of the gunpowder.

"Now we close up the tube, and we have our shot ready. Shall we try this one and see if we've got enough powder in it before we make another?"

"Sounds good to me!" Phil was sweating in his woolen Confederate uniform, but he was grinning. Handing Spider his tools, he headed for the cannon.

"You have to stay by the truck, Sister Minnow," Spider cautioned as he hefted a plastic pail full of water from the back. "That's the job of the powder monkey. When I call for the shot, you bring it to me."

Setting the bucket of water down by the swab and ramrod, Spider suggested, "Since this is the first time, I don't see that we need to go through the whole ordeal."

"It'll be good practice," said Phil, pulling on the welder's gloves. "Help us get the routine down."

"Okay," agreed Spider, so while Phil held his gloved finger over the hole, Spider went through the motions of cleaning out the barrel and swabbing it down. "Let's have that shot," he called out.

Sister Minnow brought it to him and then bustled back to her post. Spider loaded the charge into the barrel and tamped it down with the ramrod. "How hard do I tamp it?" he wondered.

"I think it needs to be right to the end, so hit it pretty good."

Spider did and then reported, "Ready, sir."

Phil reached for one of the caps, but Spider reminded him that he needed to pierce the bag of powder first, so he did that, thrusting the ice pick in up to the hilt.

"We need to tie the lanyard on, too," Spider added. He took his pocket knife and cut the loop of lace that Sister Minnow had sacrificed, tying one end to the hammer and measuring off a dozen feet.

With trembling hands, Phil put the primer in the hole. He straightened and looked at Spider with a serious expression. "This is it," he whispered.

"Yeah. But before you pull the lanyard, I wonder if we shouldn't raise that barrel just a bit. We don't want to take out your Grandpa's fence by accident."

"Good idea." Together Phil and Spider raised the barrel a notch. "I think maybe we should have done this before we loaded it," Phil muttered.

"Okay," said Spider. "I'm supposed to stand here by the wheel and cover my ears and you're supposed to stand away to the length of the lanyard. When we're ready to fire, you jerk it, and Katy bar the door!"

Spider took his place and Phil walked slowly to the end of his lacy tether. "Ready . . . Aim . . ." he called.

Spider covered his ears.

"Fire!" Phil yanked the lanyard, and there was a sound like a thunderclap, a huge roaring report that reverberated sharply on Spider's protected eardrums. All three watched in awe as smoke and fire belched from the muzzle of the cannon and, after a delay much longer than they thought it should have been, they heard the crashing of the ball as it landed deep in the forest beyond the pasture.

"Oops," Spider said. "Too far. What'ya think? Too much powder, or was the barrel too high?"

"What? I can't hear a word you're saying," Phil shouted.

"Too much powder," Spider shouted at Phil. "Put in less this time, Sister Minnow."

She saluted. "Yes, sir!" and turned to her appointed task.

"Cover the hole," Spider shouted to Phil. "The hole. Cover it."

It was only when Spider demonstrated, that Phil understood. "I can't hear a thing," he shouted as he covered the hole with his glove.

When Spider was sure that the air supply to the barrel had been cut off, he stepped warily in front of the gun and plied first the corkscrew and then the swab. Calling for the shot, he took it from Sister Minnow and gingerly slid it into the barrel, then rammed it securely down.

Stepping to the side, he shouted to Phil, "Cannon's loaded, sir."

Phil lifted his hand from the hole and stabbed the ice pick into it. Then he placed the primer and stepped to the end of his lanyard. Reaching over his head with his free hand, he covered the ear nearest the cannon. "Ready. Aim. Fire!"

Again the giant thunderclap sounded through Spider's hands, and he wondered how loud it actually was. He uncovered his ears, and through the smoke he saw the top of a tree shear off before the ball went crashing into the woods just a bit nearer than before.

"Barrel must be too high," Spider opined. "Let's drop it a notch."

"What?"

Spider made downward motions with his hands. "Let's drop it a notch. We're shooting too far," he shouted.

While he and Phil worked at lowering the barrel, Spider noticed a low pitched humming in his ears. "Let's only do one more," he shouted at Phil. "It's too hard on the ears."

Phil frowned. "What gears?"

"Ears!" Spider shouted, pointing. "It's hard on the ears!"

"I know. I can't hear a thing."

Spider could. The humming was growing louder and was coming from the woods opposite the road. It was a diesel engine. Sounded like a piece of heavy equipment, and it was getting louder. Spider turned to scan the woods and caught a flash of yellow moving through the trees. "We've got an audience," he said, but Phil was putting on his gloves and didn't hear him.

A backhoe emerged from the woods as Spider went to the muzzle with his corkscrew. He could tell by the sound that the hoe was approaching in high gear, and as he plied the tool he glanced over his shoulder. "When's he going to slow down?"

Phil, standing with his finger on the hole, didn't answer, but he had also heard the roar of the motor, and his eyes were getting bigger as the yellow behemoth bore down upon them.

"Is he going to stop? I don't think he's going to stop!" Spider shouted, scrambling away as the hoe roared past, between him and the cannon.

The backhoe did stop, just beyond them. At the controls was a grim-looking fellow dressed in blue coveralls with a wild mop of black, curly hair and intense dark eyes. He backed up to the cannon, and the backhoe bucket, which was equipped with a thumb, reached out and grabbed the cannon.

"Hey! What are you doing?" yelled Phil, but he was drowned out by the roar of the engine. He grabbed onto the dangling tongue of the carriage as the cannon was lifted off the ground. "You can't do this!" he hollered, setting back on his heels.

Spider intercepted Sister Minnow who was running to help and sent her back to stand by the pickup. Phil, still clutching the wagon tongue of the caisson, was being towed along as the backhoe rolled toward the woods. "You can't do this!" he shouted again, vainly planting his feet.

Spider trotted over to admonish Phil to give it up, but the stubborn soldier kept his post, resisting manfully as the speed of the backhoe increased. By the time they reached the woods, Spider was striding briskly to keep up and Phil was mostly being dragged. The hair on the back of Spider's neck prickled at the way the man at the controls glared fiercely down at them. "Let's leave it be!" he shouted to Phil.

Phil was tenacious. His face was grim, and this Johnny Reb fought all the way. Spider kept pace as they passed through a strip of woods into a semi-open field where there were a number of deep holes dug, with a mound of fresh earth beside each. The backhoe rolled to the edge of one of the pits, and Phil finally let go when the cannon dropped ten feet down. The fight just went out of him, and he stood unbelieving as the backhoe started pulling dirt in on top of the cannon.

Sister Minnow came running up, shaking her finger at the man on the backhoe. Spider couldn't hear what she was saying, but when he suggested to Phil that they needed to get the lady out of the way, he nodded and, shoulders sagging, shambled behind as Spider escorted Sister Minnow back to the pickup.

"You want me to drive?" Spider asked.

Phil still looked dazed, so Sister Minnow took his hand and led him to the passenger door. Spider gathered up the tools from the former artillery emplacement and stowed them in the back of the truck. Then he got in and towed the empty trailer around in a wide turn and headed back to town.

They were a silent trio. Phil sat like a grieving parent, and Sister Minnow patted his hand sympathetically. Spider drove to Cy's house and was glad to see that his Stevens County cruiser was in the driveway. "I think we'd better report this," he said. Phil looked at him blankly and then nodded.

Spider exited the truck and went around to open the door for his crewmates to get out. They followed him up the walk to the open front door, standing anachronistically on the porch as he rang the bell.

They heard Cy's shuffling approach through the screen. "Hello, Phil," he called from mid way. "Hello, Agnes. Is the South rising again?"

"We've come to make a report," Sister Minnow said. "Someone stole Phil's cannon."

"Beg pardon?"

"We were out shooting off the cannon that Phil made, and this lunatic came up with a backhoe, picked it up, and buried it. Right under our noses!"

Cy opened the screen door. "If it wasn't you talking, Agnes, I'd think you'd been hitting the sauce. Oh, hello, Spider. I didn't see you there. Do you understand what she's saying?"

"It's pretty much what she's been telling you."

Cy shuffled aside. "Well, come in. Sit down. It looks like this is going to take a minute."

When all were seated, Spider told the story. Cy listened intently, taking notes. "And this was completely unprovoked?" he asked.

"Unless he took exception to the fact that the shots landed in the woods beyond. But he wasn't in that area. I don't know that he even knew that's what happened."

"Where were you at? Where is this field located?"

Spider looked to Phil for the information. "We was out on Brown Road, just past High Valley," Phil supplied.

"Brown Road? Tell me again what the man looked like."

Spider described him, and Sister Minnow added that he looked like a maniac. Cy jotted down some more notes and then stood. "I'll go out there and talk to him. Spider, if you'll go out with me, I'd appreciate it. Phil, why don't you take Agnes on home. We'll do what we can to get your cannon back. I think we may be able to manage it; although, if the balls landed on his land, and if he had it posted for no hunting, he may have a legal leg."

"Do you know him?"

"If it's who I think it is, yes, I do. I'll go talk to him right now."

"Spider can show you where it is," Phil said. "Can't you, Spider?"

Spider shepherded them to the door. "Yes, I can. Sister Minnow, why don't you take Phil home and maybe fix a real good supper. I'm sure he'd like that, and I would too."

She nodded and marched out the door, a woman with a mission. Phil looked a little less wobbly and managed to help her get her petticoats stuffed in the cab before getting in and driving away.

Spider turned to look at Cy. "What have you got up your sleeve?" he asked. "You know something. What is it?"

"How do you know?"

"I don't know. Something about your eyes, or the way you're almost smiling. What is it?"

"Well, the fellow on the backhoe, Tommy Hobson. The one that buried Phil's cannon . . ."

"Yes. What about him?"

"He's the fellow who wrote those other letters to Greenchem."

SPIDER AND CY WERE IN THE Stevens County car headed out of town when Spider said, "Say, Cy, you want to run by Minnow's and let me pick up that picture? Maybe after we talk to Tommy Hobson we could go up to old Cougar Wilson's and have him tell us that Stan Lucas is Steve Greene."

"Sounds like a plan," Cy agreed and made a U-turn in the middle of Main Street to drive back to Minnow's.

Spider dashed in and returned with the picture. As he settled back in the passenger seat, Cy asked, "Everything all right in there?"

"Phil's working at getting on the outside of a piece of chocolate cake. I'd say he's feeling better."

Cy chuckled and pointed the car toward the highway again. "The thing that Phil doesn't realize is, he couldn't have chosen a worse place to shoot off a cannon."

"No?"

"Uh-uh. Tommy Hobson was in Vietnam and got shot up pretty bad. He's . . . well, we used to call it shell shocked. Now they call it post traumatic stress syndrome. He's a good fellow—hard working and kind, normally, though pretty much a loner. He goes to therapy and, in his words, he's all right as long as he takes his 'wacko pills.' But, I would imagine that he wouldn't cotton to someone shooting off a cannon in his front yard."

"Mmmm. I see." Spider's brow wrinkled. "So, if he's hard working, what does he work at?"

"He's a stone mason. A bricklayer. I don't know that he works steady. There's not too much building going on in the county right now."

"He doesn't do any backhoe work?"

"Until you mentioned it, I didn't know he had a backhoe."

"Why would he be digging holes in a field?"

Cy considered. "Maybe he's just learning to operate. Maybe the backhoe is another thing to keep him busy when he's not laying brick."

"Makes sense. So, he's out practicing, and he hears artillery going off . . ."

". . . and he's back in Vietnam and takes it out, single handed," Cy finished.

"So he's hardworking, kind, and brave. How about forgiving? Think he'll give it back?"

"We'll know soon. Is that the field?"

"Yeah. Turn in on that lane there. That's where we had the howitzer."

"Is that what it was?"

"Yeah. It's called a mountain howitzer, used from 1849 to 1890. Never heard anything so loud in my life."

They bumped along the lane and through the woods to the field beyond. "We need to make sure we ask him about why he wrote to Greenchem, too," Spider murmured.

"I've got an uneasy feeling about that," said Cy. "We'll deal with the artillery piece first."

Tommy was still on his backhoe digging holes, but he noticed the county car and waved. Turning off the machine, he set the bucket on the ground and climbed down.

Spider got out, and as he waited for Cy to emerge he studied the approaching Tommy Hobson. He's about my age, Spider thought. That could have been me. Spider remembered the relief he felt, back in the sixties, when he found that married men were no longer being drafted. He had been glad, then, that he didn't have to go to Vietnam. Now, almost thirty years later, he had the feeling that he should have gone, that he had let others take his lumps. It was odd, and odder still as he contemplated this unkempt fellow with the dark laser-eyes who was pointing his finger.

"I know who you are," he said to Spider. "You were here with those other two. I'm sorry about your big gun. I guess I went a bit wacko for a while."

"It's not mine," said Spider. "Belongs to Phil Duke, the fellow in the uniform."

"That a Civil War uniform?"

"Yeah. Same with the gun. It's Civil War, too."

"You tell him if he comes out here tomorrow, this time, he'll find it back out where it was, and no worse for being buried. That's a promise. Only, maybe he can find another place to do target practice."

"That's for sure!"

Tommy looked at Cy. "I hope he's not going to harbor any ill feelings or try to bring the law into this," he said anxiously.

"I don't think so. Since the balls landed across the fence, that's someone else's land, and it's posted no hunting."

"I didn't think of that," Tommy said. "That's my land."

"There you go. You've both got a beef. Call it even."

"Even it is," said Tommy. "You tell him to come tomorrow and get his gun. I'll fix it so he'll never know it was buried."

"I'll tell him," Cy promised. "Say, Tommy, where'd you get the backhoe?"

"I bought it."

"When'd you buy it? I didn't know you had a backhoe."

"I've had it for three, four years. It was new when I bought it."

"It's a nice looking one. What you doing here, practicing?" Cy walked closer to look at one of the holes.

"Practicing what?"

"Digging." When Cy saw that Tommy was still puzzled, he said, "Why are you making these holes?"

"I'm burying barrels," Tommy said.

Spider got a sinking feeling in the pit of his stomach. "What for?" he asked.

"'Cause they pay me to."

"Who pays you?" Spider and Cy asked the question at the same time, knowing the answer already.

"A company called Greenchem."

"Uh, and what's in these barrels?" Spider tried to keep his tone conversational.

"It's chemicals," Tommy replied.

"It's toxic waste," said Cy.

"No, it's not!" Tommy was vehement. "I wouldn't do that. It's chemicals that, if they're kept at about fifty degrees, will degrade into water. Then, by the time the barrels rust through, all that goes into the earth is water, which is needed for the aquifer anyway. Instead of building a storage building and running refrigeration to keep it at the right temperature, he just pays me to bury them. It's cheaper for Greenchem and helps me out, too."

"Who told you about the chemicals turning into water?" Cy asked.

"It was the owner of the company. Steve Greene."

"He came and talked to you?"

"He comes a couple times a year. He likes to make sure everything is going the way it should."

Cy and Spider looked at one another, and while Cy continued talking to Tommy, Spider went back to the car and got his folder. Holding the picture so that his thumb obscured the signature, he approached Tommy. "Do you recognize this fellow?" he asked.

"That's Steve Greene." Tommy looked puzzled. "What are you doing with a picture of him?"

"He's disappeared, and we're trying to find him."

"Maybe that's why I didn't get my check," Tommy said. "He's almost a month behind in what he owes me. He's never been behind before."

"Did he give you any documentation on the makeup of what's in the barrels?"

"Yes. I've got it over at the house. I wouldn't have done this if it was going to do harm."

"Tommy, I want you to find that documentation," Cy advised. "I think that this man lied to you, and the chemicals aren't going to turn into water. I'm going to bring out the EPA in the next day or so, and they'll want to have all the barrels dug up. Do you know where they all are?"

"Yeah. I marked each place with a stake. It'll be easy to find them all."

"You're not in any trouble, Tommy," Cy assured him. "If anyone is, it's this fellow." He indicated the smiling face of Stan Lucas.

"I thought he was a straight shooter," Tommy said sadly. "He always paid me on time, always made sure that I was happy doing this for the company. This is hard to believe." His eyes grew moist.

"I know. Well, you don't have to dig any more holes."

"I'm going to kind of miss it." Tommy wiped his nose on the sleeve of his blue coveralls.

"You could always hire out to dig people's basements and septic tanks," offered Spider.

Tommy brightened. "Never thought of that. Maybe I will."

"I'll be in touch, Tommy." Cy shook his hand.

Spider offered his hand as well. "Don't forget you're going to dig up that howitzer."

"I won't."

"I'll be in touch. Soon," Cy repeated. Then he and Spider walked back to the county cruiser.

As they drove out through the woods to the lane, Spider sighed. "I guess we don't have to go see old Cougar now. Does this clear anything up?"

"It lets us know what kind of a slimy snake Stan Lucas was, but does it tell us why he disappeared?"

"It gives him a motive for making himself disappear. The contract with Greenchem is about up for renewal. He's been clearing at least a hundred thousand dollars a month on this scam. Over four years that's . . ."

"Almost five million dollars."

"Great Suffering Zot," Spider breathed.

"And," Cy added, "it's also a pretty good reason for Brick Tremain to want him out of the way. If he was onto the scam, he might be mad enough to do him in."

Spider grimaced. "I don't see that. These two guys are going to blow the whistle some time if they don't get paid, and then the EPA will get involved and Brick will be in a world of trouble."

They were both quiet a moment, thinking. Then Spider mused, "Unless Brick doesn't know about this wrinkle. Maybe he thinks that Stan found someone to take care of the toxic waste for forty thousand, and Stan set up a way to charge a hundred twenty, and pocketed the difference. It still adds up to a chunk of change."

They spent the rest of the ride each lost in his own thoughts. When Cy pulled up in front of Minnow's, Spider said, "I'm flying out first thing in the morning. I'll call and let you know what I find out. Can you delay calling in the EPA for one day? I'd like to go talk to Brick and let him know so he's prepared to deal with the mess."

"I probably wouldn't be able to get ahold of them today, anyway. It's getting on towards closing time. I'll wait until four o'clock tomorrow afternoon to call."

"Thanks. I don't know if I'll be back. If I uncover something there that says he skipped with the loot, there's no reason for me to come back. Brick will have to deal with what's buried up at Tommy's." He held out his hand. "It's been a pleasure."

Cy's eyes crinkled as he smiled and warmly shook Spider's hand. "The pleasure was mine."

"I'll call you to see if you found anything about Stan leaving Las Vegas on public transportation. I wonder, can we track someone going across the border?"

"I don't know. I never had to do that. I'll see what I can find out."

Spider got out and ambled up the walk, his mind still sifting through all that he had discovered that day. As he passed the Yukon, he spotted the crumpled bike still in the back.

"Shoot. I forgot about that," he muttered. Spying Phil through the window, he had an idea and walked briskly toward the house to try it out.

Entering the kitchen, the astringent smell of camphor assailed his nostrils. It seemed particularly strong around Phil, who had changed from his woolen uniform to khaki pants and a yellow, short-sleeved shirt. Sister Minnow had put off her long dress and petticoats and was working at the stove in a short muumuu.

"I've got news," Spider said. "The fellow who buried your howitzer is named Tommy Hobson. He said that if you come tomorrow at about this time, your gun will be sitting out in the field again, none the worse for wear."

Phil grinned and said, "How about that!"

Sister Minnow, already pink from standing over the stove, grew pinker still and waved the chicken leg she had just speared with a cooking fork. "Hallelujah!"

Spider continued, "He apologized. The thing is, he was in Vietnam and suffers from post traumatic stress, so when he heard the cannon, it was like he was back there and he just reacted."

"Wow! He's a pretty brave soldier to come and take out a howitzer all by himself," Phil said.

"Well, you weren't bad yourself. You weren't going to give up without a fight."

"I sure didn't want to lose that cannon," Phil admitted. "Thank you, Spider."

"Thank Cy. He's the one who made the deal. Say, Phil, do you know anything about bikes?"

"Bikes? Bicycles? A bit. Sure."

"I'm leaving tomorrow—"

Spider didn't get a chance to continue because Sister Minnow wailed, "Tomorrow! You can't leave tomorrow! You just came!"

"I know, Sister Minnow. I took the room for two weeks, and I'll pay you for that. It's just that I have to go back to Las Vegas, and if I find there what I think I'm going to, there's no need to come back."

"Who's going to help with the cannon?" worried Phil.

"I imagine you'll find someone. Why don't you ask Smitty, up at the mine. I think he'd be a good man to have on your crew."

"That's not a bad idea. Now, what were you saying about bikes?"

"Come outside. I want to show you something." Spider led the way to the SUV and took the bike out of the back. "I wrecked this the other night."

"Is that how you got your arms all bungled up?"

"Yeah. My knees too. But the thing is, it's not my bike. Do you think you could get a new fork and put on it? Put it to rights? I'll be glad to pay you for the work and to pay you to ship it to my son in Seattle, too."

Phil looked critically at the bike. "I think I can do that. I'll just wheel it in to Agnes's garage. I can come over here and work on it. She's a nice lady. I like spending time here."

Spider closed the hatch and followed him to the garage. "She's a good cook, too."

"That uniform was too hot, so she got me some of her . . . some of Earl Minnow's clothes to put on. Me and him're about the same size. Or he was, anyway."

"She's been letting me use Earl's lunch box. She's a good woman."

Phil nodded. "And she's a good cook." He leaned in close and whispered. "A person that's thinking of marrying her would have to think about bein' a Mormon, wouldn't he?"

Spider glanced up at the kitchen window and answered in a whisper. "Well, you'd have to talk to her about that, but I know it would make her happy to have you think about it."

"Maybe I will."

"Supper," sang Sister Minnow through the open window.

"Did we mention that she's a good cook?" Spider asked, grinning.

"I believe we did."

Agreed on that point, Spider allowed Phil to go first and followed in his redolent wake to the dining room where Sister Minnow had fried chicken on the table.

THOUGH SPIDER ARRIVED AT the Las Vegas airport at seven-thirty in the morning, when he stepped out of the terminal the heat was already oppressive. Pulling his hat brim down against the slanted early-morning rays, he watched for the shuttle to the el cheapo rental car lot and wondered if Brick Tremain would thank him for standing in the sun to save a few dollars. I've been in the Northwest too long, he thought. Can't take the heat any more.

The shuttle was air-conditioned, as was the midsized car he rented, and by a quarter after eight Spider was sitting in a near-vacant parking lot in front of a nondescript strip mall wondering how he was going to get into the unit that had the address the Mailboxes lady had given him. Closed Venetian blinds covered the windows, but as Spider pondered, he became aware that through the glass door he could see that the lights were on and someone was moving around inside.

The only other car in the lot was a 1975 Ford LTD, a boat of a car that had once been sky blue but had oxidized to an overcast gray. On its door was a magnetic sign that said, "Al's Commercial Cleaning."

"Huh," Spider grunted, tapping his fingers on the steering wheel as he weighed his options. Finally he got out, walked purposefully across to Greenchem's office, and tried the door. It swung open, and Spider found himself face to face with a thin, sallow-looking man with sunken cheeks and wispy black hair who was winding up a vacuum-cleaner cord.

It was the cleaning man who spoke first. "Mr. Greene?"

"Uh, you must be Al. How do you do?" Spider stuck out his hand and shook the janitor's.

"I've cleaned every two weeks, like you wanted, though lately it's looked like no one's even been here. No trash in the wastebaskets, mail piled up in front of the mail slot. I began to wonder."

"No, no one's been here," Spider said, looking around.

The office was sparsely furnished: desk, four-drawer filing cabinet, phone, fax. An apologetic cough drew Spider's attention back to Al, who was fiddling with the plug on the end of the vacuum cord. "I hate to mention it, but I didn't get my last check."

"You didn't? Well, I'll look into it and make sure that you get all that's owed. Are you about done?"

"I was just going to clean the bathroom, though it doesn't look like it's been used at all in the past two weeks."

"It hasn't. Don't worry about that. Let it go for today."

"You're sure?"

"Yeah. Don't bother."

"Thanks." Al finished winding up the cord and looked at the watch on his skinny wrist. "I'm a bit late this morning, and my next job is supposed to be done by nine." Picking up his vacuum and a tray of cleaning supplies, he headed for the door. Spider held it open and nodded. "Don't worry about that check. I'll see you get taken care of."

"Thanks, Mr. Greene." He was off across the parking lot to stow his vacuum in the cavernous trunk of his powdery, blue-gray boat.

Spider waved and let the door swing closed as he turned to survey the office. "What am I looking for?" he muttered as he ambled to the desk and sat down. Pulling open the top drawer, he found a book of deposit slips.

"Well, this will do for starters." Taking the pen from his shirt pocket, he lifted the cover and looked at the top carbon copy, dated January of this year and depositing $400,000 to Bank of America. Using the pen to pick up the next page, Spider looked at February's deposit. It was again $400,000. "Great Suffering Zot!" he breathed, looking at March, then April, and then May. "Great Suffering Zot!" he repeated. "That's two million dollars just this year!" There were no deposits after May.

There was nothing else in any of the desk drawers besides a few pens, paper clips, and a pad of sticky notes. Spider leaned back in the chair and surveyed the desktop. A daily calendar lay opened at May 29, but as Spider leafed back through, turning the pages with the point of his pen, he found no notations on any of the pages. Stuck to the base of the calendar was a small sticky note with a number written on it, and next to the note was a compact telephone answering unit flashing the numeral eleven. Spider clicked the button marked listen and heard Cougar Wilson's message of the day before. Then there were four messages from Bob at Value Car Rental concerning a car that had been rented in Spokane that had not been returned. As Spider listened to the messages from last to first, he found an interesting continuum: Bob had been businesslike at first, then pleading, then angry, then threatening. Taking a sticky note from the back of the pad, Spider wrote down Bob's number, though after hearing it repeated in varying tones four times, he doubted if he would forget it. There were also three messages from Tony DeYeso and three from the purple-haired clerk at Mailboxes and More.

Spider was just about to get up when his eyes again fell on the fluorescent sticky attached to the calendar. Rubbing his chin in thought for a moment, he finally dragged his handkerchief out of his back pocket and used it to gingerly pick up the telephone receiver. Carefully punching the buttons with his pen, he waited for the burr of the ringing on the other end of the line. Finally it came, but at the same time, Spider became conscious of a phone ringing close at hand.

What is that? he wondered, looking around, but it appeared to be coming from outside. The ringing stopped, and he heard a breathy voice say, "Hello?" At the same time, through the phone and from outside, he heard the jingling of keys, and then the door opened and Bev, cell phone to her ear, stepped inside the door.

"Is that you, Bev?" Spider asked, looking at her but speaking into the receiver. He could tell that it was by the way she looked from him to the cell phone she held in her hand.

"What are you doing here?" Both asked the question. Neither answered. As before, their eyes locked, but this time it was Bev who looked away first.

She put her cell phone back in her purse and put her keys in her pocket. "What are you doing here?" she asked again.

As Spider replaced the phone on its cradle and put his handkerchief back in his hip pocket, he wondered how such a soft voice could be so cutting. Before he could frame a reply, she spoke again.

"What happened to your arms?"

"I got tangled up with a cougar."

"You're lying."

"All right, I drove a bicycle off a cliff."

She sneered, and it twisted her handsome face into something sharp and ugly. Spider looked away. "Uh, I have to tell you, Bev, that you turning up here this morning looks mighty bad."

"What do you mean?"

"Well, there's been a crime—a swindle—perpetrated from this office, and your being here implicates you. Your boss, Brick Tremain, is the one who was swindled, and you might want to have a pretty good reason ready for him and the police about your being here with a key to that door."

Bev looked like she was ready to say something, but the hoods came down over the eyes and she turned to go.

"Uh, before you leave, I'd like to have your key," Spider said.

"And who gave you authority to ask for my key?"

"After a manner of speaking, Brick Tremain did." Spider held out his hand.

"I'll give my key to Brick, along with any explanation he might need. I'll give you nothing."

Spider dropped his hand. "You headed Brick's way right now?"

"You mean am I going to work? Yes, I am."

"Well, I'm right behind you."

Bev shrugged. "Suit yourself. Your movements don't concern me in the least."

"Before you go, I'd like to have that key."

"And what are you going to do? Take it from me?"

"If I have to." Spider eyed the tall redhead. He didn't want a tussle over the key.

"I'll cry rape."

"I don't think that would fly. Remember, you're implicated in a crime. I would think you'd want to cooperate with the investigating authorities."

"Investigating authorities." Bev spat out the words, but she dug the keys out of her pocket, separated one from the ring and flung it on the floor. Then she turned and with a violent thrust pushed open the door and strode out.

"I'm right behind you," Spider called. His inclination was to linger, to investigate further, but he had an uneasy feeling in the pit of his stomach and decided he'd better reach Heritage Tower soon after Bev.

Wondering if she had thrown the right key on the floor, he picked it up and tried it in the door. It fit. Standing in indecision for a moment, Spider finally decided to take the book of deposit slips with him, so he took the time to fish the book out with his pen and wrap it in his handkerchief, tying it up like a hobo's pack. Then he turned out the lights and locked the door behind him. He used the drive to Heritage Tower to do some mental math. *Two million in five months. Greenchem had a four-year contract. Great Suffering Zot.*

As Spider pulled in beside Jade's Yugo he wondered if the young man had solved the problem that had caused two thugs to lie in wait in the parking garage. Casting a wary glance around, he strode to the elevator and rode up to the lobby, carrying his hankie-pack with him. An elevator was open, and he slid through the doors just as they were closing, only to find when he went to push the button for the twenty-fourth floor that there wasn't one. Feeling a little disoriented, he asked a well-dressed woman next to him about it, and after glancing at the package he was carrying, she explained that the elevators on this side only went to the fourteenth floor. He needed to ride back down and take an elevator on the other side of the lobby.

Spider sheepishly moved to the back of the elevator, and when the sharp dresser exited at the fourteenth floor, he rode back down, crossed the lobby and rode the elevator that serviced floors fifteen through twenty-four. Then he transferred to the private elevator that went to the offices of Brick Tremain Enterprises.

Erin, at the desk, brightened as she saw Spider step out of the elevator. "Good morning, Mr. Latham," she greeted as he approached.

"Good Morning, Erin. I'm here to see Mr. Tremain."

Erin glanced first at the scabs on Spider's arms and then at the bundle in his hand. "He's in a conference right now and can't be disturbed."

"How about Bev?"

"Um. She's also in conference."

"Was it Bev who called and said Mr. Tremain wasn't to be disturbed?"

"Yes, it was."

"Thought so." Spider strode down the hall to Brick's office door.

"You can't go in!" Erin called. "He's in conference!"

But Spider already had the door open and was greeted by startled looks from Brick Tremain and Bev Compton. Brick was in his chair behind the desk and she was in a side chair pulled up close. Her right hand lay on top of the desk, and his larger one lay clasped on top of it. She had a handkerchief in her left hand, and her shiny eyes testified that she had been weeping. Brick gave her hand a squeeze and then released it and leaned back in his chair. "Come in, Spider." He didn't smile. "Sit down."

Spider entered and closed the door behind him. Setting his bundle on the edge of the desk, he pulled up another chair, took off his hat, and sat.

"When I called you in to help," Brick said sternly, "I didn't mean for you to start accusing employees."

Spider felt himself redden. He rubbed his thumb along the grosgrain ribbon inside his hat band and thought for a moment. Then he looked Brick in the eye. "I don't recall accusing anyone," he said, keeping his voice even. "I just discovered that Stan Lucas used an office about a mile away to bilk you out of about sixteen million dollars."

"Sixteen million dollars!" Brick's eyes got big and he almost shouted the number.

"Bev had a key to that office, and in fact I found her there this morning. What I said to her was that it looked bad."

"Sixteen million dollars!" Brick repeated. "I don't understand."

"I think that you were right to send me to Chewelah to look into Stan's disappearance. You remember I called and asked if you had received the memo about the difference in the cost of handling toxic waste—the difference between Greenchem and other companies?"

"I remember you asking," Brick said. "I never got the memo."

"Well, Stan was the one who negotiated the Greenchem deal. You know that. What you didn't know was that Stan was Greenchem."

"Stan was Greenchem?"

"He set up a company, rented an office, hired people, and billed BTE to handle toxic waste. Not only at Snakewater, but at other mines too, I assume?"

Brick nodded.

"He did it—at least in Chewelah—under the name Steven Greene. Someone in Chewelah identified a picture of Stan as Steven Greene of Greenchem. Snakewater does business with a Spokane address, but I was able to find out that the main office, if that's what you want to call it, is here in Las Vegas. I went there this morning and the janitor let me in. Ten minutes later," Spider nodded in Bev's direction, "she showed up with a key to the place."

"She's explained that. She said she got a call from Stan last night."

Spider's eyes narrowed and he watched Bev closely.

Brick continued: "Stan said he was sending her a key and he wanted her to go and get something out of the file cabinet and mail it to him. He said he wouldn't be able to come back ever and that she was to tell Opal and me how sorry he was."

"What did he want her to get?"

Brick turned a questioning look on Bev. Her chin came up, and though her eyes were still moist, her soft voice was steady. "He wanted me to get a list of people who worked for him. He didn't pay them their last check. He wanted to pay them and tell them that Greenchem was out of business."

"Big of him," Brick said dryly.

"Where did he call from?" Spider asked.

"He didn't say. It wasn't a great connection, but it could have been from anywhere."

"Where were you supposed to mail it to?" Brick asked.

"Somewhere in New York. I'd never heard of it," Bev replied.

"The key." Spider said. "How did you get the key?"

"He sent it to me. It arrived yesterday. It was in the mail when I got home."

"Where was it mailed from?"

"There was no return address. I tore through the post mark getting it open. I don't know."

"You tore through the post mark?" Spider was incredulous.

"I didn't know who it was from," she said wearily. "I didn't know until he called why I even got it."

Brick clarified: "So you got this key in the mail with no letter, no return address, and until you got the call, you didn't know who it was from?"

"That's right. I didn't ask to be involved in this."

"Why didn't you call Brick or Opal to let them know Stan was alive?" Spider asked.

"He called late. It was about midnight, and he woke me out of a sound sleep. I figured it could keep eight more hours." Her eyes welled up again, and she rested her forehead in her hand. Her hair fell forward in a fiery cascade. "I'm sorry, Brick. Sorry that he's done this to you. Sorry that I didn't call, if you think I should have."

Brick shook his head. "No, no. That's all right, Bev. You go along now and have a cup of coffee and take a minute to get yourself together. I'll discuss a few more things with Spider and then you and I can talk about the rest of the day."

Bev dabbed her eyes and then stood. Brick and Spider stood as well, and she managed a small smile. "You don't have to get up. I'm fine. Really." She opened the door to her office and disappeared inside.

Spider sat down again and waited.

Brick sat, too, lost in thought. Finally he asked, "What do you make of it all?"

"You mean about Bev being involved?"

Brick waved the idea away. "No. Bev's not involved with this. I know her too well. If she says that the key came in the mail and she got a call from Stan, then that's what happened."

"Well, about the other. I think that Brick Tremain Enterprises is in big trouble with the EPA."

Spider had Brick's undivided attention. "What do you mean?" he asked sharply.

"Well, Stan didn't set up a real toxic waste disposal system and overcharge. He overcharged and buried the waste."

"What?" Brick was in shouting mode again.

"At Snakewater Stan hired a fellow to pick up the chemical and drop it off at a loading dock out in the middle of nowhere. The fellow was a bit of a misfit, a loner who kept to himself. All anyone ever saw him do was pick up the barrels at Snakewater in a nice looking pickup that said Greenchem on the door. He got paid well for that little bit of work, and he got to keep the pickup. Then another fellow—again, a loner who didn't mingle much with other people—would pick up the barrels and bury them on his property. He had been told that the chemicals would degrade to water. He has documentation that he was told that."

"So for the past four years the toxic waste has been buried?" Brick's face was flushed, and he was having a hard time keeping the decibels down.

"'Fraid so. The local deputy sheriff is going to call the EPA, but not until this afternoon. I don't know if it would be better for you to get in touch with them rather than them getting in touch with you. He said he'd wait until four to call."

Brick wilted. "And you think that Snakewater's not the only one?"

Brick began untying the handkerchief bundle. "Well, I know that he was banking four hundred thousand dollars a month. That didn't all come from Snakewater. Don't touch the tablet, please. His fingerprints will be on it, and that's evidence. But look." Spider lifted the pages, one at a time, with his pen.

"The way I figure it," Spider said, "is that he planned to leave once the contract was up. When Tony DeYeso wrote you that memo about alternative toxic waste handlers and what they would charge, I imagine Stan figured the jig was about to be up. So, he just didn't come home. There's a message on the answering machine there at the Greenchem office about a rental car rented in Spokane that hasn't been returned. I talked to the airlines, and they were pretty sure he was on that flight to Las Vegas, though they wouldn't swear that he couldn't have boarded and then got off. Looks to me like he did get off. He rents a car and makes for the Canadian border—it's less than a hundred miles from Spokane. He's there before his suitcases reach Las Vegas."

Spider laid the key on Brick's desk. "I don't know how you want to handle this. I think I've done what you asked me to do. I didn't find out where Stan is, but I did find out why he left."

Brick pushed the key back to Spider. "You're not done yet. We need to find the double-crossing whelp. I don't imagine the police will expend any more energy at finding him now than they did before. I want him found."

"Uh, there's a couple of things. First, there's Opal. Are you going to tell her about this? That he's alive?"

Brick sighed. "I'll tell her as gently as I can."

"And there's another thing. There are three people that are owed money by Stan. I promised they'd be paid."

"You've got your nerve. The man cheated me out of sixteen million dollars!"

"Well, I gave my word. I'll pay them myself if you won't."

"I won't."

"I'm going home," Spider announced, standing. "My mother is in failing health, and I'm going to spend the night with my wife. I don't know that I'm the one to find a fugitive. Seems to me it's more a job for the police. I'll go think on it and let you know tomorrow."

"I'll pay your people," Brick said, leaning forward. "Please. I need you to stay."

"I wasn't making a threat to make you pay them. I was just explaining how things are."

"I know. Go on home, Spider. Let's talk tomorrow."

Spider picked up his hat. "I'll leave this deposit book and key with you, if that's all right. I'll pick them up when I go back to that office, if that's what you decide you want me to do. You sure we don't go to the police about this right away? They could probably access that account, tell you if the money's been taken out of it. That could maybe help in finding Stan."

"No. Trust me in this." Brick rose and walked Spider to the door with his arm around his shoulders. "Go home and take a break. You've done well. I'm the one that fouled things up, bringing that snake on board."

Spider found himself standing in the hall with a frown on his face and an unsettled feeling in the pit of his stomach. He saw Erin eyeing him warily, so he didn't linger outside Brick's door, but instead approached the reception station and asked where the mail room was. Following her directions to a remote corner of the maze of offices, he found a large, unwindowed-but-brightly-lit room that was neat and orderly. A counter shared one wall with a copy machine, and a bank of tall filing cabinets marched along the opposite wall. Spider stood in the doorway and watched a young woman seated at a desk as she bent over a stack of papers, considering each before writing something on the bottom.

She was small and plump with a dark complexion, high cheekbones, and black hair cut short and trim along the neckline. She must have sensed his presence because she looked up from her work. Spider was aware of dark eyes and lashes and a smile that sucked away all the discontent he had been feeling. "You're Maria," he said.

"Yes?" Just the hint of an accent, a very subtle *j* before the *y*.

"I'm Spider Latham."

Again the incandescence of that smile. "Yes! I know who you are. What happened to your arms?"

"Uh. I got tangled up with a bike. Kid stuff. Is Jade around?"

"He went to courier something across town. He'll be so sorry to miss you."

"Yeah. Me, too." Spider looked at the stack of papers at Maria's desk. "Is that mail that just came in?"

"Yes. My job is to open the mail and route it to the person—or persons—that need to see it."

"I see you've made copies of everything. I remember Brick saying that you did that and filed the copies."

"I do. The originals don't always make it back to me to go in the files, so I find that if I copy it right away, nothing gets lost."

"I don't suppose you keep a log of the correspondence that comes in, do you?"

"No, but that's a good idea. I always stamp it with the time clock so we know when it was received. But I don't log things in—too time consuming. Why do you ask?"

"Uh, Bev said that something came in just before Memorial Day—something that Stan Lucas was looking for before he went to Chewelah. She said it came in the mail, but she couldn't remember what it was."

Maria's eyes widened just a fraction. It was reflexive and instantaneous, and then she looked away.

"What were you thinking?" asked Spider.

"Um." She shook her head in embarrassment. "It was an unkind thought."

"Tell me. It may be important."

"Um. I was thinking that Bev forgets very little. She has a memory like an elephant."

"How's your memory?"

She turned on the smile again. "Pretty good." Getting up, she walked confidently to a file drawer marked Personnel-Snakewater and opened it. Extracting a folder, she brought it over to her desk. "I'm showing you this because I know that Mr. Tremain has given you access to everything at Snakewater," she explained. "Jade told me."

Spider set his hat on the counter and picked up the folder, noting that the name on the tab was Tony DeYeso. Opening it he saw that the top document was a letter from Lester Bealman, Private Investigator, and addressed to Stanley Lucas. In terse prose, Lester related that, under the freedom of information act, he had been able to determine that Tony DeYeso had served two years at Deuel Vocational Institution at Tracey, California, for four counts each of burglary and breaking and entering and had been released five years ago. His whereabouts were unknown, having presumably left the state. Spider checked the received stamp: May 28, 1993. "This came in the Friday before Memorial Day?"

"Yes. You can see that this is a copy. I never got the original back."

"Huh. Did you give this to Stan Lucas?"

"I didn't hand it to him. I routed it to his in-box. Our file clerk acts as messenger, moving things between offices. Because it's a personnel issue and confidential, I put it in an envelope."

"You sent it to Stanley? Not to Bev?"

She shook her head. "Anything addressed to Mr. Tremain goes to Bev, but I always send Stan's correspondence directly to him."

Spider frowned. "Was Stan in the office this day? How would I find that out?"

"Bev would probably know. But maybe not. That's a long time ago. Maybe Erin would know."

"I'll ask her. Thanks, Maria. You've been a big help."

"It was nice to meet you. Jade has spoken about you."

Spider picked up his hat. "Tell him hi. Sorry to miss him."

"I will." She picked up the folder and smiled one last time.

Spider walked back down the hall with a lighter step, intending to quiz Erin about Stan Lucas's whereabouts on May 28, but she wasn't at the reception station. He waited, thinking she would soon return, until the lingering effects of Maria's smile began to fade, and the uneasiness began to return. Muttering, "I'm going home," to the empty air, Spider headed for the elevator.

C H A P T E R

SPIDER MADE ONE STOP BEFORE he left town, begrudging the time.
But it was for Laurie, so he found the right store and spent the time to
select just the right product. Then he was on the freeway heading for the
turnoff onto Highway 93 that ran past Alamo and through Caliente and
nine more miles to the gravel road that would take him home. Each mile
that he traveled lightened his spirits and each bend in the road was like a
familiar friend.

Spider felt like he had been gone a month, and driving over the cattle
guard, even the sight of his beat-up pickup was welcome. He got out of
the car and hurried up the steps to the back porch, hanging his hat on the
peg by the kitchen door and calling, "Anybody home?"

"In here," Laurie called from the back of the house.

Spider walked through the kitchen to the hall just as Laurie came out
of Mother Latham's bedroom. He was surprised at the dark circles that
were under her eyes, but her smile of welcome was warm, and she almost
bowled him over in her haste to give him a hug.

"You're back!" she squealed in his ear. "I'm so glad you're back."

"Me too. How's mama?"

"Come and see. I don't know that she's doing too well." Laurie led the way to the bedroom door and pushed it quietly open.

Spider stepped inside and almost didn't recognize the gaunt figure with hollow cheeks lying in the bed looking at him fixedly. Her eyes reminded him of Tommy Hobson's.

"She's not eating much of anything," Laurie said softly. "She's just melting away."

"Great Suffering Zot," Spider breathed.

Laurie spoke in a normal tone. "Look who's here to see you, Mother Latham. It's Spider."

"Hello, Mama." Spider walked over and clasped the bird-claw hand resting on the bedcovers.

Rachel Latham didn't return the pressure. Her intense blue eyes followed him, but she didn't say a word. "Hello, Mama," Spider said again and leaned down to kiss her on the forehead.

"She usually takes a nap about this time," Laurie said. "I think if we go, she'll drop off to sleep. Did you have lunch? Maybe I can find something for you to eat."

"I'm gant as a gutted snowbird," Spider confessed. "I didn't want to take the time to stop and eat." He patted Rachel's hand and then followed Laurie to the kitchen.

"What on earth happened to your arms?" she said as she put slices of bread on the counter.

"Uh. I was out riding Bobby's bike and didn't look where I was going."

"Well, it must have been some spill you took."

Spider grinned. "It was."

"So tell me. Did you find what you were looking for?"

"I think I did." Spider told her about talking to Cougar Wilson and how Tommy Hobson took Phil's cannon and buried it.

Laurie sliced Spider's sandwich in two and then, still holding the knife, stood with her hands on her hips. "Are you making this up?"

Spider raised his right hand. "I swear."

"Okay. Go on." She set his sandwich in front of him and filled a glass with milk.

Spider continued, telling how he and Cy had discovered the buried barrels and how he had come back to Las Vegas to find the main office of the bogus company.

"So you're saying that—what was his name? Stan? Okay, so what you're saying is that Stan set up a company to handle toxic waste, only he didn't handle it."

"Nope. He had people bury it."

"But how could that happen? Isn't someone going to know?"

"He chose loners. People who don't mix with other people. And he let them think that if they told other people about their 'jobs' that other people would try to get the jobs away from them. Heck, it had gone on for almost four years, and if I hadn't happened onto that box of mail, it would still be going on."

"Isn't that something! A bit of luck there. So what happened to Stan?"

"He's hiding out somewhere. I figure he acted like he was coming home—you know, boarded a plane, checked his luggage. Then he got off the plane before it took off and rented a car and made a run for it. Maybe he went to Canada. Maybe he went to Mexico. Bev says he called her last night."

"Yeah, that's what you said. Do you think that's really so?"

Spider shrugged. "I don't know."

"And you walked in while she and Brick Tremain were being . . . cozy?"

"He was holding her hand. She was kind of moist around the edges."

"And he doesn't want you to go to the police?" Laurie cocked an eyebrow. "Does that sound right to you?"

Spider shook his head. "I felt weird about it all morning. Unsettled, you know. I'm not much of a mind to go back, though Brick's pretty set that he wants me to keep looking until I find Stan."

"Well, listen for that still, small voice," Laurie admonished. "Don't be getting into something that you'll wish later you hadn't."

Spider shook his head. "I'm not even going to think about it right now.

I'm just going to enjoy being home. You got somewhere you want to go? Want to get off your tether for a while? I'll stay and take care of Mama."

"Oh, Spider! How wonderful! I can go on the hike tonight."

"What hike?"

"Well, last week I got on my soapbox about combined activities and said that the Young Women would be glad to do merit badge stuff with the boys. Remember? I told you about it. I suggested a twenty-mile hike. They must have planned this to humor me. It's a hike from the church up to the spring and back. It's all of two miles up there, but for an evening hike, that's all right. I didn't think I was going to be able to go. Annie's the only one I've had come in and sit with your mother, and she couldn't come tonight."

"Well, now you can go." Spider frowned. "What is today? Isn't tomorrow night Mutual?"

"Usually, yes, but the Primary is having Activity Day at the spring tomorrow night, so they decided to hike up there today." She looked at her watch. "I wonder where my swimming suit is. I haven't been swimming in I don't know how long."

"You've got a while before you have to go. Come and see what I got you."

"You got me something?" Laurie's brown eyes sparkled, and she clasped her hands over her heart. "What is it?"

"It's out in the car. Wait and I'll get it."

Laurie hovered at the window as Spider ambled out to the rental car and got a plastic bag out of the backseat. She met him in the kitchen on his return, smiling and eager. When he clunked the sack down on the table she blinked and asked again, "What is it?"

"It doesn't look like much," Spider said, taking a box and a roll of wire out of the sack. "What it is, is an electric eye."

"An electric eye?"

"Yeah. We'll put it up in mother's room so it will sense when she gets up. I can run a wire into our room to your side of the bed, and I've got a doorbell here, see? That way, you can sleep in your bed, and you'll know when she gets up because the doorbell will ring."

Laurie stared at the wires and gadgets stacked on the table so long that Spider began to feel uneasy. Then, without speaking, she walked to the sink, got the bucket of chicken scraps from underneath, and strode out the door.

Spider went to the service porch and watched her determined gait and the way she flung the contents of the bucket over the fence, causing the chickens to squawk and scatter. "Oops," he muttered. When she disappeared into the barn, he turned and began searching in the service cupboard to see if there was an electric drill there.

Spider worked in his bedroom installing the doorbell and stringing wires up through the attic until his mother woke. Then he worked in her room, installing the photoelectric cell and connecting it to the bell.

Laurie stayed outside until just before it was time to leave. She came in and heated up some leftover stew and set it on the table.

Spider responded to her to her flat-toned call to supper. "You're not going to eat?"

"I'm not hungry. I've got to find my suit and get on my way." Clunking a can of dietary supplement down on the counter, she said, "See that your mother drinks this." Then she left him alone with his leftovers.

Spider was looking in the bread drawer when she passed through the kitchen and went out with a single-syllable farewell thrown over her shoulder. With a dried up heel of bread in his hand, he watched her drive over the cattle guard, ramrod straight behind the wheel of the crumpled pickup. Sighing, he took his dinner in to eat by his mother's bedside.

Rachel plucked at the covers with her thin fingers, and the tendons in her neck stood out as she strained forward. "You need to stay there, Mama," he said. "You need to keep your legs up."

Under her fierce gaze Spider ate a bit of his dinner, but then he set the plate aside and began reciting a familiar family story of how, when he was a little boy, she used to get the tram operator to let her ride in an empty ore bucket from Jackrabbit over the hill to Castleton so she could buy things at the company store. Her fingers gradually grew still, her eyes softened, and she lay back on her pillows as he talked.

When he finished that story, Spider segued into another about how his dad built shelves in the Empress mine, just a stone's throw from their back door, so that the cool air in the mine could keep the milk and meat cold, since they didn't have a refrigerator.

Spider coaxed Rachel into drinking half the nutritional supplement. Then he told more stories until it got dusk. Turning on a lamp, he began to sing, "You're Rachel Latham, your husband's name is Bill . . ." as Laurie had done. He was on the twentieth verse and back two generations when he heard the kitchen door.

"Laurie?" he called.

No answer.

"Laurie?" Picking up his dish, he carried it with him to the kitchen where Laurie was standing in the dark, weeping.

"Laurie, Darlin', what's the matter?" Spider ditched the plate and pulled his sobbing wife into his arms. "I'm sorry about the present," he murmured. "It should have been something better, I know. I'm sorry. Please don't cry."

Just as well ask the wash to stay dry when a thunderstorm hits the slick-rock country to the east. The flood will come, and you'd better be out of the way, because it's a wall of water, Spider thought. Laurie was carried away on such a flood, weeping in great, gusting sobs that wracked her small frame and wet Spider's shirt where her face was pressed.

"Shhh, shhh, shhh," he whispered. "Never mind. I'll make it right. I'm sorry."

Laurie shook her head and tried to gain command of her voice. "It's—it's—it's not that," she managed.

"Well, what happened?"

She only shook her head, but the weeping was subsiding.

Spider continued to hold her close, whispering "Shhh, shhh, shhh," at intervals. At length she was quiet.

"It's just so frustrating," she said in a damp whisper.

"What, Darlin'? What's frustrating?"

She sighed. "I just want what's best for my girls. I just want to follow the program."

"I don't think there's anyone who will argue with that."

"I just thought it would be an efficient and effective way to deal with Brother Bingham's not wanting to let his Scouts do things with the girls if we all did some merit badge thing together."

"Mmmmm. You said that. Let me guess. There weren't any Scouts there."

Laurie disengaged and took a napkin out of the napkin holder on the table to blow her nose. "Oh, there were Scouts there all right. I think every one of them came and brought a buddy. It was a great turnout."

Spider waited.

"There just wasn't a single priesthood leader there. Not one."

"Did you have a problem managing the kids?"

Laurie blew her nose again and shook her head. "No, they were great. Just great."

"So why the tears?"

Just then the doorbell rang. "What was that?" Laurie asked.

"Mama must be up."

They both hurried in and found Rachel Latham tottering toward the doorway, trailing a damp, partially-unwound ace bandage from her ankle.

"I've got it," Laurie said, and stepped in to steady the fragile widow. "Do you need to go to the bathroom, Mother Latham?"

Spider watched their slow progress down the hall, and when the door was closed on him, he went to the kitchen to wash his dish.

★   ★   ★

It was late by the time Laurie and Spider finally got to bed. They had turned off the air conditioner and opened the bedroom window wide and lay spooned together with Laurie's head just below Spider's chin. He kissed her on the top of the head. "I didn't realize it took so long to get Mama ready for bed," he murmured. "Do you do that every night?"

"Well, I want her to be clean, and I like to give her a back rub, since she's been lying down most of the day. And I always change her bandages at night. Yeah, it usually takes that long."

They lay in silence for a while, and then Spider said, "You never got a chance to tell me why the tears tonight."

Laurie sighed. "I don't know that I know. I certainly was on a crying jag, wasn't I? Maybe it's because I care so much, and when none of the men showed up it was like they didn't. Or maybe I thought it was a payback for messing with their program."

"More probably they'll all show up tomorrow night for Mutual, having forgotten that the day was changed."

Laurie yawned. "Do you think so?"

"Yeah. But there's natural resistance to what you're wanting to do. You have to remember that men are linear. We'll do this first and that second, and after that we'll do the third thing. When you try to get us to do two things together, it throws us for a loop. Women are naturally better at multitasking."

"Seems that way, doesn't it?" Laurie yawned.

"Uh-huh. So when you put them together you get a dynamite combination. Like you and me. I'm the thinker, you're the doer. Take that idea of doubling the fast offering. I can think about it and talk about it, but you're the one that does it. I sometimes wonder if that wasn't the way it was in the Garden. There's old Adam talking away about the commandments that God has given, and pontificating about how it's necessary to keep them, and on and on, and Eve's busy making an apple pie." He chuckled, but there was no answering laugh from Laurie. She was sound asleep.

"Bless your heart," Spider whispered, and kissed the top of her head again. "You're plumb tuckered out." Then he gently pulled his arm out from under her and turned over. Pulling the sheet up around his shoulder, he was determined not to think about the Snakewater puzzle. Instead, he set himself to remembering the names of the third generation of Lathams, just in case he was called upon to sing them.

Spider didn't get past the fourth of seven children before he fell asleep. Sometime in the night he dreamed he was riding his old bike, the one he had as a child, only it was tiny and he had to hold his knees out to pump the pedals. He came flying down Endless Agony Road with his legs straight out in front of him, free wheeling off the cliff and sailing through the air. Then the bike was gone and he was flying like Superman, one arm out in front and one leg flexed, until he passed a flag pole. He grabbed the top of the pole with one hand, and the momentum of his flight swung him around and around the pole in a dizzying circle as he descended. He was almost to the bottom when the pole turned to the aerial of a blue sedan, but he was still twirling around and around. Every time he made a revolution somebody rang a bell. Ding-dong. Ding-dong. Ding-dong.

Spider woke to the sound of the doorbell ringing. His mother must be up. Stumbling out of bed, he made his way in the dark to the hallway where a nightlight was burning and then on in to his mother's dimly lit room. There she was, looking like an off-kilter specter in a white cotton nightgown, listing a bit to the right as she made her way toward him with hands outstretched.

"Hello, Mama," he said softly. "On your way to the bathroom? Let me help you."

He put his hand under her bony arm and helped steady her, but at the doorway she turned and headed back to bed. Spider stayed beside her and then tucked her in, stroking her hair and speaking softly to her in a soothing tone of voice. When he thought she was settled he found his way back to his own berth. The air coming in the window was cool, so he pulled the blanket up under his ears and sighed, letting himself drift back to sleep.

The doorbell rang again. Wondering how good an idea the apparatus really was, Spider got up and repeated the same scenario. When he got his mother back to bed this time, he lingered at the doorway a while to see if she would stay. She did, so he went back to his warm nest under the blanket.

The third time was a replay of the first, though the dream changed a bit. The bike was full-sized, and the antenna didn't start out being a flagpole. Spider flew off the cliff and grabbed the antenna of the blue sedan parked in the trees. Around and around he twirled, hanging onto the metal rod while the bell rang, ding-dong, ding-dong.

Spider finally surfaced and realized what the sound was. Throwing back the covers, he mechanically took care of the re-bedding task and was back in his own place before he was really awake.

The rest of the night was uneventful, and Spider woke early enough to drive to Caliente in time to be there when Kosloski's Department Store opened. He returned with a bedside commode and an aluminum walker. As he carried them in he was glad to see that Laurie was looking more rested. Mother Latham was still asleep.

They had a leisurely breakfast. Spider told her more about his trip to Chewelah, and Laurie said that she had decided to call Bishop and ask to be released as Young Women President. "I can't do it justice," she admitted. "This is my season to take care of your mom, and the Young Women season is over. I need to concentrate on this calling. Maybe that's why I was crying last night. Maybe I was grieving."

Spider smeared some jam on a piece of toast, taking care to get it clear to the edges. "You're not going to be able to keep her alive, Laurie," he said, involved in his task. "I don't know that she'd choose to stay alive if she had the choice. You talk about seasons—this is her season to leave, I think." Finally he looked up and met her gaze. "Maybe it's time to let go."

Laurie's eyes welled up with tears. "When it's time, she can go. But I'm not the one that decides. Until the decision is made, I'll do what I can to keep her comfortable."

The telephone rang, and Laurie rose to answer it, clearing her throat on the way, so she could sound normal. "Hello?" She listened for a moment, frowning, and then held out the receiver to Spider. "It's someone from Blue Sky Airlines who says she has some information for you."

"WHAT WAS THAT ALL ABOUT?" Laurie asked. "First you try to put her off, saying you don't need to bother her, and then you're saying 'Great Suffering Zot.'"

"Uh, it's too much to explain right now. Things have been knocked into a cocked hat." He looked around the room, looked at his watch.

"You need to go back, don't you?"

Spider shook his head. "I don't know. I need to stay here, but yet . . ."

"Go," Laurie said. "I'm sure your mother will still be here when you get back. The doctor said people of that era, with constitutions like hers, don't die easy. She's still able to be up and around, even if she's unsteady."

"Yeah, but . . ."

"I'm truly grateful for the doorbell and for you getting up with her last night. After a good night's sleep I'm ready for another week. You can leave. We'll be all right."

Spider looked at his watch again and then examined the toe of his boot.

"Anything I can do to help?" Laurie asked.

Spider shook his head. "I'm trying to fix it so I accomplish two things at once. I don't think I can do it."

Laurie laughed and began clearing the table.

Spider picked up the phone and dialed BTE, asking for the mail room. "Hello, Maria? This is Spider Latham. Is Jade there?"

There was a pause while Jade came to the phone, and then Spider said, "Jade, I need your help. But, uh, first I need to ask you a question. You'll probably want to go to another phone where you can be private to answer it. Do you want to call me back?"

"I don't have any secrets from Maria," Jade said, and Spider could tell he was smiling. "I know what you want to ask. It's about those guys that waylaid you in the garage, isn't it?"

"Bingo."

"That was Maria's dad and brother," Jade said. "I had been dating Maria—we were getting pretty serious, and they didn't think my intentions were honorable. They're a pretty . . . a pretty traditional family. They were issuing me a little warning. Unfortunately, they got you instead."

"I thought it was something like that. You said it had been taken care of."

"We got married the day I dropped you off at the airport. The 'Forever Special' at the Little White Chapel on the Strip. It was pure Las Vegas, but we're going to try to make it something more."

"Does your father know?"

"I'm of age."

"Uh, yeah, I guess you are. Okay, I've got something I want you to do. It's about the Snakewater affair, and it's pretty important."

Spider outlined what he needed Jade to do and received the young man's assurance that he would cover the base. Just as he was about to hang up, Jade said, "Hey, Spider?"

"Yeah?"

"I figured out how that folder got in the Yugo."

"What folder?"

"You said that when you put your suitcases in the trunk there was a folder from Snakewater there."

"Yeah?"

"It must have been in Stan's suitcases—maybe stuffed in a front pocket. If he was in a hurry and forgot to zip it, it might have fallen out in my trunk."

"But how did you get the suitcases?"

"When the airlines called Opal, she asked me to go by and pick them up. I did and took them to her house."

"But I got an inventory from the police."

"Well, yeah. They came and got them from her when she finally got their attention. She had left them in the entryway, right where I set them."

"I see. Thanks for clearing that up."

"Sorry it took me so long to remember. And don't worry—I'll take care of this other thing for you."

Spider said good-bye and hung up. Satisfied with that detail taken care of, he called Blue Sky reservations and found that he could get on a flight out of Las Vegas in four hours. Otherwise he'd have to wait until evening. "Book me on it," he said, grateful that he hadn't yet completely unpacked.

"I've got to leave right now," Spider said to Laurie. "If I miss that flight I'll be cooling my heels for about six hours in the airport."

"I'll help you pack." Laurie went to the wash room and got socks and Levi's that had been folded but not put away. When she got to the bedroom, Spider was putting the last of his toiletry articles in. "Shirts?" she asked.

"Got 'em." Spider laid the copy of the information that he had gotten from Maria on top of his clothes and zipped the suitcase shut. "I'll just tell Mama good-bye."

Rachel Latham was still asleep. Her jaw was relaxed, allowing her mouth to gape, and she was slightly snoring. Shrunken and diminished, she didn't look like his mother at all, but he kissed her brow and touched her hand.

Standing by his side, Laurie whispered, "We'll be fine. Don't worry."

She walked him to the car and embraced him, patting his cheek and saying again, "We'll be fine."

She was still there at the edge of the driveway as Spider rolled over the cattle guard and turned toward the highway. Watching Laurie in his rearview mirror until she disappeared, he offered a silent prayer that the Lord would watch over his household while he was gone.

★　★　★

Standing in line at the car rental counter in the Spokane airport, Spider was surprised to hear a familiar voice. "Dad?"

Turning around, Spider saw Bobby, shiny-eyed and mouth set in a straight line, standing outside the roped-in enclosure. Leaving his place to the next person, Spider hurried to his son.

"Bobby! What are you doing here?"

Bobby's chin began to quiver. Folding his arms across his chest, he turned away and walked behind a sign advertising Gold Card Service. Concerned, Spider followed. "You all right, Son?"

Still hugging himself, with tears streaming down his face, Bobby looked at his feet and shook his head.

Mindful of passersby, Spider stood so as to shield Bobby from strangers' stares and waited for him to get hold of himself. After a moment he asked, "Were you coming to see me?"

Bobby nodded.

"Well, wait here. Watch my suitcase. I'll get a car and we can get on our way, talk in the car."

Bobby nodded again. Spider dragged his handkerchief out of his pocket and pressed it into his son's hand and then went to make arrangements for a car.

As they drove toward Chewelah, Spider let Bobby find his own time to tell what was on his mind. They were well clear of the urban area and driving through tall pines when Bobby finally sighed and said, "Do you remember what you said to me just before I left you last Sunday?"

"Uh, I don't know that I do."

"You said that I could hide from you and mom, but there were others, and my unborn child was among them, that I couldn't hide from. What made you say that?"

"I don't know. I just said it."

"Wendy left me."

Spider looked over at his son, but Bobby was staring out the window. He thought it best to say nothing.

"She said . . ." Bobby began.

Spider waited.

Bobby continued looking at the trees. "She said that I wasn't the man she married. She said that I wasn't the man she wanted as the father to her children."

Spider reached over and gripped his son's shoulder.

"She's pregnant."

"Oh, Son!"

They drove in silence. Bobby took a ragged breath. "I went to see the bishop."

Spider nodded, eyes straight ahead, and Bobby continued, "I prayed to God for a sign that I could redeem myself. All I could think of was that I had to come and see you. This morning I prayed for a sign, and then there you were in the airport. It was like God telling me that I can hope."

"Huh. I wasn't even in Chewelah. I wasn't going to come back, but then something happened, and I felt I should. Huh."

"Do you think I can win her back?"

"I think you should do whatever you do for you, not for her. If you've gone to the bishop, it needs to be because you want to change your life, not because you hope to impress Wendy."

"But a child, Dad! I'm going to be a father."

They continued in silence, contemplating the import of that statement. Father-to-be and grandfather-to-be, each lost in the wonder of a child to come.

Spider stopped at a hamburger joint along the highway, and they ate supper in an awkward companionship. Bobby asked about the scabs on

Spider's arms, and Spider told him about the disastrous mountain bike ride, making it sound far more amusing than it really was. Bobby laughed, but he also looked searchingly at his father.

When they were in the car and rolling again, Bobby asked his father why he had gone home, and Spider filled him in on the developments thus far.

"Mind if I tag along?"

"Glad to have you."

They were coming into Chewelah, and Spider drove directly to Cy's house. Cy was home, and when he got over the surprise of finding Spider and Bobby on his doorstep, he invited them in.

"I was going to call you tonight," Cy said. "I finally found out that Stan didn't fly out of Las Vegas, either under his own name or Steve Greene's."

"Yeah, I know. We're operating on a different premise now. Do you have time to go with me on a little expedition?"

"Where are we going?"

"Up by Snakewater. There's a road called Endless Agony up there."

"Care to tell me what we're going to find?"

"Uh, I'd rather tell you after we find it. I'm operating purely on a hunch, and I'd be mighty embarrassed if it doesn't pan out."

"That's rough country up on Endless Agony. You haven't forgotten that I'm not as spry as I used to be."

"I think we've got that base covered." Seeing Cy eyeing Bobby speculatively, he said, "No, you're not going piggy-back. We need to get going if we don't want to lose our daylight."

They snailed out to the rental car, and Spider was glad to see Bobby patiently holding the door for Cy to get in the passenger seat before occupying the back. On the way up the mountain Spider told Cy about his investigation in Las Vegas the morning before.

"So, what do you make of it?" Cy asked. "Do you think this gal, Bev? That her name? Do you think she's on the level?"

"I'll know more when we get through today."

Spider drove up Endless Agony and turned into Honor Wise's

driveway, crossing his fingers that she would be home and not out gathering specimens.

She was home, and she came out to meet Spider as he got out of the car. "Hello, stranger. How are you faring?"

"Fair to middling. How—" Spider was interrupted by a call from Cy.

"Honor? Is that you?" Cy had the door open and was struggling to get out of the car.

"Cy? Cy Chamberlain? Spider, did you know?" Honor's graceful, loose-limbed strides took her around the car, and before Cy could get his crutches out she was embracing him.

"Know? Know what?" muttered Spider.

"What a nice surprise!" Honor was smiling, and Cy was glowing.

"Don't tell me!" Spider broke into a grin. "Is this the one that married and moved away?"

Cy nodded and whispered something to Honor, who still stood with her arm around him. She laid her head on his shoulder in another short embrace.

"Well, I hate to break up a reunion, but we've got something to do here. Honor, I wonder if you'd mind bringing your four wheeler, let Cy come with you, and you take us back up to where you and I had the face-off with that cougar. Bobby and I can hike."

"What cougar?" Bobby asked from the backseat.

"Can you find it again?" Spider asked.

"Sure," she said to Spider. In an quiet voice she asked Cy why he was on crutches. He murmured an answer, and they spoke softly to one another until Spider cleared his throat.

"We're going to lose our daylight. We need to be on our way," he admonished.

Honor laughed. "I'll get the ATV. We can all ride."

She was as good as her word, and presently, with Cy's legs dangling in front and Spider and Bobby precariously sharing the tray in back, she headed out the driveway and up the hill. "It helps not to have too much pride," mentioned Spider. "I wasn't feeling particularly manly the last ride I took on this beast."

"So what are we going up there for?" Honor asked.

"Uh, I'd rather wait and have a look-see."

They left the road and bumped along a path for a ways, and then Honor turned off and went through the woods, picking her way around, and sometimes over, fallen logs. Spider had one hand holding on under the driver's seat and the other gripping the edge of the tray. It was a precarious perch, and it was all he could do to stay on.

"How you doing there, Cy?" he asked.

"There better be something at the end of this trail!" Cy said through gritted teeth.

"I'm feeling the same way myself."

"It's not too much farther," Honor said. "We could have taken the shorter route, the one Spider took. Duck!"

Spider didn't duck in time and he was hit in the back of the head with a larch limb. "Ow! You want to call out a little sooner?"

"What shorter way?" Bobby asked. "If there's an easier way, why didn't we take it?"

"I said shorter, not easier. Your dad drove off the side of the road and dropped about forty feet. It's a wonder he's alive."

"Is this . . .? I can't believe it!" Bobby exclaimed.

"Yeah, well, it wasn't my finest moment," Spider admitted ruefully. "But it may have been providential."

"Here we are," Honor announced and stopped the ATV.

Spider hopped off and looked around. "I landed about right here," he mused and looked up through the trees.

Bobby came to stand beside him and look up as well. "Geez," he breathed. "You must have really been moving. The road is way over there."

"Uh, now that we're here," Spider said, "I'm a little embarrassed at what I have to confess. I, uh, I had a dream the other night—kind of relived the flight, the one on the mountain bike, you know? In the dream, down below me, about right in that clump of bushes, there was a car. It was a blue sedan."

"You're kidding!" Cy sputtered. "You dragged us clear up here because you had a dream?"

"No, wait!" Honor said. "It makes perfect sense. Spider was unconscious when I got here. He probably lost some memory of what happened just before he landed. But he was processing it in his dream."

"Uh, there's more. When I got to the Greenchem office in Las Vegas there were a bunch of messages from a rental car company. Seems someone—Stan, in fact—had rented a blue sedan in Spokane, and it never got turned back in. I thought that Stan had driven it across the border and abandoned it, but I don't think so now."

"Well, there's one way to find out," Cy declared. He wiggled off his perch and began shuffling forward.

Honor started up the ATV. "If Spider and Bobby will walk ahead and pull the brush out of the way, I think you can ride, Cy. You're the law, and I think you should be there when it's found, but we want to get there before dark."

Cy laughed and agreed, and they began their push through the dense thicket.

Bobby and Spider concerned themselves with creating a hallway in the brush for Cy to ride through.

"I feel like Moses parting the—" Spider stopped in midsentence and looked where Cy was pointing. There, wedged between two young larch trees, was a blue sedan.

"WHA'DYA KNOW!" CY BREATHED, looking at the car sitting between the trees in the clump of bushes. "It musta' come down the same way you did, Spider, but it's not in too bad a shape. How do you suppose that happened?"

"Well, I imagine it just rolled over the edge—it wasn't screaming down the hill like I was. There's enough of a slope there that it probably was able to keep a bit of traction and not come a-tumbling. Hitting some small trees would slow it down, and when it didn't quite make it through those two, the friction just stopped it. I've never seen anything like it. Never heard of anything like it either."

"So," Cy wondered, "you got any more surprises, Spider?"

"Yeah, and I'm sorry to say that you're the one that's going to get this one, Cy. Like Honor said, you're the law, here. I think that you'll find Stan Lucas in that car."

"Get out of town!"

"No, I think he's there. Let's get a little closer." Spider started clearing brush again, and Bobby followed suit, with Honor inching Cy forward on the front of the four-wheeler.

Finally Cy called for her to stop. He gingerly climbed down and laboriously approached the driver's window of the car. The other three hung back, waiting.

"He's here, all right," Cy called.

"Is it Stan?" asked Honor.

Cy shrugged. He was looking green around the gills.

"I imagine the body is all bloated," Spider murmured. "Probably has started to decompose." To Cy he said, "Got any sign of a cause of death?"

"Go on over and look, Dad," Bobby said. "You're a deputy, too."

"Thanks, son, but Cy is quite capable. I've got enough horrible images in my mind to deal with. I don't need this one."

Cy was peering through the window. "I can see that his skull has been caved in."

"That could have been from the ride down the hill," Honor commented.

Cy shook his head. "It's in the back. He's pitched forward, and something or someone has made mincemeat of the back of his head. We'll have to wait for the pathologist's report, but just looking at it from here, I'd say it was a crime of passion. Went way beyond what it took to kill him."

"While you look around here, Cy, I'm going to go up on the road, see if there's anything up there," Spider said.

"I'll go with you, Dad."

"I'd look out for cougars," Cy cautioned. "There's scratch marks on the door here that looks like there's been one window shopping more than once."

"All right." Spider headed off at a brisk pace with his son right behind.

When they began the climb up the embankment, Bobby looked up. "Geez, dad! You made it sound funny, flying off the edge of the road."

"Well, in retrospect it is a bit humorous. At the time I thought I'd well and truly bought the farm."

Bobby looked back. "The brush is so thick there that already we can't see the car."

"Yeah. Careful, now. Make sure you have a good hand- or foot-hold before going on."

"I've been doing rock climbing at the gym, Dad. I know how it's done."

"Rock climbing at the gym?" Spider muttered as he hauled himself up the steep incline.

They made the top and looked around, both panting and out of breath. "So, what do you think?" Spider asked. "If you were going to roll a car off the road with a body in it, where would you start?"

"Haven't a clue. Am I going to just let it go, or am I going to do like they do in the movies and jump out at the last moment?"

"Well, let's think about it. The windows were all rolled up, and the doors were all closed. I would imagine whoever did it stopped by the edge, turned the wheels to the right, and got out. Then a nudge from the back would have sent the car over."

"Then it has to be right above where we found it, or nearly so," Bobby figured.

"I'd say so."

"How did he know that it would land where it couldn't be seen from the road?"

Spider considered. "Don't think it mattered. How many people come up here before deer season? It would be quite a while before anyone spotted it, even if it was in plain sight. By then, whoever pushed it off could be long gone."

"Do you know who did it?"

"I've got an idea, but my ideas haven't been holding water lately. We'll wait and see." Spider went to the edge to look for evidence of tire prints.

Bobby wandered up the road with his hands in his pockets and looked at the boulder that had fouled up Spider's descent. He kicked it and then stood surveying the vista out over the valley. "This is a steep old mountain," he commented, turning to look uphill. "Reminds me of home."

"Yeah. They've got more water, though."

"I wonder what that is," Bobby mused.

"What?"

"Up there." Bobby pointed at something that looked like a yellow ball.

The bright color stood out against the gray-brown of decaying larch needles. Bobby climbed up to it and was reaching down to pick it up when his father yelled, "Don't touch it!"

Bobby paused, hand still reaching toward the earth, and looked up questioningly.

"Don't touch it," Spider repeated. "Can you see what it is?"

"It's a rubber glove. One like you use to do house cleaning. It's wadded up in a ball."

"Wait. I'll be right there." Spider scrambled hastily up. "Look around. Do you see another one?"

"Over there. Looks like someone tossed them up here from the road."

"Possibly." Spider bent down and picked up a couple of twigs and tested them for sturdiness. Giving one to Bobby, he took the other and rolled the glove-ball to a place where he saw the hand hole, poked his stick in, and picked it up. "I'll carry this one; you get the other."

"Let me guess," Bobby said, picking up the other glove. "We don't want to mess up any fingerprints."

"Yeah. I don't understand it, but they can find prints way after the fact on the darndest things, so it just makes sense to take the precautions."

"But why would the person get rid of the gloves right here?"

Spider headed toward the edge of the road. "I don't know. Maybe they figured since they wore the gloves it would keep prints off the car, but didn't know that the gloves themselves could have prints. Besides, we still have to connect the gloves with the car."

"Well, gee," Bobby said. "Gloves on road; car off road at the same place. Duh."

"Careful, now," Spider admonished, as they dropped over the edge. "Okay, okay. You practiced at the gym. Sorry. I can't stop being a father."

Each made a careful, one-handed way down the slope, grabbing at a bush or a branch for balance at a particularly steep passage, each holding his evidence-on-a-stick up and away for safety.

They had almost made it to the bottom when Bobby slipped on a piece of moss and went down, turning his foot underneath him. He let out a yell of pain, but he didn't lose his glove.

Spider came right behind him. "What happened, Son?"

"Turned my ankle," Bobby said through clenched teeth. "It hurts like h . . . , like blazes!"

"Can you get up? Here, let me hold your stick." Holding the two together like lollypops, he gave Bobby his other hand and helped him to rise. "Lucky you waited to do that 'til we were almost down. Lean on me."

"That's what I get for feeling impatient with Cy," Bobby muttered. "God really has a way of teaching, hasn't he?"

"If you're ready to listen, he does."

Bobby found it impossible to put any weight on his right foot, so they made a slow and careful progress down the slope and through the brush together. Bobby had his arm around his dad's shoulders and, with that help, made his way by hopping.

Halfway to the thicket where the car was they stopped to rest. "This whole situation is just fraught with metaphors," Bobby panted.

"Life is fraught with metaphors, if you're looking."

"I'm looking! I'm looking!"

Cy and Honor were sitting on the four-wheeler, deep in conversation, when father and son made their three-legged approach. "What happened? Whatcha got there?" Cy asked.

"Bobby turned his ankle, and we found some rubber gloves right about where the car went over. Could be something."

"Could be," Cy agreed.

"I've got some plastic bags we can put them in when we get to my house," Honor offered. "And we'll look at your ankle when we get there, too."

"This seems to be your week to cart injured Lathams off the mountain," Spider observed. To Cy he said, "What's next here?"

"I can't do anything until the forensic team comes out and goes over the car."

"You've got a forensic team?"

Cy nodded. "We'll get the pathologist out, hear what he says."

"You got a pathologist?" Spider repeated, thinking of Lincoln County's coroner, old Doc Goldberg, with his wispy, flyaway hair and age spots on hands that were continually shaking with palsy.

"I'm trying to decide whether to have them come out tonight or wait until tomorrow, when they'll have some daylight."

"Are you going to want to be here with them?"

Cy smiled. "Darn right I'm going to be here! It's my case, thanks to you, Spider. Honor will let me bring her four-wheeler up."

"Uh, then maybe you could arrange your teams to come up later. I've got some questions I want to put to a few people, and it would probably expedite things if you were there. I want to wrap this up tonight if I can and be back on my way home tomorrow."

Cy smiled. "Wrap it up tonight? I'd say you were kidding, but after this, nothing will surprise me."

"Let's go down to Honor's. We can get some ice on Bobby's ankle and I can call the people I want to talk to and arrange for them to come by the motel."

Spider let Bobby ride on the back alone. "The lame and the halt," he commented as he followed on foot carrying the two sticks. Bobby smiled at him, and it made his heart lighter to see it.

When they got to Honor's she got out her first-aid box and had a look at Bobby's ankle. It was discolored and swollen, and he winced when she touched it.

"I'll give you some aspirin and wrap it with an ace bandage for support. We'll put ice on it and elevate it, but I think you'd better go in to the emergency room when you get back to Chewelah and have it looked at."

"I'll be all right," Bobby said.

Spider had just finished his calls. "I'll take you in," he said. "I'll drop you off and you can have it seen while I'm talking to people. You can give me a call when you're done and I'll come get you. The hospital is just a few blocks from the motel." He picked up his hat and looked around. "Shall we go, then? We've got lots to do yet."

Bobby insisted that with the ace bandage he could make it to the car unassisted. Cy hobbled along in Bobby's wake while Spider hung behind with Honor. "He said he had a good marriage but that you were the love of his life," Spider confided, looking at Cy.

"Mmm," she said noncommittally. "He's aged well."

"He's a good man. Uh, I want to tell you that I'll be talking with John tonight. Don't worry, I don't suspect him of anything. I just want to include him in the mix."

"I'm not worried. John's a good man, too."

They were standing in the doorway and Spider noticed a miniature drawing, much like the larger ones hanging on the wall, but very delicately done. "Convolvulus Arvensis," he read, stumbling over the syllables. "What is that?"

"Wild morning glory. It's one of my favorite plants. Some say it's a nuisance, but I like it. It's hardy and tenacious, and the roots go deep. It covers ugly things and blooms when nothing else will."

"Do you ever sell your flower pictures?"

"No. But I have been known to give them to good friends. Why do you ask?"

"Well, you talking about the morning glory reminded me of my wife, Laurie. I wanted to take her something. I, uh . . . I just thought . . ."

Honor took he picture off the wall and gave it to him. "For Laurie," she said, and kissed him on the cheek.

"Thanks."

"We've got lots to do yet," hollered Bobby from the car.

Spider laughed and put on his hat. "I guess that's my call."

Honor walked with him to the car and leaned in to say good-bye. She passed an ice bag to Bobby, admonishing him to put his leg up on the seat and ice it good. Then she clasped Cy's hand. "Cold hands, warm heart," she said.

"I'll be up tomorrow," Cy promised. "I'll call and let you know when."

"I'll be here." She stepped back from the car, and Spider headed down the hill to Chewelah just as the sky was turning pink with the setting sun.

SPIDER STOPPED FIRST AT THE Gunsmoke Lodge. Stella was in the office, and he made arrangements to rent Number Seven. He also asked to have the key to Number Eight, as he said that he wanted Deputy Sheriff Chamberlain to look at something in that unit.

Stella regarded him for a moment, chewing her gum in square-jawed silence. "Okay," she said finally.

"How late will you be here?" Spider inquired as he signed the registration card.

"I'll be off at ten."

"I'd like to talk to you after a while, if that's all right?"

"What about?"

"Well, I don't know if you heard, but Stan Lucas disappeared the day he left Chewelah. I'm talking to people who may have seen him that last day."

"I heard that. I seen him," Stella said. "Me and a few other people that came by the motel."

"Uh, could you maybe think about who all saw him that you know of? I've got to run my son to the hospital."

"What's wrong with him?"

"He hurt his ankle. As soon as I drop him off there, I'll be back. We're going to talk to some other people, but when we're through could you come over and talk to Deputy Chamberlain and me?"

Stella reached for a pen and turned over a registration card to write on the back. "I'll make a list."

"That'll be great. Say, Stella, are there any messages for me? Anyone call and leave one?"

Stella glanced at the pigeonholes behind the counter and shook her head. Spider thanked her and went out, leaving her hunching her square shoulders over the counter, jaw working as she listed the numerals one, two, three. He carried the key out to Cy and asked him to go on in and greet anyone who showed up.

"You going to tell me who's going to show? Or is this another surprise?"

"Uh, no. John Nelson, Tony DeYeso, and Carmen Gage. After we talk to them, we'll have a word with Stella." Spider indicated the office with his thumb. "She may have some information for us."

Cy climbed out of the car, dragging his crutches after him, and Spider headed to the hospital. It was an old building, but in good repair, run by the Sisters of Charity. A crisply efficient gray-haired lady in a modern habit frowned at Bobby for walking in and immediately coerced him into a wheelchair. Assuring Spider that she would call when Bobby was through, she wheeled him through double doors marked Emergency Room.

Spider returned to the motel, noting that a Snakewater pickup sat in the parking lot. When he knocked at the door of Number Seven, it opened to reveal the large frame of John Nelson. Spider had forgotten how impressive his physical presence was. He held out his hand and grasped the superintendent's huge paw. "Hello, John. Thanks for coming."

Spider shut the door behind him and looked from John to Cy, who was sitting on the edge of one of the beds. "Has Cy said anything about why I asked you to come over?"

"He said it was your show, all the way."

"Uh, sit down, John. Uh, first, I want to impress on you that what we tell you tonight is confidential. We'd appreciate it if you don't discuss it with anyone else for a while."

"I don't have loose lips," John said brusquely, sitting down on a hard chair. "Now what's this about?"

Spider sat on the other bed. "Stan Lucas never left Chewelah. We found his body tonight."

"Never left Chewelah? But—What happened?" John swallowed and his eyes darted back and forth from Spider to Cy.

"We're treating it as a homicide, and we're talking to people who may have seen him that last day."

"That last day being Friday or Saturday?"

"I'm working on Friday now. If I find someone who says they saw him on Saturday, we'll revise our thinking."

"I saw him Friday," John said, looking down at his hands. "He came to the office in the morning." There was something about the inflection of his last word that made Spider think he was going to say more, but he didn't.

"And is that the last you saw him?"

There was a long pause, and then John said, "No. I knew he was leaving early the next morning. I came by here to see him."

"What about?"

"It was a personal matter. I . . . I wanted to ask his intentions about Carmen. I wanted to warn him to leave her alone."

"And did you?"

John looked up as another car drove in. Through the window he saw that it was Carmen at the wheel of her Snakewater pickup. He shook his head. "No. She was already here talking to him. I could see them, because they were standing just outside the door. She left here and went to the Mountain Aire for supper. I followed her and acted like I met her by accident. We spent the evening together—she spent the whole time telling me how wonderful Stan was, and how he was going to divorce his wife and marry her. He was going to leave the company, and they would go away together."

John's eyes followed Carmen as she parked the pickup and pulled the mirror around to check her makeup. "We must have stayed at the lounge until one in the morning. She got a little tipsy, so I drove her home and tucked her in bed."

"Then you went on home?"

John finally looked at Spider. Then his gaze dropped and he shook his head. "No. I slept on her couch. That's the best I could hope to do, and I somehow felt that if I could be even that near her, it would be enough. It was stupid, and I'm ashamed to say it because it makes me sound like a moon-calf. But it's the truth. That's what I did."

Spider stood. "I'm sorry, John. It's hard to have to pry like that. I don't think I'll ever get used to it."

John stood as well. "That's all, then? Do you want the name of the bartender at the Mountain Aire?"

"Cy knows who it is." Spider opened the door and offered his hand. "I enjoyed working with you. I'm sorry it's had this kind of an ending."

"Yeah. Me, too." John stalked across the parking lot, pausing to say something to Carmen, who glanced over at Spider. John got in his pickup and watched Carmen slowly approach the door that Spider was holding open.

"Hello, Carmen," Spider said. "I don't know if you remember me."

"You fixed the conveyor."

"Uh, yes. And you know Deputy Chamberlain?"

"Yes. Hi, Cy."

"Hi, Carmen." Cy attempted to rise, then thought the better of it.

"Won't you sit down," Spider said gently, indicating the side chair. "Carmen, the reason I came to Chewelah was because Stan Lucas disappeared just after he was here. Did you know that?"

Carmen's eyes were big, but she answered, "Oh, yes," in a confident manner.

Spider blinked. "And how did you feel about that?"

"Well, I knew he was going to have to go away, and all."

Spider sat on the edge of the bed, opposite Carmen. "You did?"

"Well, yes. When he divorced his wife, his father-in-law wasn't going to keep him on with the company, now was he? Stan knew he'd have to move on."

"What did he plan to move on to?" Spider asked. "Where was he going?"

"He thought he'd have to do something foreign. Maybe go to South America or the Middle East."

"Was he planning to send for you?"

She nodded. "Yes. He was going to put an ad in the personal section of the Spokane newspaper. He gave me money to buy the plane ticket. The ad would tell me the flight number and date that I should fly. He'd meet me at the airport, and we could be together."

Spider looked at the floor for a moment, remembering her daily search of the personals column. "Did you expect to hear from him by now?"

"Well, yes. But he said it might take a bit of time, and all. I don't mind waiting."

Spider looked up and met her eyes. "When did you last see Stan, Carmen?"

"It was Friday night. Why is that important? If he's disappeared, surely it's his own business. He didn't take the company payroll with him, did he?"

Spider ignored her question. "Tell me about your meeting. It was here at the motel, wasn't it? Did he ask you to come?"

"Well, no. In fact, he was a little put out. He said he had lots to do and that I needed to let him do it. He wouldn't let me come into the room. I asked him if he was hiding something, because usually when I came we . . . well, you know, I stayed a little while. But he said he was getting his papers in order and had them spread all over the bed and didn't want to get them messed up. He told me to check the newspaper every morning, and watch for the date and time. He asked me where I put the plane ticket money and said he'd send for me. He said I needed to believe in him. I told him I did."

"It's been a month," said Spider.

"It could be a year. I'd still believe in him," she said passionately.

"Did he kiss you? That last time you saw him?"

For the first time, Carmen showed confusion. Color rose in her cheeks, and she looked down at her hands. "No," she said in a tiny voice. "But I kissed him. He didn't seem to like it very much. Said it was too public."

"What did John say to you in the parking lot just now?"

The color in her cheeks deepened. "He said that it was important that I tell you the truth, no matter what you asked."

"What happened after you left here, that day after you saw Stan?"

"I went to the Mountain Aire for supper. John happened by, and we went into the lounge for a drink. I'm afraid I drank too much, and he took me home. I don't know what he thought was going to happen to me, because he slept on the couch."

"And you never saw Stan again?"

"No. Why? Is he in some kind of trouble?"

"Uh, he's dead, Carmen. We found his body this afternoon. He never left Chewelah."

The color that had suffused Carmen's cheeks drained away. "Dead?" she asked, only no sound came out when she mouthed the word.

"We're very sorry. I don't know what he had planned, but something went wrong. We're sorry."

"Dead?" she said again, and this time she managed a whisper.

"Yes," Spider said gently. "Do you have someone, a friend, that you can go to right now, be with?"

"A friend?'

"Someone you can be with. I know this is a difficult time for you."

"John. John said he'd wait. John can be with me. I want John."

Carmen jumped up and fled, wrenching open the door and running across the parking lot into the waiting arms of the superintendent. Spider watched as he gently helped her into the pickup and then climbed up after.

She had her face buried in her hands as he put the truck into gear and quickly drove away.

"So, what did you make of that?" asked Cy from inside the room.

Spider closed the door and shrugged. "About what I thought."

"So what are you looking for?"

"A motive."

"He wasn't the best-liked man on the planet," Cy observed dryly.

"Yeah, but it takes more than dislike for a person to turn someone's skull to mush. A crime of passion, you said."

"Did I say that? I can imagine old John wanting to turn his skull to mush, but I can't imagine him doing it."

"Me neither. Ah. Here's Mr. DeYeso." Spider went to the door and held it open while Tony got out of his car and walked toward him. "Thanks for coming, Tony."

Tony shook hands. "What's going on?"

"We need to ask you a couple of questions. You know Deputy Chamberlain?"

"Not officially. How do you do, sir?" Tony shook Cy's hand and sat where Spider indicated.

"Uh, you told me about bringing that memo and personally giving it to Stan. I need to ask you some questions about that. Did you say that as you came, Carmen was just leaving?"

"Yes, I did."

"And was Stan inside or outside of his room?"

Tony raised his black brows at the question. "He was standing in the doorway."

"And when you spoke to him, did he invite you into his room?"

"The conversation wasn't long enough for that. I handed him the memo, and he said a few pithy things about me knowing my place, and I left."

"Was he alone?"

Surprised, Tony said, "As far as I know."

Spider considered the toe of his boot and then asked, "Do you trust me, Tony?"

"Well, yeah."

"I need you to tell me explicitly what he said to you. Verbatim if you can."

Tony's olive complexion grew sallow and he swallowed as his eyes held Spider's. Taking a deep breath he launched in: "He said he recognized me from Deuel, knew I'd done time. He also knew I didn't say anything about it when I was hired at Snakewater. He said I needed to stop sending memos and keep my nose out of where it didn't belong. He said if I said one more thing about toxic waste he would make sure that I was down the road with a bad recommendation."

"So, how did you get out of the background check? It's a policy that everyone is fingerprinted."

"Luck, I thought. John told me to do it, but I put it off and put it off. I couldn't go, and I couldn't tell him why. But no one checked up on me—I was the only one in the office at that time, and there was no one to make sure that it was done. I thought I might get away with it, until Stan said he remembered me."

"And then Stan disappeared," Spider added.

"My good luck."

"Uh, Stan's dead. We found his body tonight up near Snakewater."

"Was it an accident?"

Spider shook his head.

The color drained from Tony's face, and the area around his mouth took on a bluish hue. His eyes all of a sudden looked sunken and bleak. "I guess that looks bad for me," he said.

"The thing that's bad for you is that you didn't tell Brick Tremain about your record in the first place," Spider admonished. "You wouldn't be the first ex-con that he's hired. I'll see what I can do to straighten that out with him, and I imagine John will help. But you have to be up front with him about it."

"Isn't it a bit too late?"

"I don't know. I think it will help that you didn't back off about the Greenchem thing in spite of what Stan said. Talk to Brick. I think you'll find he's fair. He believes in second chances."

"Does this mean that you don't think I had anything to do with Stan's death?"

"I'm not accusing you. I'm just on a fishing expedition. I want you to think. Was there anything odd about Stan that evening? Anything amiss? Different?"

Tony's brows knit in concentration, and then he shook his head. "He was himself. Shallow. Abrasive. Determined to put me down. I didn't see anything different."

"Okay," Spider said, handing Tony a folder. "This is how Stan confirmed that you were at Deuel Vocational Institution. He apparently saw you there when he was doing time and remembered."

"It's my wretched nose," Tony said with a rueful smile. "It certainly isn't conducive to a life of crime."

"That document is in your file. Brick hasn't seen it yet. Might be good if you're the one that shows it to him."

Tony looked over the letter from Lester Bealman. "Thanks, Spider. I'll take your advice."

Spider stood. "Somehow your memo never got to Brick. I'll make sure that he gets a copy of it so he knows what you did for him." He opened the door and held out his hand. "How's that baby?"

"I haven't had to take her on a drug run since I punched you in the face."

Spider threw back his head and laughed, clapping Tony on the shoulder. Then he rubbed his jaw and said, "Did you do some boxing at Deuel?"

"Matter of fact, I did." Standing, Tony turned to Cy. "Glad to meet you, sir." He stepped through the door and called, "I'll let you know when I talk to Brick," over his shoulder as he went back to his car.

Still smiling, Spider closed the door.

"What's this about a drug run?" asked Cy.

Spider was dialing the phone and said, "Just a minute." He asked

Stella to come over for a moment, and then told Cy the story about Sister Minnow sending him to Tony's in the middle of the night. Cy enjoyed it hugely, and he and Spider were both grinning when Stella knocked.

"Come in," Spider invited.

Stella at first only peeked in, but seeing their smiling countenances, she opened the door and entered with the note card in her hand.

"Thank you for coming," said Spider. "Won't you please sit down? You know Deputy Chamberlain, don't you?"

"Oh, we go way back," said Stella. "Hi, Cy."

"Hi, Stella. Whatcha got? A list?"

"Yeah, I made this for Spider. The people I saw talking to Stan Lucas on that last Friday he was here. Two of them was here tonight."

"And those two are?" Cy questioned.

"Carmen and that beak-nosed fellow. Only times I've ever seen him. Looks like a Turk."

"You've got someone else on the list, don't you? I see a number three."

"I don't know her name. It was the woman in the scarf and sun-glasses."

"Who?" Both Cy and Spider spoke at once.

"I don't know her name. She came in a blue car."

Spider tried to ignore his racing pulse. "Uh, when did she arrive? Before or after Carmen?"

"Before. I have a mind that's why he wouldn't let Carmen in the room. Already had the other one in there. It did me good to watch him doing the fancy dance out on the sidewalk with Carmen, trying to keep her from knowing about the lady inside."

"And the lady inside? Did she know about Carmen?"

"She'd have to be blind and deaf not to. I was outside having a smoke, acting like I didn't see what was going on, but I saw plenty. The curtains were open. I imagine the mystery lady saw plenty, too." She chuckled. "It sure did me good to watch him dance around in hot water."

"And you don't have any idea who the 'mystery lady' was?"

"No, but I've got the license number of the car."

Cy and Spider looked at each other. "How did you manage that?" Spider asked.

"Company policy. If you stay in a room, we get the license number. I figured she was staying, so I jotted it down on the card. I looked it up in the files after you said you wanted to talk to me."

"Stella, you are a gem!" exclaimed Spider. "This is going to be a big help. One more thing. Can you remember what the mystery lady looked like?"

"She was tall and thin. Well dressed, except for the scarf. I mean, no one wears one of those triangles tied under your chin any more. Who did she think she was trying to be, Jackie Onassis?"

"Here's a long shot," Spider said. "You clean the rooms. Did any rubber gloves go missing from the cleaning cart about that time?"

Stella shook her head. "There are several pairs on the cart, and someone's always robbing them for some other job. I couldn't say about that. But I'll tell you what did go missing, and that was the rug in front of the fireplace in Number eight."

Spider and Cy looked at each other just as the phone rang. Cy answered it. "It's for you," he said, holding it out to Spider.

Spider thanked Stella and took the card with the license number from her before walking her to the door and shaking her hand. Only then did he come and take the receiver from Cy. "Hello? Oh, hello, Jade. What news?"

Spider listened for a moment and then looked at his watch. "Okay. Call me when you know, but don't cut it too close, okay? Where are you calling from? Give me that number." Taking a pen from his pocket, Spider wrote it down. "And give me a number to call." He was just writing down the second number when there was a loud and insistent knock on the door.

"Who could that be?" wondered Cy.

Spider said good-bye to Jade. "Maybe it's the mystery lady," he murmured as he opened the door. There was Bobby on crutches with his ankle in a splint and a huge grin on his face. Behind him was a serious-looking young man in a white lab coat with a stethoscope slung around his neck.

"Hello, Dad. Have I got something for you!"

"What are you doing here? You were going to call!"

"I'm fine. Don't worry. Dad, this is Dr. Smythe. Dr. Smythe, this is my dad and Deputy Sheriff Cy Chamberlain."

"Spider Latham," Spider offered, extending his hand. "Glad to meet you."

Dr. Smythe shook Spider's hand and nodded to Cy.

Bobby hobbled over to the bed and plopped down. "I was talking to Dr. Smythe while he was looking at my ankle, and we were talking about Chewelah. He's never lived in a small town before, and we were talking about small towns, the pros and cons. I told him a story about Panaca, and he told me a story about his first night here in Chewelah." Bobby looked at the young doctor. "Please tell my dad what you told me."

"I feel really foolish," the doctor said.

"If Bobby thinks it's important, I hope you will tell us. Please sit down."

Reluctantly, Dr. Smythe sat. He pulled the stethoscope from around his neck and began fiddling with it. "My wife and I stayed here our first night in Chewelah. By 'here' I mean in this very room. We were dead tired, but the people in the next room were arguing, and it was hard to get to sleep. We couldn't hear the words plainly, but the tone showed lots of anger. At one time the woman screamed—and I mean screamed—'You said you were going to send for her.' Then a man shouted something back. Something short, because then it was all over. I figured they finally realized they were keeping everyone awake and toned it down. Or maybe they decided to kiss and make up. Whatever. I was glad to be able to get to sleep. Anyway, I must have been nervous about my first day at work because I was having heartburn, and I got up about one o'clock to get an antacid. I heard the door open and close in the next room. I was curious, so I looked out the window and saw the woman—I guess it was the one who had been screaming. She was putting suitcases in the trunk of a car."

"Do you remember what kind of car?"

Dr. Smythe nodded. "She was putting them in a GMC Yukon. I noticed the car when we came in."

"Did you get a good look at her?"

"It was dark, but the lights in the parking lot were on. She was tall and slender."

"Yes?" Spider said encouragingly.

"She had hair that went down past her shoulders."

"Could you tell the color?" Spider asked, leaning forward.

"Yes. It was red."

"Bingo," said Spider. He picked up the phone and handed it to Cy, pointing to the numbers he had just written down. "Can you call the Las Vegas police and have them pick up Bev Compton? She's just getting ready to leave the country. If they will call Jade Tremain on his cell phone at that number there, he can tell them where she is now. He's prepared to tackle her if necessary to keep her from getting on the plane to Mexico City, which she intends to do in about three hours."

"And what do they charge her with?" asked Cy.

"The murder of Stan Lucas," Spider said. "It was indeed a crime of passion."

IT WAS EVENING OF THE NEXT day by the time Spider got home. Bobby came with him, and they traveled together in easy companionship. The black cloud of despair that had hung over Bobby seemed to have lifted. "I looked into the car, Dad," he confided. "It made my stomach turn, but it snapped a lot of stuff into perspective for me."

"What kind of stuff?" Spider wondered.

"Oh, moth and rust stuff. Lucas was chasing after the things of the world, and what did it get him? When he disappears, they have to pay someone to care enough to search for him."

Spider nodded, but in his mind he saw Opal's pale countenance. She cared. Stan didn't deserve it, but she cared.

The sun was going down as they drove across the cattle guard and Bobby looked at his watch. "Sure gets dark early here," he commented.

"Depends on what season you're in. There's your mother. I hope she's got something for supper."

Laurie gave them the last of the leftover stew, but she had made fresh bread to go with it. After dinner, Bobby volunteered to sing to his grand-mother while Spider helped with the dishes.

"I don't understand," Laurie said as she wiped down the counter and hung up the dishrag. "You have to take me through it all. What made you suspect Bev?"

"Come into the living room. It seems like I've been away forever. Let's go sit, and I'll tell you."

Spider pulled off his boots and put his feet up on an ottoman. "Okay, here goes. It took me a while to tumble to it, but Bev and Stan were having an affair."

"But I thought he and Carmen . . ."

"He was. He seems to have been a man of enormous appetite. And slick! He had an easy answer for every question. He told Opal that he was flying out Memorial Day evening. Bev picked him up, supposedly to take him to the airport, but the gal at Blue Sky airlines told me he flew out the next day. I guess that was a way to get a night together where he thought no one would know. It wasn't until I looked at the two pages of notes I'd made at different times, trying to put all I knew down on paper, that I saw the differences in the dates."

"Okay," Laurie said. "So he and Bev are having an affair. Did she know about Greenchem?"

"She says she didn't, but I think it will be easy to prove she did. Old Cougar Wilson said that when he called in once, a woman called back and took care of things for him. I think the police will be able to find a con-nection. They may even find that she was latching onto the money before heading out to Mexico. I don't know. I would think she would try to get a hold of it."

Laurie shook her head. "But I still don't understand how she did away with him and fooled everyone."

"I think that the plan was that she was going to help Stan disappear and probably join him at a future time. We know that she created a driver's license with her picture and her name as Stanley Lucas."

"But that's silly! Stanley is a man's name."

"It is," Spider agreed, "unless you've got photo ID and a gal making jokes about being named after her father and what that's done to her life."

"Is that what she did?"

Spider nodded. "I just about shut that Blue Sky agent down when she called. I thought I'd got the problem solved. But then she went on and said that she certainly remembered giving out that boarding pass because she had never seen a woman named Stanley. Well, that made me sit up and take notice. Then she described her as a redhead, and everything fell into place."

Laurie frowned. "But, how could she do that? Make a driver's license?"

"With her computer. She took my license and made an ID for me in about three minutes. Laminated and everything."

"Okay. So she flew to Spokane—"

Spider picked up the narrative. "And rented a car as Stanley Lucas. The car was to be turned in at Boise. That's another thing the gal at Blue Sky told me. Stanley was booked to fly from Spokane to Las Vegas in the morning, and he was also booked from Boise to Los Angeles that evening. He had a connecting flight from Los Angeles to Mexico City, she said. She thought that was curious."

"Well, I do too."

"I think the plan was that Bev would fly to Vegas with the luggage— just as she did—and make it look like he disappeared."

Laurie nodded. "Just as she did."

"Stan would then take the rental car on to Boise and fly from there to L.A. and on to Mexico."

"I see," Laurie said. "Nobody is going to check on him going out of Boise."

"Not when he definitely flew out of Spokane that same morning."

"Okay." Laurie's brows knit. "So she was in on the Greenchem thing. Must have been."

"Yes. And I imagine that after doing her part, she was going to join Stan in Mexico or wherever."

"And live happily ever after?"

"Huh," Spider grunted. "Until Stan's eye started roving again."

"Okay. I understand that. So, she flew to Spokane, got the car in Stan's name, and drove to Chewelah in a scarf and sunglasses so no one would recognize her."

"Yeah. I asked her once if she had been to Chewelah, and she told me she hadn't."

Laurie plowed on. "And when she gets there, Stan has visitors to the motel room."

"Both of them stir her to action," Spider added. "She gets furious with Stan for telling Carmen that he's going to send for her. And, she's warned by Tony about the memo he's sent. She makes sure that Brick never gets a copy of it. If he hadn't sent me to Chewelah, he may not have known anything about it until the contract ran out."

"Or until the barrels of toxic waste started piling up because Cougar Wilson never got his check."

"There is that," Spider agreed. "It may be that she was going to wait until just before the contract came up for renewal to pull up stakes. Maybe the reason she went to the Greenchem office that day was to pay the fellows so they would keep on with the process. There was half a year to run, which would be another two million dollars. I imagine when she saw me there she figured she'd better get out while the getting was good."

"So you asked Jade to keep an eye on her? Why didn't you say something to Brick?"

"I was pretty sure about Brick. Ninety percent sure of him. But I didn't want to risk the ten percent of him being in on the whole deal. Or at least, of him being involved with her."

"Okay," Laurie said. "Let's go back to Chewelah. They argued about Carmen, and she got so angry she—what?"

"There was a fireplace poker in the motel room. I think she caught him in the back of the head with it and knocked him out. And then she didn't stop beating him with it until he was beyond dead. She waited until everyone in the motel was asleep, and then she put the suitcases in the Yukon and put the body in the blue car."

"How big was Stanley? Could she do that with dead weight?"

"She's strong. She lifted me up once when I was down, and I was surprised at how strong she is."

"And she drove him up on the mountain and ran the car off the road. How far is that?" Laurie asked. "Is that possible? How did she get back to the motel?"

"She ran. It's only seven miles, all down hill. Don't forget she runs marathons. If she made four or five miles an hour, she could be back at the motel by four, five in the morning. She gets in the other car, drives to the airport, checks the bags and boards the plane. It's doable. She did it."

"Spider, it sounds fantastic! Are you going to be able to prove it?"

Spider nodded. "I think so. Cy felt that they could get a print off the rubber gloves. They dusted Stan's room for prints, and before I left they had found a couple that matched hers on the doorframe. That put her in the room. They'll look pretty closely at the poker as the murder weapon. And the car rental fellow positively identified 'Stanley Lucas' as a tall, slender, red-headed woman."

"And Bobby helped you out, you said?"

"Yeah. He found an eyewitness who put her at the motel. We had several lucky turns here, though they usually involved a Latham getting hurt." Spider sighed and leaned his head back. "It's sure good to be home."

"Mmm. I'm glad you're back, and glad Bobby could come say goodbye to his grandma." Laurie paused and listened to Bobby's husky baritone singing, "And should we die before our journey's through, Happy day! All is well."

She cocked her head and a frown knit her brow. "By the way, why did Bobby go back to Chewelah?"

"Uh, he's having a hard time right now. He and Wendy are having a bit of a rough go, and I guess he wanted some family support."

"I've been worried about him."

"Worried? How so?"

"Oh . . . It seemed he was growing away from us. From what he'd been taught. But he seems all right now. Listen to him in there."

They stopped talking and heard Bobby singing, "Your name is Rachel Latham, and I am your grandson, Your husband was my grandpa Bill . . ."

"What was that you said, the other day, about the Lord being efficient and accomplishing more than one thing at once with blessings and trials?" Spider asked. "I think Bobby's doing more than reminding Mother who she is, right now. I think he's reminding himself."

They were quiet for a moment, listening to the melodic genealogy that Bobby was chanting.

"I prayed for him," confessed Laurie.

Spider looked at her and smiled, remembering that ride up Endless Agony. "So did I."

LIZ ADAIR graduated from Arizona State College and taught school for several years, becoming a reading specialist. The author of two previous Spider Latham novels, *The Lodger* and *After Goliath,* she has also run a specialty wholesale bakery and been a full-time wife and mother to her husband, Derrill, and their seven children. The Adairs live in Ferndale, Washington.